Hope for Georgiana

Hope Series Trilogy
Book 3

By Jeanna Ellsworth

Dedication

Excepting those rare, natural-born social butterflies, we all have a certain level of introversion within us. Perhaps it is that timid part of our hearts that craves books with strong female leads—bold women like Elizabeth Bennett and Scarlett O'Hara.

These strong female characters—the ones who stand out in the crowd, the ones who speak their minds, the ones who refuse to accept the rules placed on them by others, the ones who advocate for the weak or less popular—are easily admired.

The irony is that even as we read about strong women, we are often blind to those same qualities in ourselves. By reading stories about strong women, you are honing your inner strong female lead for your own story's climactic finish.

I believe *you*—along with everyone else—are attracted to these ladies because you feel a private kinship to her. You may think it is because you admire, in others, the qualities you lack. But in truth, it is because you admire those same qualities that you possess in abundance.

I suppose most of you just dismissed that claim, at least to some degree. But the truth is, every woman must make the journey to find her voice, her moral platform, and to draw the line in the sand when it comes to letting others crush her passions. It is a hard road, but do not dismiss the power of hope, or minimize this powerful tool, by calling it wishful thinking.

So I dedicate *Hope for Georgiana* to the introvert in *you*, knowing that if I could read the book of *your* life, I would be equally inspired by your journey, equally amazed to see you discover your own quiet fortitude. I hope you know that the gentle side of your soul—your inner strength—although perhaps less publicly celebrated, is equally admired.

Acknowledgments

I once believed Georgiana Darcy's reserved nature made it easy for readers to undervalue her power to engage the reader, but I no longer feel that way. Many people contributed to my current understanding of Georgiana's character, however, none contributed more than Jessica Dotta, the author of *The Price of Privilege* trilogy. Mrs. Dotta was the first to make me fall in love with a timid heroine, very similar to Georgiana Darcy. After finishing the last page, I had an intense emotional reaction. I remember it well because it was the most profound book hangover I had ever had. I closed the book and put my hands on the table and just sat there, letting the hurricane of emotions flood my person, knowing instinctually to also let them flow from me as readily as the tears did from my eyes.

I must also acknowledge the Latin Proverb, *"adhuc abyssus aquarium deduxit"*, which translates to, "Still waters run deep". I know now that there is no requirement of dramatic heroics for a reader to fall in love with the hero, but that depth of character and integrity are vital, for that is what makes a real hero.

I must also acknowledge my brother Ted Putnam. Though younger than me, he has been the same protective, loving, empathetic, wise, and ever-supportive brother to me that Fitzwilliam Darcy is to Georgiana. He never gave up hope for me to find a man who was worthy of me. And I must say, he is a good one to have in your corner, for when I need a fast pass for my prayers to reach Heaven, Ted is the one I call.

CHAPTER 1

26 August 1813

It was two days before Charlotte Collins was to marry Georgiana's cousin, Colonel Richard Fitzwilliam. The whole household was up and breakfasting early. Richard had already relocated to his new townhouse, but he had called on Darcy House that morning early enough to share the meal with everyone. Georgiana took a moment to look around at the faces of all those she loved most. There was her brother, Fitzwilliam Darcy, and his wife, Elizabeth, along with Charlotte and Richard. They were people she loved dearly—people whom she could never live without.

I would do anything to make them happy, she thought. When her eyes landed on her brother, he smiled wide enough to show his dimples. *Especially William.*

Catching her eye, her brother put down his napkin and addressed her. "Georgiana!" he announced, with a bit of excitement in his tone.

Georgiana was not the only one who noticed her brother's jubilance. Elizabeth and Charlotte both looked up from their plates. There was a bit of a sparkle in her brother's eyes. It was curious, perhaps even mischievous. "Yes, William?"

"Do you remember Henry?"

She studied his face a bit more. For the last few weeks, with the approach of the London season and her coming out, her brother had often been found deep in thought; she could even describe him as preoccupied. He had brought up the names of several gentlemen after these long, silent, brooding moments. One time he had asked her about Mr. Griffith, and almost in the same breath, inquired whether she minded men who were bald. Mr.

Griffith was bald. Another time he blurted out in the middle of dinner the name of an earl in the neighboring county. Was his name possibly Lord Henry? She couldn't remember. But nevertheless, her brother had that same look again in his eyes now.

The look that said he knew exactly who she was to marry.

She groaned inwardly.

She wracked her mind, attempting to recall all eligible bachelors of that name. "Henry Hastings?" she asked.

Elizabeth looked perplexed. "Who is Henry Hastings?"

Darcy very nearly rolled his eyes, "He is an old mate from Cambridge who just inherited a baronetcy. But no, that is not who I meant. I meant Henry Darcy!"

"Our cousin who moved to the Americas?" Bringing up their cousin in the middle of breakfast definitely piqued her interest. Perhaps he was *not* trying to find the perfect match for her at this particular moment.

"Manhattan, New York, to be exact. He is coming to visit!"

Georgiana smiled. "Splendid! I have not seen him since I was a little girl. What brings him to England again?"

"He says he wants to get back to his roots. True Englishmen always come home, you know, and he has always been a fine fellow. I am sure the two of you will get along magnificently."

Dread filled her bosom.

Elizabeth came to her rescue. "William, dear, we have talked about this. Georgiana is nervous enough to have her coming out. There is no reason to push her toward a match—be the gentleman English, Irish, or American."

Darcy tucked his chin back in shock and obvious horror at his wife's statement. "Of course her husband will be an Englishman!"

Georgiana would turn eighteen exactly one month from today, on September 26. It seemed her brother could think of nothing else besides her coming out and arranging a marriage for her. Charlotte made a comment to appease William about how all the finest gentlemen were Englishmen and Georgiana was sure to meet many of them without her brother's interference.

The only one who had not said anything yet was Richard. Georgiana looked in his direction and caught his eye. He smiled at

Georgiana kindly and gave her a subtle shrug as if there was nothing he could do to change William's mind.

Richard, you share guardianship with my brother. Say something! Richard just smiled and turned to say something to Charlotte. Georgiana sighed. If the war hero felt unequal to this particular skirmish, there was little hope of tactical success.

It was as if she were trapped in a burning building, yet no one seemed concerned enough to call for the fire brigade. The idea of her brother—no matter how beloved he was—arranging a match for her was terrifying. And yet everyone at the table seemed content to carry along with normal conversation. She looked once more at her cousin, Richard, and tried to plead with her eyes for him to intervene. But it seemed this battle would be one she would have to fight on her own.

Georgiana twisted the linen napkin in her lap and looked around the table. Next to her sat William and Elizabeth, who had a beautiful relationship that stemmed from mutual respect. No one could ever doubt it was a love match. Elizabeth did not come with any dowry or connections to speak of, yet William had not hesitated to choose the woman who completed him. And across from her sat Charlotte and Richard. They too had fallen in love without a thought in the world to money. Why could William not grant her the same fate?

For a brief moment she cursed her thirty-thousand pound dowry. She was grateful for the security and comforts it offered, of course. But it also had the rather unfortunate side effect of ensuring every bachelor in the country would see her as a financial prize to be won. Would anyone ever see the worth of her heart? How in the world would she ever trust that a suitor *truly* loved her and wasn't simply after her dowry? Her stomach tightened, and she pushed the food around on her plate.

Her brother was apparently oblivious to her distress. Georgiana realized the conversation must have continued on without her notice. "Now, Elizabeth," William responded jovially, "I will have no argument on the issue. Georgiana deserves a wealthy, titled *Englishman*. Cousin Henry's father, my dear late father's first cousin, may not be titled, but he still owns half of Nottinghamshire. Well, perhaps not half, but close to it."

Georgiana made one last desperate attempt to engage Richard's assistance, and the colonel braved his way into the skirmish.

Finally.

"So, Darcy," Richard interjected, "when will the prodigal second cousin be arriving?"

Georgiana frowned at Richard. *Hardly the reinforcements I was hoping for, Cousin.*

When Darcy made no reply, she then looked to her brother and saw a smile form on his face. "I am usually not very good with surprises, but I must confess that I sent a carriage to Liverpool a few days ago to fetch him. His ship came in last Wednesday, and he will arrive at Darcy House this afternoon. Just in time for your wedding, Richard! Oh, and Mr. Pastel said he had some business in London, so he will be riding along with him. I really think it is just an excuse to be present for your wedding, Charlotte."

"Mr. Collins's old solicitor?" Charlotte replied. "I hope there is nothing wrong with the inheritance again. I thought everything was settled four months ago, before our engagement." Charlotte's first husband, Mr. Collins, had squirreled away a large sum of money that was withheld from her until she spent a full year in mourning. There had been several other stipulations as well which, as Georgiana understood, Charlotte had been mostly ignorant of. But by her innate loyalty—a loyalty that Mr. Collins certainly had done nothing to deserve—Charlotte had been awarded a large sum of money after strictly obeying a full year of mourning.

"I am not entirely sure what Mr. Pastel needs," William replied. "His letter only said he needed to meet with me about a changing of the guards. It seems his brother would like to switch offices and run the Liverpool business instead." He directed his gaze back at Georgiana. "What do you think about Henry Darcy coming to stay with us, Georgiana?"

She smiled politely at her brother and said, "It is wonderful news, of course. I am happy to welcome our cousin back to England."

Her brother sat back and folded his arms with a smug look on his face. He then looked at Elizabeth and raised an eyebrow.

It was the look of success. Her fate was as good as sealed.

*****

Charlotte Collins had arrived on Mr. Darcy's doorstep last year as a pregnant widow with nothing but a few black dresses and a single trunk of belongings. Georgiana had barely known Charlotte then. But now Georgiana was helping one of her dearest friends pack the last of her belongings into a much larger trunk. It was hard to believe how much had changed.

Georgiana opened Charlotte's wardrobe and took out a bundle of letters from her late husband, William Collins. Charlotte had explained how Mr. Collins had written them to her before they were married. She had told Georgiana that they spoke nothing of the man that he had been after the marriage. Instead, they contained a subtle gentleness. They had given her a few shreds of hope during those months when she endured his abusive wrath. Charlotte was saving them for her son, Isaac Byron Collins, so he would know that his father was not entirely devoid of morals or kindness.

Georgiana wordlessly handed the letters to Charlotte, who placed them neatly into the trunk. They rarely spoke about her first husband. Mr. Collins seemed to have had a dual personality. In public, he seemed a bumbling fool, always praising and giving special attention to those of higher rank, but only making himself look ludicrous. Although she had never met him, Georgiana had once heard her brother say that Mr. Collins was "an utter fool". Well, he had utterly fooled a lot of people. No one was aware of what went on behind closed doors except his wife. Even after his death, she had stayed mute on the subject until she fell in love with Colonel Fitzwilliam and learned to trust again.

The wedding was still two days away, but Georgiana was so excited she could hardly stand it. She couldn't have been happier to know that her cousin Colonel Fitzwilliam and her friend Charlotte Collins had learned to master their fears. It was all so romantic! Her cousin was a decorated war hero, having lost his left arm in the battle of Queenston Heights, and Charlotte was a penniless pregnant widow who didn't know whom she could trust. For over a year, Colonel Fitzwilliam had secretly been pining for her. Despite his well-known reputation as a ladies' man,

Georgiana's cousin proved quite inept at winning Charlotte's heart. But the magic of the story did not end there.

Charlotte had fought her own demons while Colonel Fitzwilliam was overseas fighting for England. And even after they fell in love, there had been still more obstacles to face. Mr. Collins's obsessively detailed will attested to his wish to control Charlotte in every way imaginable. It had even stipulated that Charlotte's son could not be legally adopted until he was one year old. And so the couple had chosen a lengthy four-month engagement. Georgiana suspected Charlotte also preferred a longer engagement and more time to get to know each other. Charlotte had come a long way in the past year, but Georgiana knew her friend was still wary. Charlotte had been fooled once by pretty words and promises of security. She was determined not to make the same mistake again.

Georgiana opened a drawer and picked up a white crocheted shawl. "I have never seen this before, Charlotte," she exclaimed. It was exquisite in its craftsmanship. "How beautiful!"

"I worked on that the first few months of my marriage. It was going to be a present to my daughter if the baby was a girl. You may have it if you wish."

"Oh no, I could not take something so fine. Where did you learn to do needlework like this? Did your mother teach you?"

Charlotte took the shawl and examined it closely. "Actually no. It was my good friend Deborah. She ran the orphanage in Meryton for many years until her eyesight made it impossible. In her nearly blind state, she would feel my stitches and tell me what I was doing wrong. She would show me each new step in the pattern. She did it all by touch.

"This shawl brought me a great deal of comfort during those months I was married to Mr. Collins. Ironically, crocheting this numbed me from the sorrows I felt. It became natural to spend an hour or two a day working on it. Even on the days that my body ached from the injuries Mr. Collins's anger inflicted, it allowed my soul a respite from the life I had learned to accept."

"How can you even consider parting with it if it means so much to you?" Georgiana asked.

Charlotte smiled and said, "Let me ask you a question. Why do you think I no longer crochet?"

"I suppose because you are not being injured anymore."

"Plausible answer, and yet incorrect on several fronts." Charlotte raised the shawl and said, "A single knot does not make this beautiful. In fact an entire row of knots do not. It is layer after layer of repeated patterns that create this masterpiece. During my marriage to Mr. Collins, nothing in my life was predictable. I never knew what to expect. Life was not a recipe of perfect proportions. Some days I had too much of one thing and too little of something else."

"Like fear or trust."

"Or happiness or sadness. Sitting down and doing something that required a predictable pattern brought me stability. But when I came to Pemberley to live with you, Elizabeth, and Mr. Darcy, I found that my need for predictability in my life had diminished. Life itself became predictable. At first it was hard. But it became clear that life with the Darcys had a calming routine to it. Instead of finding peace in the predictability of each stitch, I had dear friends who never wavered in their love for me. This shawl literally kept me warm at night while I was married. Now I have replaced it with dear friends like you and Elizabeth and the loyalty of Mr. Darcy."

Georgiana fingered the delicate white stitches. "Do not forget Richard," she smiled.

"Yes, and my Richard. So you see, I am warm from the inside out now. I have no need of a shawl. I would really like you to have it. It would mean a great deal to me if you kept a part of me with you. It truly represents what I felt on the inside back then: I was all tied up in knots. I know when Richard and I marry we will only be a mile away from Darcy House, but I will miss you a great deal, Georgiana. It is the faithful friendship that I shared with you and Elizabeth that taught me to believe in love. You two were the stability and predictability that I needed."

Georgiana was moved to tears. Charlotte had come so far in the last year! "I would be honored to take this shawl," Georgiana replied. "I will cherish it always."

"Thank you. Now let us finish packing. Hand me that box."

Georgiana did so and asked, "What is this?"

"It is the only heirloom that my son will receive from a father he never knew. Open it."

It was a small box, about the size of her fist with a single clasp at the front. She undid the clasp and opened it to see a gold pocket watch with an inscription that she could not read. "This looks like real gold."

"It is. Mr. Collins wore it every day. You can see the little dents and nicks in its metal."

"What does the inscription say?"

"It is a quote in a foreign language. I believe it is from John Heywood, an English author and playwright from the 1500's. Mr. Collins told me once what it said; I believe it was something like 'The harder I work, the more luck I have,'" Charlotte explained.

"How fitting that you will give it to your son."

"Yes. The General will most likely have to work hard in life even though we will have my inheritance and the money Richard made off the bet with your brother. I still am shocked that Mr. Darcy would honor a bet on such a large of a sum of money."

"But that was the whole point, Charlotte," Georgiana teased. William bet Richard his annual income that Charlotte did not feel the same way as she did before Colonel Fitzwilliam left for the war. The wager proved very effective in encouraging Richard to pursue her again. "I think it will make a rather nice wedding present."

"A rather *extravagant* wedding present, I would say." Georgiana only smiled at Charlotte. It would probably be years before Charlotte would ever feel worthy of Colonel Fitzwilliam's love. "Nevertheless, when the General reaches maturity, I shall give him the pocket watch."

Georgiana handed the box to Charlotte and continued to hand books to her. She smiled at the way her friend still called her son "the General". It was the nickname that Richard had employed before departing for the war in Canada. Charlotte still enjoyed using it, perhaps because she wished to avoid any thought of the child's namesake—his deceased father. Unsurprisingly, the day after her betrothal to Richard, Charlotte had confessed to Georgiana her deep desire to have Richard adopt Isaac and have the boy's name changed to Isaac Byron Fitzwilliam. Georgiana had encouraged her to discuss it with Richard, knowing her cousin would be honored by such a request. A few hours later, Richard, who loved the General like a son, had met with this solicitor to have the papers written up. As soon as they were married, the adoption would proceed. And Charlotte would be rid of the name Collins forever.

They heard a knock on the door, and Charlotte stood to open it. The nursery maid, Sally, stood there with the General and said, "I'm ta tell ya that Mr. Henry Darcy is here, and Miss Darcy is needed right away. And Isaac wanted to kiss ya before I put 'im down for 'is nap."

Charlotte took the baby, who was nearly a year old, and said, "I will put him down. Thank you, Sally." She then turned to Georgiana and said, "What do you remember about Mr. Henry Darcy?"

"I was but five when he moved away!" she replied with a slight laugh. "I daresay I cannot even recall the color of his hair."

"How much older than you is he?"

"Five or six years. I can't imagine he is five-and-twenty yet."

"Well, let us go meet the man! I will put the General into his crib on the way down."

Georgiana followed Charlotte to the nursery, which would only house the General for two more nights. The wedding was the day after tomorrow, and the nursery was really rather crowded now with two cribs and two nursery maids. The plan was that Sally would take care of the General at Richard's new townhouse while the happy couple enjoyed their two-week wedding trip. The Fitzwilliam's townhouse was on the outskirts of the Mayfair neighborhood and just a mile walk from Darcy House. It would be nice to have them so close. Charlotte had become like family, and now she would literally be a cousin.

Elizabeth was rocking her son in the corner. Georgiana lowered her voice and asked, "Oh, Elizabeth! Are we disturbing you and little David?" David Harrison Darcy was born just seven weeks ago, and he was the greatest blessing in the Darcy household since Isaac was born. He stubbornly made them all wait on pins and needles for his birth. One never can predict the exact day a baby will be born, but from the size of Elizabeth's abdomen at the beginning of July, they all expected him to be born any day.

But he had waited until July 8—making it a very long week for all parties concerned. The midwife said she had never seen such a healthy, robust baby. Elizabeth had some trouble with the delivery because of his broad shoulders. When the anxiety of the birth died down, Colonel Fitzwilliam quipped that God gave him big shoulders because He knew the lad would have to carry the weight of the Darcy legacy.

William was a proud father. David was the only thing that divided her brother's attention from arranging the perfect match for her. For this reason, Georgiana was especially grateful toward her new nephew.

"No, you are not disturbing me," Elizabeth whispered. "I just finished feeding him. He seems to grow by the second. The stockings I made last month will not fit a day longer. This little bundle brings me more joy than I could have ever imagined."

Georgiana stepped closer and reached out for him, "May I?"

"Only for a minute. I understand our guests have arrived, and I fear my husband's wrath if I unnecessarily delay the introductions."

"Oh, William will not mind our delay so long as David is the cause of it."

Charlotte put the General down in his crib and tucked a light blanket around him. "There now. Sleep, little one." Isaac fussed for a moment then rolled over. "I am going to miss him. I am glad we waited four months to get married, because that allowed me time to wean him. Leaving him here was a bittersweet decision, but taking a baby on one's wedding trip does seem . . . a little unorthodox."

Georgiana rocked David but couldn't help but giggle. "Do not worry, Charlotte. We will look in on him every day. I will have Sally bring him over at least three times a week."

"Yes, Charlotte," Elizabeth said. "If William thinks he can keep me indoors in such fine weather, he is surely mistaken. A walk through the neighborhood will do me good. We will all look after the General. Now let us go meet this American cousin."

Georgiana rolled her eyes and put David down in his crib. In a perfect imitation of William, she declared, "Henry Darcy is an *Englishman!*"

They all shared a few giggles at that. Elizabeth said, "Be patient, Georgiana. He is just very worried right now."

"But the season is still months away!"

"I know, dear, but my husband is nothing if not meticulous. You remember when Mr. Collins died? He begged for tasks. He was so efficient in completing them that Mr. Collins had a tombstone within a week!"

"His meticulousness is what I fear the most," Georgiana fretted.

Elizabeth then said the only thing that could have calmed Georgiana down: "You know as well as I do that his heart is in the right place. Just give him some time. He will soon see that you need to find your own love, just like we did."

CHAPTER 2

Georgiana followed Elizabeth into the sitting room, and her brother immediately started introductions. "Georgiana, this is Henry Darcy."

She curtsied and looked up at her long-lost cousin. He was taller than her brother by an inch or so but had the same wavy brown hair, just like her father. *It must be a Darcy trait.* His eyes were a light brown, nearly golden, and he had long eyelashes. Georgiana admitted he was quite handsome. He had a slight tan and the subtlest hint of freckles. He swept a hand through his hair and then flashed a brilliant set of perfectly white teeth, which seemed only whiter against his brown skin tones.

"How do you do, Georgiana?"

She felt a sudden rise in color in her cheeks, not only because he had used her Christian name, but because his voice was deeper than she expected. *Well, it's safe to assume he sings a bass part, I daresay.* "I am well. How do you do, Mr. Darcy?"

"I'll have none of that, Georgiana! I'll go by Henry or nothing else. I may be born an English gentleman, but in America, families calls each other by their first names."

Georgiana was too surprised to say anything at first. How could she call him by his Christian name so soon when her brother wished for a match between them? She looked to her brother for guidance on the matter, but he seemed to be pleased with the suggestion. "Very well, H . . . H . . . Henry. I do hope your travels were pleasant."

"Oh yes! Mr. Pastel kept me quite entertained!" Henry Darcy jubilantly exclaimed.

She curtsied to Mr. Pastel and said, "Good afternoon, Mr. Pastel. It is a pleasure to see you again."

"Thank you, Miss Darcy. The pleasure is entirely all mine. I would not miss the wedding; I know how long awaited it is." He then looked to Charlotte and said, "Congratulations, Mrs. Collins. It pleases me to see such a joyful end to this last year."

"Thank you, Mr. Pastel," Charlotte said.

Elizabeth motioned for everyone to sit down. Georgiana took a seat next to Elizabeth, foreseeing that she would need her sister-in-law's strength to get through this tea. Elizabeth could converse easily with just about anyone, a talent which was probably one of her best qualities. It was highly desired, but harder to come by for Georgiana, and Georgiana knew it. Talking with unfamiliar people took herculean effort on her part, and Mr. Henry Darcy certainly fell into the category of unfamiliar. The sum total of things she remembered from their youth amounted to only two scant details: he was always cheerful, and he never teased her. And, of course, his brilliant smile against his tanned face and his smoldering eyes made the act of conversing even harder.

"So tell us a little about yourself, Mr. Darcy," William began.

"Not fair, Cousin. I cannot allow you to call me Mr. Darcy if Georgiana is not allowed to. Besides, it just is not the American way."

"But it is the English way." William seemed pretty confident in his rebuttal.

"You forget, Fitz, I have only ever been called Mr. Darcy by strangers. If you call me Mr. Darcy, I will assume you are summoning my father back in New York!" Georgiana tried not to giggle at the nickname that Henry had for her brother. William never enjoyed being called Fitz. In fact, Richard sometimes used that to his advantage when William was being particularly annoying.

"And how is the elder Mr. Darcy?" William asked, changing the subject.

"Mighty fine, I'd say. Living the high life and building his empire both here and there. He just signed another contract to fund a series of buildings right on Fifth Avenue."

"Ah, I see. And this Fifth Avenue, is it prime farmland?"

"Ha! Certainly not! No, my father does not manage farmers. He manages trade businesses. It is far more lucrative. His steward still manages the estate and farms here in Nottinghamshire, of course, but they do not make nearly as much income as his businesses. After all, with businesses, one is not dependent on things like rain. There is no worry that a weather calamity might wipe out an entire year's worth of crops. He simply buys up businesses that look like they are going under, and he turns them around. I intend to do the same thing do here."

William smiled broadly as if he just heard good news. "So, you intend to stay in England, Mr. Darcy?"

"I do, unless everyone keeps calling me Mr. Darcy. Then I'll have to slap the English right out of them and set them straight!"

Everyone laughed, although her brother a little less enthusiastically than the rest. Then William said, "Forgive me, I am an Englishman through and through, but I will try to abide by your preferences. Henry it is from here on out."

"Thanks, Fitz," Henry chuckled, then turned and looked expectantly at Georgiana. "Now, Georgiana, why don't you tell me who all the rest of these lovely people are?"

Everyone waited for her to introduce them, and Georgiana swallowed hard. "This is Elizabeth Darcy, William's wife. They have been married since May last year. They have one son, David, who is seven weeks old and the light of their life. This is Charlotte Collins, soon to be Charlotte Fitzwilliam, as she is marrying our cousin Richard. You came just in time to see their wedding on Saturday. Charlotte has been a widow for a year and a half and has one son from her previous husband. We call her son the General, but his real name is Isaac. Do you remember Colonel Fitzwilliam?"

"I certainly do! Although he was not a colonel then, I recall he was excellent in outsmarting the enemy." He looked at William and said, "Do you remember that snowball fight of all fights back before I left for America? You and Richard against me and George Wickham. I swear by Jove, George couldn't hit you no matter how hard he tried. And he was three years older than me! But then he decided to put a rock in the snowball. Landed right between your eyes if I remember right."

Georgiana blanched slightly at the mention of George Wickham and noticed that William did also. He looked in her direction and put on a false smile and remarked, "Yes, I still remember the sting."

"What ever happened to George? Right smart fellow, he was."

Georgiana didn't know what had happened to him since the incident at Ramsgate. Having someone speak his name in front of her was like a branding iron to the eye. It stung enough to threaten tears.

There was a prolonged pause in the conversation as if William did not know what to say until Elizabeth finally explained, "I understand his plans were to take his talents to Australia."

"Oh," Henry replied, "did you get a chance to meet George, Elizabeth?"

She cleared her throat and said, "Unfortunately I did."

Georgiana whipped her head toward Elizabeth and caught a slight look of guilt before William stood up and said, "So, Henry, must I introduce you as my American cousin? Or can I term you as an Englishman living abroad?" It was a blatant effort to change the subject. Even Henry looked a little confused but was polite enough to follow William's lead.

"Oh no. I can't pass myself off as a true American. I may talk with American slang, I may even walk like an American, but I shall never pledge myself to anyone other than the king. My father won't either. Besides, there are loads of benefits to living in one country but claiming citizenship of another. Attracts a lot of attention. People still look at England as an established country. Old money, you know. It makes people feel we are more stable, therefore they are more comfortable investing in us. The war has made it a little tricky, but we manage to steer clear of American soldiers. Nothing like hearing this English accent of mine to get them snoopin' into my business."

Charlotte asked, "How old were you when you left England?"

"This is like the game of twenty questions! Don't worry, I don't mind as long as I get to ask the same number of each of you! But to answer your question, my family moved from Nottinghamshire when I was eleven. This is my first trip back to England for over twelve years."

Georgiana did the math in her head. That would make him five years her senior and now three-and-twenty.

"Your father has returned a few times over the years," William remarked. "Once when I was still in Cambridge, and again just before my father died. I did not get a chance to see him then as I was on my grand tour. My father adored your father. They were closer than cousins—more like brothers."

"Yes," Henry replied. "He always speaks well of the late Mr. Darcy. You have my condolences. But it seems you have done well for yourself since taking the mantle upon your shoulders. Darcy House is even better than I remember. You have a fine home."

"Thank you."

Elizabeth rang the servant's bell. "You and Mr. Pastel would probably like to freshen up." When the servant came in, she asked, "Have our guests' rooms been readied?"

"Yes, ma'am."

"Thank you," she said. Turning to the men, she announced, "I will show you the way."

"Much obliged," Henry said.

Mr. Pastel stood and bowed to Georgiana and said, "Darcy House is magnificent. Perhaps we could have a tour after we freshen up?"

Georgiana curtsied and smiled back at him. "Certainly."

*****

"Well, he certainly knows what he wants in life," Darcy said proudly.

Elizabeth came and cupped her husband's jaw with her hand. "Not too unlike someone else I know."

Darcy felt confident in their privacy even though the door to his study was ajar, so he leaned down and placed some kisses on his wife's face. "You are still my love, my life, the love of my life."

He hadn't realized what a huge part of her time having children would take. He pulled her still slightly rounded hips towards him and hungrily embraced her. It had been too long since he could do much more than that, but the doctor had cleared Elizabeth to resume intimacy as soon as she felt ready. She still got up several times a night to feed David, and he often got up with her, just to share in that precious moment. His wife was so beautiful. Her motherly figure made him very proud to be a father.

Elizabeth melted into his arms as usual, but something was making her hang back a bit. "Is everything well?" he asked.

Elizabeth pulled away slightly and said, "Yes, dear. I just feel that you should tread carefully with your plans for Henry and Georgiana."

He mocked being offended. "I do not have plans for them! What are you suggesting? Do *you* think they are well matched?"

Elizabeth took a deep breath and said, "I am trying to be serious. I know you, and I know that you wish to find Georgiana the perfect match, but I am not sure Henry is the right one."

"Of course he is! He just needs a bit of polishing up. Soon he will shine like a new penny. We just have to introduce him to the right people in the right circles. There are still a great number of people who will remember his father's presence. And from the sound of his business plans, he is intent on making a name for himself and earning his own fortune, over and above of what he will inherit."

Elizabeth reached up and put her hand on his jaw. "Be careful. Consider what Georgiana's wishes might be."

"Very well. I will not push her into it, but nor shall I limit their exposure to each other. He will be staying right here in Darcy House until he gets his feet under him in his business ventures."

*****

Mr. Benjamin Pastel was pleased Mrs. Darcy had assigned him a room in the family wing. The Darcys had become dear to him over the last year. Carrying out Mr. Collins's final wishes had been . . . difficult. In fact, sometimes it had been downright impossible. There had been so many deadlines, stipulations, and requirements; even the minutest detail had been scripted. Benjamin respected Colonel Fitzwilliam and had suspected his attachment to Mrs. Collins, regardless of his attempts to hide it. And when they were at Rosings for Anne de Bourgh's wedding to Captain Jersey, he had immediately seen through Colonel Fitzwilliam's façade. The colonel was clearly a man with a mission—who was about to ruin everything.

It had been a few days premature, but before Colonel Fitzwilliam did anything so foolish as offering marriage to the sweet, kind widow with a heart of gold, Pastel had hurried things along and revealed the truth about the will. Seeing the shock on her face when she realized she was not a penniless widow after all, but rather an heiress, had been priceless. He knew he had done the right thing. For the first time in his professional career, he had been sincerely happy to see his client's wishes so thoroughly thwarted.

Mr. Pastel ruminated for a moment about the Darcys. Elizabeth was a singular lady. She clearly had Mr. Darcy wrapped around her finger. Their special love was palpable. And Miss Darcy seemed to be the picture of perfection. She did not put on airs, and although a bit shy, when she did speak, it was always worth listening to. She was fiercely loyal to her family too. He remembered several times when she had heatedly defended Mrs. Collins's character, despite the fact that she must have known all along that her friend and cousin had tender feelings for each other. He admired that kind of loyalty.

He wished for that kind of loyalty in his own family. But his brother, Clyde Pastel, would never be a moral person, let alone a selfless one. Clyde was a man who liked the chase. He went through a cycle of chasing wealthy widows, earning their trust, rapidly draining them of their fortunes, and then moving on. This was one reason why Benjamin Pastel felt it was important that he himself manage Mr. Collins's will.

Benjamin now felt a stronger urge than ever to disengage himself from his wayward brother. His father had left his solicitor's business, Pastel and Sons, to both of them. But Benjamin knew his father would not be proud of the direction Clyde had taken the business in. For over a year, Benjamin had been trying to weed out the disreputable clients—Mr. Collins among them.

He was very pleased to see the now honest cargo ships safely transferred into Charlotte's hands. As soon as she married Colonel Fitzwilliam, the managing of the ships would fall to Colonel Fitzwilliam. It would be the perfect livelihood for him—a lucrative business that could accommodate his war injury. Admittedly, as soon as he heard that the colonel had lost his arm,

Pastel had hoped Mr. Collins's ships—and the colonel's tender feelings for Charlotte—might be of some use to the couple.

He took a look in the mirror and adjusted his cravat. He had much to discuss with Mr. Darcy. Upon leaving his chambers, he ran into Henry Darcy.

"Pastel! You clean up nicely."

"Thank you. You do too."

"I spent a bit of money in Liverpool learning how to dress like an Englishman. I have the breeches, the Hessian boots, the starched cravat and, one cannot forget, the waistcoat and vest! Americans have a little more relaxed fit than all this. Now I know why English gentlemen have such impressive posture! They can't slump their shoulders without ripping a seam in their jacket!"

Mr. Pastel chuckled and patted him on the shoulder. "You will get used to it, I promise. Do you really intend to put down roots in England?"

"You bet your bottom! Now, do you think we can find our way back for the tour?"

"Well, even if we do not, it will be fun getting lost in a house this big."

"I knew I liked you! I don't know how Darcy does it. He is full young still, and yet he has managed Pemberley and Darcy House for over six years *and* raised Georgiana. Speaking of which, did you catch that look between Georgiana and Darcy when I mentioned George Wickham?"

Mr. Pastel had noticed it, but he also knew when to let things go. Years of being a solicitor, helping people hide their deepest secrets of fortune, love, and property, left Mr. Pastel with a strong commitment not to pry into the affairs of others. Clearly there was some bad blood between George Wickham and the Darcys. But Pastel did not even know the man, and he was happy to leave it at that. Instead he changed the direction of the conversation.

"Tell me more about Miss Darcy," Benjamin asked. "She is a bit shy around me. What do you remember about her?"

"Not much beside golden locks and pink ribbons," Henry sighed. "She always wore pink. She liked to tag along with her brother and cousins. I remember once when Darcy and I nearly came to blows over a game of jacks. Georgiana put her fists on her hips and stood right between us. She stared me down as if she had the power to pummel me. It was too adorable not to laugh at, and the whole situation soon dissolved into a puddle of hysterical tears."

Mr. Pastel was pleased that his redirection had worked. It was also a very endearing story, one that verified that Georgiana was indeed a very loyal young lady. They made their way down to the foyer again where they met Georgiana and Charlotte for the tour.

*****

The tour did not take as long as Darcy had expected. Either that or Mr. Pastel had deserted the group prematurely. "How do you find Darcy House?" he asked his guest.

Mr. Pastel smiled. "You are a very lucky man, Mr. Darcy," Pastel replied. "I have known many wealthy gentlemen and have been in hundreds of fine houses, but there has never been one that appealed to the senses like Darcy House. Is it your doing?"

"It is the work of generations. When I inherited, I only refurnished a few rooms."

"It speaks of refinement, and the tastes of your parentage can only be described as classic. The colors are rich and inviting and blend well with the entire spirit of the house."

"Thank you. Now, how can I help you? Your letter said you are considering extricating yourself from your brother, Clyde."

Mr. Pastel motioned to a chair, and Darcy nodded. When they both took seats, Mr. Pastel began. "My brother and I have grown increasingly different. He attracts disreputable clients, like Mr. Collins, through gaming tables. He has made a reputation for himself as someone who can work around good, honest laws— laws that are there to protect the innocent and trusting people of the world. After finishing Mrs. Collins's inheritance paperwork, and seeing all the hoops that both she and I had to jump through just to hand over money that should rightfully been hers, I cannot stomach the prospect of continuing as his partner."

Mr. Darcy nodded. "You told me that Clyde wants to run the Liverpool office."

"He does. And at the moment, that office is entirely in my name. My hope is that I can give it to him free and clear in exchange for his claim to the new business here in London. Our Liverpool office brings in a great deal more money."

Darcy pondered this for a moment as his mind started churning. "You would sell out completely in order to start over?"

"Indeed. And I would not be entirely bereft. I may be in trade, but I have learned a great deal from the wealthy. When a client invests in a business, it is my job to ensure his financial security, and therefore I conduct a great deal of research into proving the investment is sound. I have become rather good at seeing the warning signs that made something look more lucrative than it actually is. I also think I have a knack for seeing something's potential."

"Are you saying you have also invested in these schemes?"

Pastel nodded. "At first, I was very conservative and invested only in the slow-growing investments," he explained. "But over the years, as the wealth accumulated, I have reinvested all my dividends. I live frugally, sir, and without an estate or family to support, I get along quite nicely."

"I congratulate you on your good fortune, but I am not sure what you need from me."

Mr. Pastel took a deep breath and glanced away for a moment before answering. "I hope to present my plans to Clyde before the week is over. He will need time to transfer his belongings to Liverpool. In the meantime, I think he has occupied the London office long enough for those less-than-stellar clients to find their way back there. My hope is to find a location that is nearer to downtown London. I also hope to find a townhouse within walking distance. This will all take time. Until then . . . well, I will be homeless."

Darcy smiled. "Is that all, Pastel? Of course you can stay here until you find the right suite for your office. Richard managed to find a suitable townhouse about a mile from here. I shall give you the number of the agent who helped him."

"That would be very helpful. I am sorry to show up like this hoping to be invited to stay longer, but I knew I could not simply make the request through a correspondence."

"We may be *new* friends, but you should know me better than that. I never did get around to thanking you for intervening when you did with Charlotte. I know you are a very honest businessman. And yet you found a way to ensure her financial security when it looked like Colonel Fitzwilliam was about to propose and ruin it all for her."

Mr. Pastel had the grace to look away as color rose to his cheeks. "It was nothing. She deserved to have the money, and I was not going to let a few days get in the way of that. I value loyalty very highly. And although I never met Mr. Collins, it was clear that he did not deserve Mrs. Collins's loyalty. In the end, my loyalties were with her."

"Indeed. Good to have you in Darcy House. I just received several invitations for me and my family to different events. With you living in my house, may I accept for you as well?"

"Yes, I would love to rub shoulders with those who you value and respect. It would also help me build my business here in London a great deal."

"Then it is done," Darcy said.

CHAPTER 3

The entire next day was devoted to wedding preparations. But as night fell, Georgiana was not disappointed to see both Henry Darcy and Mr. Pastel at Darcy House for dinner.

The meal went smoothly, although it was hard for Georgiana to keep a straight face with all the Englishman jokes Henry made at William's expense. A few giggles escaped. Henry was so laid back that it was nearly impossible to feel uncomfortable in his presence. He brought a new level of brightness to their home. It felt similar to when Richard visited or when her brother first brought Elizabeth to Pemberley. Henry seemed to add something to her life that she didn't know was missing. It was like a missing piece of the puzzle.

Jigsaw puzzles were not a favorite of hers. When she was young, William used to clip out newspaper drawings and cut them into various shapes and have her reassemble them. Without seeing what it was supposed to look like beforehand, the task was quite arduous. It took hours at times.

She imagined finding a husband was much the same—like assembling a puzzle without seeing the finished design beforehand. She didn't even know what he would look like. Would he be tall and dark? Would he have dashing blond curls? Would he be big and brave? Or would he have a quiet strength about him, seen only by those who knew him best? Would she fail to recognize the truth until the last piece puzzle was fitted together, or would she see glimpses of the man as each piece found its place? The idea that her future husband could be anywhere was both thrilling and harrowing. She said a quick prayer that he would be an honest man who cared nothing for her fortune.

Looking back at the times when William had created puzzles for her, Georgiana realized it had probably been his way of keeping her engaged in an activity in his study while he worked. Those first few months after her father's death had been the most difficult period of her life. She had been only an infant when her mother died. So when her father died, when she lost the only parent she had ever known, a part of her had died as well. She knew William felt the same way. Spending time together had been their only comfort, their balm of Gilead.

During those first few months, William had never turned her away, probably because he ached with the same loneliness she felt. It was strange to miss someone in your life, to know that something was missing and that you would never get it back. It was easier to put it into words now that she was almost eighteen, but she still rarely talked about the loss. She had to trust someone a great deal to discuss her father's passing. Even Lady Jane Andrews, her closest friend, knew to avoid the topic.

Occasionally, Georgiana would be reminded of her father's smell, or the way his beard stubble used to show by the end of the day. It was never the big memories that brought on the lonely tears. It was the things that made him human.

He always wiped his mouth first on the left, then the right, then down the middle before answering anyone at dinner. He was rather reserved, and this unique mannerism allowed him time to think about what he would say. Sometimes he did it to hide his smile at an especially ridiculous comment or question. Georgiana always smiled remembering those times. But her father always gave thought to his responses. He had a genuine knack for holding his tongue when necessary.

No, it wasn't the big things she remembered. It wasn't the trip to France the year before he died. It was not the extravagant eighth birthday party when he brought in gypsies to tell fortunes, clowns to juggle blazing sticks, and a menagerie with real-life tiger from India. It wasn't ever the things he gave her; it was the everyday memories that took her breath away.

And now that he was gone, she recalled her memories of him over and over again in her mind. There had likely been many lessons he wished to teach her. Now that opportunity was gone.

But she had gleaned every lesson she could from her short time with him. She had learned that spending time with someone was more important than giving a gift to make up for an absence. She learned that you should never pass up an opportunity to tell someone how special they were to you. She learned that there is no perfect human being, but there are humans who will help you be the "most perfect you". She learned that money provides opportunities, but not happiness. And one must have the courage to fight for what they want in life.

What do I want in life? The question rolled around her head, like a marble in a wooden box, bouncing from one corner to another, never really finding a place to rest. She sometimes felt jostled one way and then another in a world that promised only more speed in the form of parties, balls, and soirees.

She needed life to slow down. Maybe then she could sketch what she wanted, no, *needed* from her future husband. But she feared that her entire future would comprise of more and more faces and names than she could stomach. How would she know who would love her? How would she know which man would steal her heart? Would it happen overnight or would it be slow, like patiently climbing a peak, climbing ever higher and higher until the grand view presents itself in all its beauty? It was all so overwhelming.

They were all gathered in the music room, making light conversation while Elizabeth played. Georgiana was enjoying the music and was not truly attending to what was being said. Something about this piece in particular brought her mind back around to her father. The others in the room faded away as she listened to the notes flow effortlessly across the keys.

Her father had once told her when he was just becoming sick that she needed to learn to read people's souls. He said that some people, like Aunt Catherine, were motivated only by money and power. But Georgiana's mother, Anne, had been different. It had been a special moment for the young girl. Her father almost never discussed her mother with her. Her father had held her hand gently and said, "People are motivated by all sorts of things. Money, fame, status. Those can all be lost in an instant. But someone who is motivated by joy, honor, and integrity will always be rich beyond measure. Look for these people, my dear. Hold on to them tightly."

Georgiana had been only twelve at the time, but she still remembered the conversation clearly. "How can I tell what a person is motivated by?"

"It is simpler than you think. Pride, greed, conceit—these are the signs. The man who seeks after riches may indeed find them, but he will always have a very poor soul."

She remembered feeling like she should write these things down. "But, Father, we are rich, are we not?" She was confused whether or not it was riches themselves that make a man's soul poor or something else. Her heart couldn't give credence to that concept. Most of those she knew had wealth and status, but she loved them with all her heart. She would do anything for them.

Her father coughed and tried to sit up. It took some effort, but he readjusted himself enough to lean forward. He brushed her blonde ringlets to the side behind her ear and then placed his hands on her shoulders. "We are rich, but it is not because of the land, or Pemberley, or the income we bring in every year. We are rich because we know how to love others. I have tried to teach you this in our visits to the tenants—the widows, those who need that extra kindness, and those who are alone in life."

"Like Grandpa Jacobs." Grandpa Jacobs was not really her grandfather. He lived in a small cottage behind Pemberley. His wife had died, and he had lost his only son, a sailor in the navy. He took in students to teach drawing and the pianoforte. But as his years progressed, he lost his sight and could teach only the pianoforte. Georgiana learned to play from him. She had been only four at the time, but in his failing sight, he had tied a rope from tree to tree and worn a path through the trees that led to Pemberley. He was never late to a lesson, rain or snow. He taught her until his death when she was nine.

"Yes," her father had replied, "like Grandpa Jacobs. There was a man who knew how to love passionately. He took you in as if you were his very own."

It was true. Grandpa Jacobs had taught her much more than just music. He used to make up stories to teach her musical terms. He once invented a story about a man named Steven, who only followed where his mind led him. He was an intellectual. His friends called him Even Steven because he was so predictable and regular. But then he fell in love with Ruby, a girl who loved to skip and run and dance and jump. And Steven learned to follow his heart and to skip, jump, and halt in mid-step right along beside her. And that was *rubato* time. Georgiana smiled. She had never forgotten the romantic notion of playing a piece with *rubato*. Or the importance of following your heart.

Fatigued, her father had leaned back against the pillow and let his arms drop. "Promise me, Georgiana, to take care of your brother. He is afraid. He will need you during this time when I pass. He may think it is you that needs him, but remind him every now and again that he needs you too."

Another coughing fit came on, and the nurse ushered her out of his chambers so her father could rest.

Georgiana only spoke with her father a few more times before his death. Their conversation that day changed her. It matured her. Her brother needed her, and she, being only twelve, was not too young to help him. She had vowed as she left the room that she would seek to love passionately and seek for the things in life that made men's souls rich. It was a complicated concept. And looking back, although she hadn't been able to understand it all at twelve years old, she had never stopped trying to see what it was that made a man's soul rich.

Her brother's voice brought her back to the present, and she smiled and turned toward him. "I am terribly sorry, I was wool gathering."

William asked, "I asked if you would play. What were you daydreaming about? Anything in particular?"

Georgiana smiled softly and said, "I suppose having Henry back just reminded me of Father."

A look of concern crossed her brother's face, and she wished she had not been so truthful with her answer. It was a habit of hers that needed to be amended. She often did not behave as most elegant ladies should. What better way to spoil the lightness of a room's mood than to bring up the death of a loved one?

She noticed Elizabeth had stopped playing and had walked over to her husband. It was so very unlike Georgiana to agree to play, but she knew it would please her brother if she tried to impress Henry.

"I suppose it is my turn to exhibit." The words came out forced, and she tried to hide the anxiety that threatened to emerge. It was a poor attempt at best. She did not really wish to perform, but she knew that William thought Henry a worthy candidate for a husband. Besides, she needed practice performing in front of people she did not know well. She surely would be asked to perform in front of entire rooms of strangers when she had her coming out.

Charlotte and Richard smiled sweetly at her. "Play that musical number you have been working on for the wedding breakfast tomorrow," Richard said. "What was it called again?"

"Brandenburg Concerto No. 5 in D," Georgiana said.

Mr. Pastel replied, "I know that piece. By Bach, no?" Georgiana nodded. "Its lightness and cheer always calm me."

"Me as well. And I do need to practice it a few more times."

"Pish, posh!" Richard scoffed. "You have been working nonstop for months now. But do let us hear it. It will be our private concert."

Georgiana stood, and Mr. Pastel stood as well and accompanied her to the pianoforte. She looked at him briefly, wondering at his intent, when he whispered, "You can do this." He then lifted the lid and propped it open. It was clear that he was offering her support, support that she desperately needed, but he had made it look like he was just fixing the lid. She smiled gratefully back at him.

Turning to the others, he said, "I could not let this number be muffled. I have no doubt this will be exactly what we all need to ease our worries for the big day tomorrow."

Instead of sitting back down, Mr. Pastel stood in front of the pianoforte with one arm bent behind his back. He was not as tall as Henry, but had a grace about him that no one could deny. Even Georgiana, who rarely noticed these things, could tell he was confident with who he was. He looked very much the gentleman even though he was, in truth, a solicitor. He had broad shoulders, and with one arm bent behind his back and the other hand holding the lapel of his tailored jacket, he looked as if he could be from the finest circles.

While they were at Rosings for her cousin Anne's wedding, she had gotten to know a great deal about Mr. Pastel. He was a musician himself but preferred to listen rather than play. He was very encouraging, and his opinions were kindly given. He had a way of saying how impressed he was with her skill without making a blush come to her face. Tonight was no different. She felt his coming to the pianoforte to lift the lid was praise in itself. It gave her a sense of confidence and, for the first time, she chose not to use the sheet music. It was a long piece, but Richard was right, she had practiced it for months.

She took her skirts in her hands and made a small curtsy, then looked up. Every eye was on her, including Henry's. He had one foot propped up on the knee, and she couldn't help but smile back at his wide, brilliant grin. He gave her a subtle wink, which surprised her enough to quicken her heart. She took a deep breath and then sat down. Taking a moment to calm herself was vital. The beginning of the piece was quick and could be unforgiving. It was time to display.

She began, her fingers moving effortlessly across the keyboard. With the lid propped up, she was nearly hidden from all those in the room except Mr. Pastel. She could make out his still form to the side. As the piece slowed momentarily, she looked up at him briefly and saw that his eyes were closed and he had a pleasant look of complete satisfaction on his face. In the light, he looked quite handsome. The thought surprised her, and she nearly made a mistake. She refocused her attention to the piece. She continued playing, and as the music began the crescendo, she picked up the tempo, sending notes flying through the air at speeds she had never played before.

She was playing it with rubato.

She sensed, more than saw, that Mr. Pastel was looking at her. His body had turned just enough to indicate he was giving her his entire attention. She couldn't help but feel flattered. His opinion was always genuine, and so it meant a great deal more.

She stole a glance up at him towards the end, and with the final notes, she saw him nod slightly.

She had done it!

He walked around to the bench where she was sitting and assisted her to stand, then dropped his hands to his sides and stepped away. She wasn't sure why her heart was beating furiously in her chest. Performing always seemed to do that to her. Everyone began clapping. Henry also stood clapping and started walking over to her. Her heart started picking up speed as he took her arm and paraded her in a circle looking at her from head to toe. He then stopped her and waved with his hands up and down her person and said, "Magnificent! I had no idea that such talent existed! Oh, Cousin, you shall be snatched up quickly. I dare say that you should keep that little skill hidden unless you wish to elicit a proposal. It was truly that good!"

"Oh, Henry," Georgiana said blushingly, "do not say such things!"

"I do not lie! I may exaggerate at times, but I swear to you this is not one of those times! You will be in danger of being swept off your feet everywhere you go. Why, I doubt you will be safe walking down the street!"

"Henry!" Georgiana laughed, her blush deepening.

"It is true! Why, I know of a baker who was so talented, she fell in love in her very own shop."

Charlotte peered her eyes at him. "In a bakery? Hardly the setting of great romance."

"Oh, I do not know, Charlotte," Richard piped in. "They say sweets are the food of love."

"I believe the saying is *poetry* is the food of love," William teased. "I, for one, cannot believe anyone has ever fallen in love in a bakery. As it would be too hard to compete for attention with all those lovely cakes and buns, of course." Everyone laughed.

"Very well," Henry declared, "if none of you believe me, I will be forced to relate the entire *delicious* tale." He grinned at his own pun. "This is a very real story. And I happen to know for a fact that the baker's name was Ginny. She was known for all sorts of delicacies. A certain man came into her shop every day. He was painfully shy and would always pay a bit more for the treat and walk away without his change.

"One day, he summoned enough courage to inquire about her wares. From that day on, he made a point of talking to her every day. They got along splendidly. He asked all about her ingredients and cooking methods and recipes. And then they moved on to telling each other their struggles and hopes. But although Ginny had grown quite fond of their little chats, he never asked to see her outside of the shop—not even so much as an offer to walk her home. And Ginny started to wish that he would, for she realized she had fallen in love with him.

"So, one morning, after months of this strange, business-like courtship, Ginny made a new kind of fudge. He noticed the delicacy in the shop display, and he asked to buy a piece. And do you know what her reply was?"

Charlotte laughed disbelievingly and asked, "What?"

"She told him that it was *magic* fudge. She said that it had the ability to make someone fall in love."

Everyone laughed, including Georgiana. Henry certainly had a way with telling stories.

"At that, the man turned all sorts of red and started fidgeting with his hat." Of course, Henry was acting out the shy man, and continued the story. "Another customer came in, and he stepped away momentarily, but Ginny watched him out of the corner of her eye. He was deliberating something fierce. When the customer left, he approached her again. She boldly asked him if he would like to fall in love." Everyone laughed again. "The man looked up to Ginny and said, in a nervous stutter, 'I-I-I don't need no ma-magic fudge to fall in l-lo-ove, but if you would be so kind as to eat some yourself, I'd be much obliged to escort you home.' They were engaged a month later."

Elizabeth exclaimed, "What a *sweet* story!"

"Yes what a *treat*!" Charlotte exclaimed.

Henry said, "Truly *delectable!* And, it is true! Ginny and Marcus now have six children and are as happy a couple as I have ever seen, present company excepted."

This led the two couples to look at their partners and exchange tender looks. The room filled with palpable emotion.

After a moment of silence, Richard announced, "I should probably head back to the townhouse. I know a certain lady who intends on changing her name tomorrow."

Charlotte smiled demurely and then gave Richard a look of devotion that no one could deny. "Until tomorrow."

"I am just going to go kiss the General goodnight," Richard said. "Good night, everyone."

Charlotte murmured how she would go with him, and they both left, hand in hand.

Her brother stood to say he wished to kiss David goodnight as well, but then Elizabeth whispered something in her husband's ear. He looked surprised and glanced where Charlotte and Richard had just exited. It was clear Elizabeth was telling her husband that Richard and Charlotte should probably have some time alone. A look of awareness came to his face. "Elizabeth, may I escort you to your room?" he asked.

"I would be delighted."

William beamed with joy. They still were newlyweds in Georgiana's eyes.

After they left, Henry asked, "Your brother seems remarkably happy with his wife. How did they meet? I should like to find such a love match for myself someday."

They all naturally took their seats again.

A half a second later, Georgiana realized that she had been left alone in a room with two bachelors. Henry was family, but her brother hoped for a match with him. Had Darcy left her alone with him intentionally? The thought brought a blush to her face. At least she had Mr. Pastel. He was quite proper. He even took the seat across from her whereas Henry took the seat next to her on the sofa. Henry sat sideways with one arm around the back of the sofa and one leg casually bent in the crease of the cushion. He looked so relaxed.

She glanced at Mr. Pastel, who sat erect with his hands on his knees as if he dared not wrinkle his garments. He tilted his head in a questioning manner then subtly motioned to Henry as if to remind her of Henry's question.

Georgiana began, "I daresay I am the last one to offer advice on how to find a love match, Cousin. But I can tell you that William met Elizabeth at a public assembly ball in Hertfordshire."

"Really?" Henry replied with a grin. "Go on. I demand to hear all the details, Georgiana."

"Well, you should request to hear the story from them directly, but I can give you the highlights. At the ball, the first night they met, William declined to dance with Elizabeth, and Elizabeth overheard him explaining that she was 'tolerable, but not handsome enough to tempt' him—"

Henry laughed. "Tell me he didn't say *that*!" Utter disbelief was evident in his tone.

Mr. Pastel assured, "He did indeed. I have heard the story myself." Henry gave Mr. Pastel the same look of doubt, then turned back to Georgiana.

She continued, "Elizabeth was offended, rightly so, and proceeded to argue and tease him in every interaction with him thereafter. She was under the impression that he had sheer disdain for her. You know how my brother is."

"What do you mean?"

"Trust me, *I* do." Mr. Pastel said. "He can be quite intimidating at times."

"Darcy? He is just shy!" Henry exclaimed.

"Yes, but you only know that because you grew up with him," Georgiana explained. "For several years after Father died, he was under a great deal of pressure. I am afraid it turned him rather stern and reclusive."

"I can see how that could happen. So how did they fall in love?"

"That is the magic of the story. Miss Darcy, you tell it." Both Mr. Pastel and Georgiana scooted to the edge of their seats, which made Henry raise his eyebrow in curiosity.

"William left Hertfordshire completely besotted. He thought by distancing himself that his infatuation would cease. But as luck would have it, when he went to visit Aunt Catherine in Kent for Easter, Elizabeth was there, visiting Aunt Catherine's rector, Mr. Collins."

Henry said, "Oh, I see. And I take it that Mr. Collins was Charlotte's first husband?"

"Yes. He was also Elizabeth's cousin. Well, my brother rather wrongly assumed that Elizabeth's arguments all along had been flirtations, and Elizabeth rather wrongly assumed that William's natural reserve and broodiness had been utter disdain for her. So you can imagine the misunderstandings that erupted when he made her an offer."

"An offer of marriage?"

She nodded. "And there were other misunderstandings as well that had turned Elizabeth quite against William. Suffice it to say, she assured him he was the last man on earth she could ever be prevailed upon to marry. And so he left the parsonage completely hopeless."

Henry shook his head slowly. "It must have been a painful blow for Darcy. But, given his present state of wedded bliss, I take it that is not the end of the story."

Georgiana smiled. "Indeed not. William wrote her a letter and gave it to her the next morning."

"Proper Darcy wrote a letter and gave it to someone who had just refused his hand? Not even an American would do that! He has more guts than I do!"

Mr. Pastel picked up the story. "But what happened next is what is so important. Mrs. Darcy got ill. Quite ill, delusional even. The colonel paid a call at the parsonage and was quite shocked by her condition. In her delusional state, Elizabeth had written a letter back to Mr. Darcy and implored the colonel to deliver it. Colonel Fitzwilliam knew nothing of what had happened between them, but he suspected Darcy's attachment to her. Given that and Mrs. Darcy's illness, he *made* Mr. Darcy come see her."

"See her? In her chambers?"

Mr. Pastel continued. "No, no, of course not. She was on the sofa at the parsonage. But she was still quite delusional. She begged Darcy not to leave her. Her sudden change toward him gave him a good deal of hope. Her hallucinations increased until she believed she was in heaven and somehow Mr. Darcy was there walking in a garden with her. Mr. Darcy was so worried about her that he stayed with her late into the night."

Georgiana inserted quickly, "Let me tell this next part. William finally read Elizabeth's letter as he was walking home that evening. In it, Elizabeth apologized for refusing him. William, as you might expect was on cloud nine. And the next day, when he returned, she was again very happy to see him, regardless of the continued delirium. They even embraced and whispered tender things to one another—although Richard and Charlotte were there the whole time, so it was nothing compromising. William just wanted to comfort her in her illness. And for the first time in their relationship, Elizabeth appeared as if she desired *him,* or at the very least, for him to stay with her."

"I see. What a remarkable turn of events from the previous day!"

"Yes indeed," Georgiana agreed. "But then it all fell apart again. Elizabeth had a convulsion due to the high fever, and then she suddenly, in a moment of clarity—if you want to call it that—saw that he was holding her in an embrace, and accused him of compromising her!"

Henry looked sympathetic. "Poor Darcy! I can see the roller coaster of emotions now. Hope, no hope, hope, no hope."

Georgiana nodded. "Exactly. After that, William left. His heart could not take another refusal from Elizabeth. Richard stayed behind long enough to see Elizabeth faint and revert back to her previous delusional self, the one who was desperate to be with William. But by then, William was already gone. He departed for London within the hour. Elizabeth was so sick and weak that she did not take her leave of her bed for two weeks. But Charlotte had witnessed all of their interactions and saw that these two needed to be together, so she sent Elizabeth to London to her aunt and uncle's home. Then Charlotte risked everything by writing to Richard to let him know Elizabeth was in London too! Charlotte was not too subtle in implying that Elizabeth wished to see William."

Henry leaned back, rubbed his chin and said, "Let me guess, Richard used some battlefield tactics to get Darcy's head out of the sand. No doubt Darcy was just moping around licking his wounds."

Georgiana giggled, "Yes, indeed he was. And Richard and Charlotte's plan had worked! Darcy found where Elizabeth was staying and immediately went and sought her out to 'ensure she was well'."

Henry laughed. He mockingly said, "It was the least he could do! What a fine excuse!"

Mr. Pastel said, "Unfortunately, soon after that, Mrs. Darcy got word that Mr. Collins had died. So, Mr. Darcy offered to escort them back to Kent for the funeral."

"Them?" Henry asked.

Georgiana clarified, "Oh, Elizabeth's sister Jane was there too, and she was in love with William's best friend, Mr. Bingley, who had just found out that his infatuation with Jane was reciprocated."

"I can see this now. Two near-couples trying to win over hearts in the middle of a funeral! Sounds like it should be a classic folk song accompanied by a set of fiddles."

Georgiana let out another giggle. Henry was so relaxed and comfortable around everyone. He reminded her a great deal of Richard but with an even greater flair for the unusual. Henry didn't seem to fear what others thought of him. He seemed to be his own person. He was charming indeed. He was rather rough around the edges as well, but that only made him more interesting.

The thought came to her that if someone wanted to know more about him, all they had to do was glance at the open book. If she was going to get to know him, as her brother dearly wished, she would have to glance in his direction.

She sighed, then asked, "Are you a romantic, Henry?" It was her attempt to piece together the jigsaw puzzle named Henry Darcy.

She could immediately see he was uncomfortable. Henry appeared to fidget a little. It was the first time she had seen him nervous. His fingers adjusted his cravat, and then he glanced at Mr. Pastel and said, "Don't judge me too harshly, Pastel. I do enjoy the occasional love story, but that does not make me less of a man. I love to fence, and back home in America, we play a great deal of sports. Americans do not spend days on end like this— *lollygagging.*" He turned back to Georgiana. "But, yes, I suppose I am a romantic. When I love something, I do put my heart into it."

He threw his leg over the other in an attempt to be nonchalant. He continued, "I suspect when I love someone, I will be completely devoted. I believe my intentions will be very clear. I certainly hope so. I will try very hard not to make the same mistake as Darcy—that is to say, I hope my offer of marriage will not come as a complete surprise to the lady in question."

Georgiana was intrigued by his answer. He seemed to be a very passionate man. It was interesting to hear him admit to being a romantic and enjoying the occasional love story. She realized that she had been staring at Henry for quite some time, and the silence was growing thick.

She turned to Mr. Pastel and caught him looking at her with thick, dark-brown eyelashes. His chestnut hair was always perfectly combed back, but there was a definite wave to the longer hair that came down to his collar. He smiled at her, and it felt natural to smile back in return.

Mr. Pastel held her gaze for a prolonged moment. Something passed between them, and Georgiana could not understand it. It was as if he had a secret for her. He was about to speak, but something made her stop him and ask, "Mr. Pastel, do you judge Henry for being a romantic?"

"I doubt that would be fair, as the question implies that I am not."

She lifted her eyebrow at his statement, but it seemed that was all he was going to clarify.

Mr. Pastel broke their locked gaze and turned to Henry. "Do you wish to hear the rest of the story of Mr. and Mrs. Darcy?"

Henry jovially said, "Well, I think he just answered your question, Georgiana! It seems Mr. Pastel is just as excited about this love story as I am! What a pair of sappy men we are! Perhaps we should challenge each other to a manly duel to suppress our feminine side. I say . . . fisticuffs! Nothing could be better than a few good punches to get a man's chest hair to grow in thicker!" Henry quickly stood and stepped forward, facing Mr. Pastel with his hands in front of him in fists. He jabbed one false punch and then ducked as if he dodging a blow.

Georgiana knew he was joking, and she couldn't help but laugh. Mr. Pastel leaned back and smirked, made no effort to stand, then folded his arms in front of him.

Henry looked back down at her and winked. He dropped his fists and then stood upright and placed two hands on the lapels of his jacket and in a very thick proper English accent said, "Well played, Pastel. I see who is the better man. You are right, there is no shame in being a romantic." He then returned to his seat, and the charade was over and he returned to the slightly Americanized accent and said, "Now, do tell me the rest of the love story."

Georgiana and Mr. Pastel took turns finishing the story of how William's loving ministrations to Elizabeth during her illness had revealed a different side of the man she had once declared she would never marry, and that the gardens she had seen in her illness were really Pemberley's gardens. Then Mr. Pastel explained that they still had faced considerable disapproval from Lady Catherine and how Lady Anne had come to their rescue.

When they concluded their story, Henry sighed. "It sounds like God himself had a hand in arranging this particular love match," he mused. It was endearing to see him so invested in his cousin's happily ever after. Georgiana couldn't help but think to herself, *Maybe there is some hope of a love match for me after all.* She would just have to keep an open mind.

CHAPTER 4

Georgiana checked once more on the bride, who was wearing a beautiful silk ivory and Ile d'Aix lace dress. It was a modest gown with full-length sleeves. Charlotte had claimed the morning might be too chilly for short sleeves. But Georgiana knew she simply preferred the more modest dress.

"Oh, Charlotte!" she gasped. "Richard will not be able to focus on the vows. You are stunning!"

Before Charlotte had a chance to blush, Georgiana gave her a sweet kiss on the cheek, leaving Charlotte in Elizabeth's care.

Georgiana, her brother, Henry, and Mr. Pastel were the first to arrive at the church. Richard's parents, Lord and Lady Matlock, came next, followed by Charlotte's parents, the Lucases, who had been invited to share in the festivities with their soon to be in-laws at Matlock house for the last week. They had dinner together three nights ago. Georgiana had been impressed by the Matlocks' warm welcome of the Lucases. They all seemed to be getting along nicely.

Georgiana's uncle, Lord Matlock, came and found her at the entry of the chapel and helped to greet the guests. She was always slightly afraid of her uncle, but he was in a good mood this morning and was being warm and kind to all the guests.

During a momentary pause in the arrivals, Lord Matlock leaned over and whispered, "I do not doubt that the next wedding will be yours."

She felt the heat in her cheeks from such a thought, and she put a hand up to her face to cool them. She fidgeted slightly and looked down at the ground. It was a long moment before she could look up at her uncle and respond. "I will be hard pressed to find a partner as well matched for me as Charlotte is for Richard."

Lord Matlock smiled broadly and said, "Indeed, indeed. I cannot say I am in anyway displeased with the match my son has made. What a fine family! But you should look for someone with a title or connections. That is the only drawback to Mrs. Collins."

Georgiana felt quite uncomfortable discussing potential matches with her uncle and looked away, only to see Lady Catherine de Bourgh stepping from her carriage. If she thought her uncle had too much to say on the matter, her Aunt Catherine would be far worse to endure. She curtsied and silently turned to go find her seat.

*****

Benjamin Pastel hadn't been meaning to keep an eye on Miss Darcy, but he had been somewhat alarmed to see her walking awkwardly—dutifully, in fact—to the entry of the church to greet arriving guests. He had enough previous interaction with her to know that she would feel uncomfortable in such a large group. When he saw her blush with embarrassment in front of Lord Matlock, he felt a surge of protectiveness bubble up, prompting him to make his way along the growing crowd in her direction. He soon found Henry Darcy doing the same thing.

Henry said, "Did you see it too?"

Benjamin nodded. "I am afraid she is not in her element here. She does better with small groups or guests in her home."

Henry seemed surprised by his assessment. "How do you know Georgiana so well?"

Mr. Pastel carefully considered his words. "I met Miss Darcy last October at the Pemberley house party. Later, we spent two more weeks at your aunt's estate when Lady Anne married a close friend of mine, Captain Jersey." Henry seemed to be waiting for more explanation than that. "We were thrown in each other's company quite a bit during those two weeks, because everyone else was paired off into couples. We are merely friends." Henry raised his eyebrow slightly, but he appeared to give up; Miss Darcy was heading in their direction.

Her golden hair was pulled up into a beautiful coiffure. She looked more mature than he had ever seen her. The light danced on her delicate jaw and upturned nose. He suddenly felt uncomfortable in his dark-gray frock coat. Should he have worn his blue coat to the wedding?

She smiled brightly at the two of them, and he bowed to her, suddenly finding himself at a loss for words. Her delicate lips had a touch of delightful color to them.

Henry Darcy spoke up, "Tell me, Georgiana, am I honor bound to challenge your uncle to a duel? Lord Matlock seemed to make you quite uncomfortable!" She giggled slightly and smiled at Henry.

Why hadn't Benjamin thought of something witty to say to her? He shifted his weight and let them laugh with each other over it. Henry commented how lovely she looked, and again Benjamin wished he had said something on that topic as well.

A familiar-looking lady, whose name he could not place right away, was headed in their direction. She had dark-brown locks, and her eyes were curiously examining Henry.

The mystery woman stopped right behind Miss Darcy and touched her elbow. Miss Darcy turned around and saw the lady, which elicited an excited squeal of glee. The two ladies embraced, and then Georgiana turned to them and made the introductions.

"May I introduce Lady Jane Andrews, my dearest friend! This is my cousin, Mr. Henry Darcy, who has been away in the Americas."

Of course! Benjamin had met her briefly at Pemberley's house party.

Henry bowed deeply while keeping his eyes fixed on Lady Jane Andrews's face. He stood and reached for her hand and bowed a second time, kissing it. Lady Jane beamed with pleasure, and then she looked at Benjamin.

Miss Darcy said, "And you remember Mr. Benjamin Pastel, from the house party last October at Pemberley. He is a friend of my brother." Benjamin tried not to notice how she had introduced him as her brother's friend instead of hers.

Regardless, he bowed to Lady Jane and said, "How do you do, my lady?"

"I am well, thank you."

"I am so pleased your father let you come!" Georgiana squealed. "I need a bit of moral support. I cannot decide if I am losing a cousin or gaining one!"

Lady Jane laughed. "Well, I should confess it did not take long to convince my father to attend the wedding of Lord

Matlock's son. You know how my father is with strengthening connections."

"Oh, yes!" They giggled as if they had girlish secrets they had pinky sworn to keep between them. "Forgive us, Henry and Mr. Pastel. It is just that we have not seen each other for so long! Lady Jane has been at Hawthorn Hall these last four months, and we have not seen each other for two months before that!"

Benjamin asked, "Is that Hawthorn Hall of Derbyshire? You would not be related to the Earl of Porterhouse?"

"Why, yes, he is my father! Do you know him?"

"I have done business with him." Lady Jane gave Mr. Pastel a curious look. "I am a solicitor," he explained. "Your father did business with my late father for at least twenty years. I am no longer his main solicitor, but we still keep in touch. If I am not mistaken, your father is planning on a very large remodel of Hawthorn Hall. I should like to hear about it after the service."

"I would be delighted," Lady Jane replied.

Benjamin could sense Georgiana looking at him, and he glanced her way. She quickly averted her eyes. He wondered at its import. He was slightly distracted and was not fully attending the conversation that ensued.

The music started, and he noticed that people were taking their seats. Henry paid a well thought-out compliment to Lady Jane and offered to escort her to her seat. At first, Benjamin was frustrated with himself for not offering to do so himself. But then he realized that meant he could offer his arm to Miss Darcy, and that thought delighted him.

Without delay, he did so, and was rewarded with a genuine smile. A gentle rosiness had come to her cheeks. They walked toward the front of the chapel. He suddenly realized he did not know where she wished to sit. "Would you like to sit on the bride's side or the Fitzwilliam side? I know you were debating the issue before dinner last night."

"Yes, I was. Since the Fitzwilliam side is so well attended, I shall sit with Charlotte's family."

He placed a hand over the one on his arm and patted it. Of course she would choose to offer support where it was needed most. That was just like Miss Darcy.

Georgiana tried to pay attention to the services. She couldn't believe how beautiful Charlotte was. After considerable debate, Richard had chosen to wear his false arm for the wedding. Charlotte loved him in spite of losing his left arm in battle, however, Richard did not wish to stand with Charlotte at his side and not be able to escort her down the aisle.

"Dearly beloved," the pastor began, "we are gathered together here in the sight of God, and in the face of this congregation, to join together this man and this woman in holy matrimony; which is an honorable estate, instituted of God in the time of man's innocence . . ."

Georgiana looked around and saw the many friends and family who had all waited so patiently for this moment. Richard, especially, had faced tremendous obstacles in winning Charlotte's heart. He had never been uncomfortable around ladies before, but even the brave warrior had been nervous in the face of true love. But looking at him now, he was not nervous in the slightest. He looked at Charlotte with so much devotion and tenderness that Georgiana had to look away.

The pastor continued. "First, it was ordained for the procreation of children, to be brought up in the fear and nurture of the Lord, and to the praise of his holy name. Secondly, it was ordained for a remedy against sin, and to avoid fornication; that such persons as have not the gift of contingency might marry, and keep themselves undefiled members of Christ's body. Thirdly, it was ordained for the mutual society, help, and comfort, that the one ought to have of the other, both in prosperity and adversity. Into which holy estate these two persons present come now to be joined. Therefore, if any man can show any just cause, why they may not lawfully be joined together, let him now speak, or else hereafter forever hold his peace."

Out of the corner of her eye, Georgiana saw Lord Matlock put a firm hand on Aunt Catherine's arm, stilling her.

Georgiana smiled, and Mr. Pastel, who was sitting next to her, looked up at her. She realized that his brown eyes were the color of well-toasted almonds. He smiled briefly at her and looked back to the front. *He is really rather handsome.* For some reason, the thought brought a blush to her face.

She turned her attention back to the front. Colonel Fitzwilliam looked to the pastor as the clergyman said, "Wilt thou, Colonel Richard Fitzwilliam, have this woman to be thy wedded wife, to live together after God's ordinance in the holy estate of matrimony? Wilt thou love her, comfort her, honor, and keep her in sickness and in health; and, forsaking all other, keep thee only unto her, so long as ye both shall live?"

Colonel Fitzwilliam looked at Charlotte again and smiled handsomely. "I will," he vowed.

Georgiana couldn't help but feel goose bumps at how romantic it all was. Every look and every word spoke of their love and devotion.

"Wilt thou, Charlotte Collins, have this man to thy wedded husband, to live together after God's ordinance in the holy estate of matrimony? Wilt thou obey him, and serve him, love, honor, and keep him in sickness and in health; and, forsaking all other, keep thee only unto him, so long as ye both shall live?"

"I will."

The pastor asked, "Who giveth this woman to Colonel Fitzwilliam?"

Sir William Lucas acknowledged his part, then, upon the direction of the pastor, Sir William placed Charlotte's hand in Richard's. The couple turned toward each other, and the ceremony continued.

"Repeat after me. I, Colonel Richard Fitzwilliam, take thee, Charlotte Collins, to be my wedded wife, to have and to hold from this day forward, for better, for worse, for richer, for poorer, in sickness and in health, to love and to cherish, till death us do part, according to God's holy ordinance; and thereto I plight thee my troth."

Richard recited the vow and then the pastor had Charlotte do likewise.

Then Richard repeated the next part after the pastor: "With this ring I thee wed, with my body I thee worship, and with all my worldly goods I thee endow." Richard put the ring on the fourth finger on her left hand. Georgiana had a sudden flash of anxiety. Where would Charlotte put his ring? He had no left hand!

Charlotte smiled at him and then put the ring on the fourth

finger on his right hand, giving it a subtle squeeze. They both turned to the pastor.

"Forasmuch as Colonel Fitzwilliam and Charlotte Collins have consented together in holy wedlock, and have witnessed the same before God and this company, and thereto have given and pledged their troth either to other, and have declared the same by giving and receiving of a ring, and by joining of hands—I pronounce that they be man and wife, together. In the name of the Father, and of the Son, and of the Holy Ghost. Amen. Colonel Fitzwilliam, you may now kiss your wife, Mrs. Charlotte Fitzwilliam."

Richard smirked wickedly, and Charlotte gave him a look of warning. He was obviously planning to embarrass her, but he brought her hand to his lips and kissed it instead. At first, Georgiana was disappointed that they did not kiss on the lips, but then she was relieved for Charlotte. Propriety was very important to her. Richard understood that and respected her for it. Richard had told Georgiana many times about his proposal the night of his hero's welcome ball. She loved hearing about how he had told Charlotte how he loved her. He had told her, "You are a mother, a friend, a sister, a daughter, and if you will do me the great honor of accepting my hand, you will be a wife."

But Georgiana's favorite part of the story was when Charlotte tearfully told her how he much he respected her for triumphing over so many adversities. "Your character is that of a war hero."

Charlotte had confessed to Georgiana that she had never known a man could be so tender with his words.

And now, as he tenderly kissed her hand in front of all of their friends and family, Georgiana once again realized that they had the kind of marriage that she wanted. The kiss was the perfect ending of a ceremony that was really just a beginning!

*****

They all headed toward Matlock House for the wedding breakfast. Benjamin was pleased to escort Miss Darcy again to the Darcy carriage. Mr. Darcy handed his wife in and then reached for his sister. Benjamin was a little disappointed in missing the opportunity to help her in himself. He was about to enter the carriage when he realized that Henry was just then coming up behind him.

"My apologies," Henry explained. "I hope you were not waiting long. I thought Lady Jane Andrews could use help getting into her carriage."

"We were not waiting at all," Benjamin said. He had been so preoccupied with escorting Miss Darcy that he had not noticed that Henry had slipped away from them. They both stepped up into the carriage, and Mr. Darcy tapped on the roof. The three Darcys were sitting across from the bachelors.

Mrs. Darcy exclaimed, "What a beautiful ceremony!"

"Oh, I agree, Elizabeth!" Miss Darcy said, her eyes bright and vibrant. "And what wonderful weather we are having today."

Henry agreed, "I'd say! One of the few things that are similar between Manhattan and London is that blue skies should be noticed and appreciated, because they do not happen every day!"

Mr. Darcy said, "Truly? I did not know that England and the Americas shared a similar climate."

Mrs. Darcy said, "Oh, William, I am sure rain happens everywhere. What is the weather in New York like at this time of year?"

"Don't get me wrong, there are stark differences in climates. Our summers are hotter, and our winters are fierce. But you are right, Mrs. Darcy—the rain is the same. Autumn in New York is my favorite time of year. The trees on the east coast are a sight I will miss. We have aspens that turn daffodil yellow and maples that are brilliant red. A whole spectrum of color drops from the canopy above you like never-ending gifts from God. October is a month of vibrant colors. With brisk winds to tickle the trees, one is in the presence of a constant rainbow shower of leaves."

Miss Darcy sighed, "That sounds lovely."

Benjamin couldn't help but be delighted, not in the leaves around them, but in the soft voice of Miss Darcy. Its tone was silky in nature, making him want to reach out and touch it; it drew him to her every time she spoke. He wondered how a woman who said so little could influence him so much.

CHAPTER 5

Elizabeth had begged Charlotte to let her host the wedding breakfast at Darcy House. She knew that Charlotte and Richard's townhouse would have only the barest of servants until the couple returned from their wedding trip. Lord and Lady Matlock had offered to host a breakfast, but Elizabeth insisted. After all, she still owed so much to the newlyweds for their help in bringing her and Will together.

Elizabeth watched the guests arrive and greet the happy couple. The joy that radiated from the newlyweds' eyes made her ache with an overwhelming gratitude. Charlotte's first husband had used force to coerce her to his will. Richard found that there was a much better use of the sheer grit that Charlotte possessed. Her strength was one of the things that Richard loved most about her.

Georgiana's soft voice whispered behind her, "They really will be quite happy."

Elizabeth had caught the wistfulness in her voice. She turned to Georgiana and replied, "I do believe so. And you shall too when the time is right."

"I am not so sure about that."

"I am."

"How do you know?" Georgiana glanced across the room towards Henry who was laughing gaily with her friend Lady Jane Andrews.

Elizabeth saw a deep-seated insecurity flash across Georgiana's face. "Georgiana, your fate is not written in ancient granite tombs. It is yours to decide."

Still watching Henry, Georgiana took a deep breath and sighed. Her voice came out shaky and unsure. "I fear leaving the decision up to *me* might be part of the problem. Perhaps I really should let William arrange something for me. Look at how deceived I was by George Wickham."

Elizabeth glanced around. There was not a soul in hearing

distance. It was the first time Georgiana had ever mentioned Wickham to her. She knew Georgiana had confided in Charlotte to some extent, but Georgiana had never opened up to Elizabeth about him. But she could see by the distant look in Georgiana's eyes that the young woman was reliving those fateful weeks in Ramsgate two-and-a-half years ago when she was fifteen. William had told Elizabeth how Wickham had secretly courted Georgiana there and wooed her until she agreed to an elopement. Luckily her brother had surprised her with a visit the day before their planned departure, effectively preventing it from taking place.

Elizabeth took Georgiana's elbow and quietly guided her toward the door. They both smiled and greeted visitors along the way, who were standing around enjoying the breakfast foods.

As they entered the library, Elizabeth closed the door behind her. "Georgiana, I am not going to say I do not know to what you are referring. William told me what happened between you and Wickham. But I do not think you should question your own judgment because of it. After all, it must be remembered that *you* revealed the plan to your brother. Your choice showed deep love and devotion to Will, as well as good judgment in knowing what was right. I do not think you would have actually gone to Gretna Green."

Tears welled in Georgiana's eyes. "But I would have!" she exclaimed. And with less force, she added, "I do not know exactly when—it may not have been that day, but I would have gone. It is true that I had already begun to think of excuses to delay it, but I think, eventually, I would have married Wickham. He would have worn me down until I had no other choice." She bowed her head, "That is why I cannot be trusted to know what love is when it comes around."

"Oh, Georgiana! I can imagine how you must feel, my dear. I know you must be afraid of being deceived a second time. You opened your heart to Wickham, and he rewarded you with only selfishness and greed, all because he wanted your dowry. But it is not your fault. George Wickham is conniving and intelligent, and he cares for no one but himself." The thought of Wickham filled her with an all-too-familiar nausea. *He fooled us all, not just Georgiana. To think that I . . .* She imagined Wickham's cold eyes searching a crowd, hunting for his next pretty prey, for the next girl who might bring him some fun. Elizabeth shuddered. She tried to be a good Christian woman, but she admitted the news of his death had come as a relief.

Elizabeth would like nothing better than to put the whole business far from her mind, but she knew she had a duty to help Georgiana. She reached for the young woman's hand. "You must not blame yourself, my dear. For Wickham preyed on you as surely as a wolf pack stalks its weakened prey." Georgiana looked away. "Did you know that a wolf pack sometimes follows an injured animal for miles before they attack?"

"Truly?"

"Indeed. They fight using their heads. How else could they bring down an animal as strong as a moose? Goodness, a moose is five times their size! And they have fearsome, sharp antlers that can pierce a wolf hide. But a moose never battles a single wolf, does it?"

"I suppose not."

Elizabeth took Georgiana's shoulders in her hands and made her look at her because what she would say next was very important. "You are like the moose. Graceful, beautiful, and elegant. You are practically the royalty of the forest. Wickham used an entire team of wolves to convince you to elope."

Confusion highlighted Georgiana's features. "What do you mean?"

She appeared to truly not understand what Elizabeth meant. Elizabeth paused, uncomfortable with the realization that Will had never told Georgiana the entire truth. "Georgiana, Wickham and Mrs. Younge worked together to deceive you."

Further shock flashed in Georgiana's eyes, followed by awareness. "Is that why William dismissed her? I thought it was because she did not do her job to protect me as my companion. I had no idea that she was part of the plan. Oh, dear!"

"You must not blame yourself. Will was deceived by her as well. He selected her to be your companion, not knowing of any connection between Mrs. Younge and Wickham. He has berated himself for it ever since. But it was more than the two of them that were dishonest. Why do you think she asked you to leave Tessa, your lady's maid, here in London? Mrs. Younge carefully chose servants which would turn a blind eye to your growing relationship with Wickham."

"How do you know this?"

"Will told me," Elizabeth admitted. "After Ramsgate, he was terribly upset. He made a thorough investigation of how an unmarried man could have been repeatedly admitted to the house and seen around town with you, without anyone alerting him that something was amiss. In the end, he dismissed more than Mrs. Younge. Two footmen and a maid were sent away as well."

"I had no idea," Georgiana murmured. The young woman seemed stunned by the information. "But why did they help her? Why risk losing their position?"

"It seems they were each promised a bonus at month's end."

Georgiana took a slow, deep breath.

"Honestly, I feel sorry for them. Will is fairly sure Mrs. Younge never intended to pay them. But they could not remain in the household after that. Not after such a breach of trust."

Georgiana stepped to the side and walked to the window. It was a prolonged moment as she stared out at the street. She finally said, "So, he hunted in a pack. I was fooled by more than just him. And I was not the only one fooled."

"Yes," Elizabeth confirmed. "I am sorry to bring up such painful memories. I only tell you this to explain why you are not to blame. He preyed on you, Georgiana." Elizabeth followed her to the window and watched her.

"I really did think I was in love." Shadows darkened Georgiana's eyes.

"Do not doubt your ability to recognize true love when it appears on your doorstep. Because I am here to tell you that when love knocks, it takes your breath away. There is no denying its influence on you."

Georgiana nodded and turned around again slowly. "May I ask you one more question?"

"Of course."

"What does it feel like?" Georgiana asked.

"Love? What does it feel like to be in love?"

Georgiana nodded.

Elizabeth hesitated, unsure how to reassure her. Describing love was like trying to describe the color green to a blind man.

Would her description be adequate? She somewhat murmured this thought out loud.

She then paused before answering. "It starts off slow," Elizabeth began, "like a sunrise. And just like a sunrise, you do not notice how it warms you from the inside out. But, little by little, things become clearer as the sun burns off the fog and lightens the landscape. It is a slow process. So slow in fact, that it is hard to say when the sunrise is over because the transition is so subtle.

"And when the sun finally does come up, what was foggy or full of shadowy confusion is seen for what it really is. The tree branches that whip in the night wind now can be understood for what they really are—moving branches. You finally understand that there are no strangers lurking in wait to attack. In short, when we fall in love, we gain vision and understanding of not just ourselves—our desires and preferences—but also the people around us and their strengths and weaknesses. Just as the sun rises slowly, bringing light and understanding of our environment, love allows us to comprehend the beauty in the world around us. Fear, sorrow, and bitterness drip away. Everything is sweeter, more beautiful, and you cannot contain your happiness."

Georgiana smiled. "A sunrise."

"Yes, falling in love is like watching a sunrise."

Georgiana closed the distance and embraced Elizabeth. "Thank you," she whispered.

Elizabeth kissed the young woman's cheek and wiped away her tears. "Now, I believe there is a lovely couple who are expecting a big musical number to send them off. Shall we return to the group?"

"Of course."

*****

Georgiana walked in somewhat of a daze back to the ballroom where everyone was gathered. She had caught a glimpse of what it might feel like to fall in love as Elizabeth described the effects of a sunrise. Those stolen minutes in the library had done much to lift the weight off her shoulders.

Could love be as subtle as a sunrise? Elizabeth seemed to imply that it was not some dramatic, life-altering event, like a knight in shining armor saving his fair maiden. And if no heroics were required, then anyone around her could touch her heart if she let them. So what did it matter if William introduced him to her? What if she met him on the street? What if it was someone she had known for years?

It could be anyone! The thought did not distress her in the slightest. In fact, it brought her a great deal of peace to know that love could happen at any time.

Was she ready? Another peaceful thought came to mind. She was not required to know whom she would marry at this time. In fact, there could be months, maybe even years, before she would clearly see the love of her life for who he was . . . her missing other half.

But for the first time, she knew, in the deepest part of her heart, that she need not worry about finding a "good match". She realized that she was wise enough to recognize a good match. And who knew her better than herself? William came in a close second, but even he did not know her deepest fears or desires. Isn't that what she wished William understood? She didn't want an arranged marriage; she wanted to find love. She just needed his patience and gentle guidance to keep her away from the wolves. All she needed was to wait for that blessed sunrise, and her match would be revealed in all his glory.

With new eyes, she glanced around the room. William had seen her come in and smiled at her, but his eyes soon lit up at the sight of Elizabeth behind her. Elizabeth walked to him and laid a gentle hand on William's face like she always did. *As it should be.* True love made them blind to the others around them.

She looked at her aunt and uncle, the Matlocks, and, for the first time, noticed how Lord Matlock put a gentle hand on his wife's lower back, making her glance at him with affection. Her aunt subtly stepped closer to her husband.

Charlotte showed her devotion with the deepest of blushes when Richard winked at her, rewarding him with that glorious smile he adored. Even her cousin Anne and her new husband, Captain Jersey, were holding hands; his subtle caress was not lost on Georgiana.

These were the examples she saw in her life. Each one, in their own time and in their own way, had stepped out into the adult world and been asked to risk their heart, their future, and their independence, just as she was being asked to. It dawned on her that they had all survived. Not only that, but they were better for it. Each of these four matches was selfless and pure, radiating the beauty of companionship and devotion that love brought into their lives.

How could she go wrong? She took a deep breath. She suddenly knew in her heart that didn't need to worry about not recognizing love when she found it. With so many examples to follow, she knew she would find it in her own way.

She smiled to herself. Perhaps finding a match would not be such a terrible thing. Perhaps she did not need to be always looking over her shoulder, second guessing herself, afraid of messing it up.

Just then she felt a gentle touch on her elbow. "Miss Darcy?"

She turned around and smiled. "Yes, Mr. Pastel?"

"I was asked to enquire if you were ready."

"Indeed I am. I am ready to play."

*****

Soon after her performance of Bach, they all gathered outside to send off the happy couple. Georgiana could not help but allow happy tears to fall from her cheeks. She clapped and giggled as Richard handed his new bride into the newly-acquired Fitzwilliam carriage.

Henry and Mr. Pastel were on each side of her. As the carriage pulled away, the children all started ringing their handbells as valiantly as they could. A good number of them raced after the couple, shouting felicitations as the carriage disappeared in the distance. Henry chuckled next to her with a deep resonance and said, "Well, Georgiana, shall we head inside?"

She watched for a moment longer as the carriage rounded the corner, until it was eventually out of sight. Joyful tears ran freely down her cheeks. When she looked down, she saw that Mr. Pastel was handing her his handkerchief. "Oh, thank you. How thoughtful!" She dabbed at her eyes and turned to follow the crowd back into the house.

Mr. Pastel asked, "Will you miss them?"

"Oh, definitely."

"You are very close to Mrs. Fitzwilliam, are you not?"

"Indeed. She has become one of my dearest friends."

"She is quite a bit older than you are though."

"Yes. Older and wiser friends are the best kind."

Mr. Pastel's voice was soft and comforting. "Young and innocent ones are good too." He offered his arm, and she willingly took it.

Henry had already reached the top of the steps, and Georgiana looked up to see her friend Jane there, smiling down at her. "Oh, Lady Jane, you missed it! They just left."

"I did not miss it. I watched it from the entryway. So they are off to the Lake District?"

"Yes," Georgiana replied. "I am afraid we will be without Charlotte and Richard for two whole weeks, my lady."

By this time, all three had reached the porch. Jane frowned slightly and leaned into Georgiana. She replied, "Surely you know you can call me Jane when my father is not around."

"I know, but *you* must know he would be very displeased to hear it. I would hate to be caught making the mistake in front of him. You are the daughter of an earl, after all."

Henry chuckled again, and Georgiana saw his lip turn up. Henry asked Jane, "And what shall *I* call you when your father is not around, my lady?"

Jane blushed brightly, and her eyes danced with delight. "I am afraid I cannot give you leave to call me by my Christian name, sir, for there would be a riot in the streets if it were heard by my father's ears. I am sorry, Mr. Darcy, but you must address me as 'my lady'."

Henry bowed deeply and when he stood erect, his face demonstrated the most absurd look on his face. It was a mixture of mirth and embarrassment. Georgiana was eager to hear what Henry was going to say.

"Well, my lady, that wasn't hard." Henry was holding back a smirk.

Jane looked puzzled. "What was not hard?"

Henry finally let out a deep chuckle and answered, "You just gave me leave to call you *my* lady! It appears we have come to an understanding in the few short hours I have known you! I'm delighted!"

Georgiana held her breath, resisting the outright laughter that threatened to escape. Jane was really quite shy, which was one of the reasons they got along so famously, and to be teased so mercilessly was new territory for Jane. Her father was the strictest of guardians. He insisted upon propriety and maintaining the proper behavior in any situation.

Georgiana could see the cogs of Jane's mind working as the seconds ticked by. Knowing Henry, Georgiana surmised that if Jane were offended, Henry would probably condemn her as prideful or, much more likely, tease her even further. If she were to scold him for such flirtatious behavior, then she would be defined as something she was not—a prude. She and Jane had had several conversations about what they hoped their first kiss would be like. If she were to show her marked embarrassment for having flirted— unintentionally as it was—with a man she hardly knew, then she most definitely would set a precedent that only encouraged him to tease further.

They all waited to see how she would respond. Finally Jane made her choice. She laughed.

She had chosen to be herself, sweet and charmingly beautiful, and, oh, so lovable. The laugh infected all four of them. As always, Jane had chosen to find the joy the moment could bring to everyone, which was one of the things Georgiana loved most about her. She was always the optimist. She had chosen to laugh outright at Henry's bold statement. Georgiana was so very proud to be called her friend at that moment.

Jane finally caught her breath and exclaimed, "Goodness, I must be the biggest flirt in the country, for I seem to insist on being everyone's lady!"

Henry offered his arm and escorted her in, "Ah, but, my lady, at this very moment, *I* am the one with the honor. Where shall my lady and I go?"

Jane was blushing brightly, and it was clear she was trying hard not to look him in the eye.

Oh my, isn't Henry a terrible flirt!

It seemed the next few months would be entertaining, to say the least, laced with laughter and memorable moments. And perhaps it would be—no, she would not allow herself to imagine what might be in store for her. She would just have to wait and see, for she had yet to see the sun rise in the east.

There might be hope for Georgiana yet.

CHAPTER 6

Benjamin Pastel entered the library of Darcy House, and, by the light of his single candle, found his way to the big mahogany desk. In the pre-dawn darkness, the small flame was not enough to light up the entire room, but it provided enough light so that he would not run into anything. He lit the sconces along the wall, and the room started to glow. He would probably only need their light for another twenty minutes or so.

Darcy had allowed him to use the desk in the library for his business while he stayed at Darcy House, and Pastel was anxious to get to work. He put down the candle and opened the file he had received from Darcy's agent. It was full of potential office sites for his business. The agent had been good enough to not only detail each and every building, including the purchasing costs, but he had also drawn a rough map of each location. Benjamin did not wish to be directly in the center of London—he knew he could never afford the cost, not if he intended to keep his prices competitive, and certainly not if he wished to purchase a second-floor apartment as well.

Hopefully one on a quiet street, without the bustle of merchants constantly at his window, but near a shopping district. A well-placed sign in the shopping district would be far better advertising than a weekly ad in the *London Tribune*. And far more economical.

The first site looked promising, but the second site wasn't even worth a thorough read through. The price alone would take all his savings and leave nothing for furniture, let alone a cushion for times when business was slow. He still had to consider reserving enough for a modest townhouse to live in as well, especially if he was ever to get married.

He sighed. Here he was, two-and-thirty years old and making plans to start over completely. He was well established in Liverpool. This decision would sacrifice everything he had built there. But he knew it was the right thing to do. He could not align himself with Clyde a day longer than necessary. He planned to meet with him today to discuss the exchange of offices.

This was why he was up so early, not that he wouldn't have been otherwise. He was naturally an early riser. At home in Liverpool, he usually took the time when the world was still asleep to read and practice his pianoforte. But he certainly couldn't play at this time of the morning, not when he was a guest.

And now Liverpool was no longer his home. He had no home. The thought saddened him deeply. He was living off the good grace of a former client.

Not that Darcy wasn't a wonderful host. He certainly was. And it had seemed like a good idea at the time. But being in Miss Darcy's presence so often was proving a little more difficult than he had expected.

There was no denying that her beautiful blonde hair and her classic blue eyes were captivating, but the more he saw her day in and day out, the more he saw a lady unlike anyone he had ever met before. She was charming, graceful, fiercely loyal, and impeccably well-mannered. And if he were ever privy to that unique look of adoration that she bestowed so generously on those she loved—the angelic expression that she shared freely with her brother and Colonel Fitzwilliam—his heart would probably stop altogether.

It was a look that engulfed her whole face. He first saw it when she spoke of her friend Charlotte, now Mrs. Fitzwilliam. He knew it so well by now that he could identify it from a hundred feet away. It wasn't just her eyes, it was her entire countenance. Loyalty and compassion emanated from her face. Her smile would push up her cheeks just enough to bring a roundness to them, and then the classic Darcy dimples emerged. Her dimples were more subtle than her brother's, but they made her entire face soft and feminine.

He saw it again when her cousin, Anne de Bourgh, married Captain Jersey. Anne had been a frail-looking woman when Benjamin first met her, but since meeting Captain Jersey, she had grown into herself. She was everything delightful and charming now. He remembered a conversation with Miss Darcy while at Rosings Park, before Anne's wedding, when Miss Darcy expressed how very proud she was of her. Her affection and devotion to her cousin was palpable.

Captain Jersey, a groom without a bride, had a bit of urgency in his gait. He stopped at the table and asked the four players, "Have you seen Miss De Bourgh?"

"Captain," Miss Darcy's soft, gentle, yet persuasive voice reprimanded, "She has requested you simply call her Anne."

The captain's smile widened. "I see she has not refrained from sharing our private conversations," he replied.

Miss Darcy, with a rarely seen level of playfulness, replied, "We might as well be sisters, instead of cousins, for all the gossip we share now." She seemed genuinely proud that she and her cousin had such fondness for each other.

"Then you should know by now," Captain Jersey continued, "that it will take a wee bit of tenacity to change the habits of an old man like me. I still cannot believe I am getting married again. I must have lost all reason! Truth is, I should question her sanity . . . it was she who consented to marry me!"

Georgiana's sweet and genuine giggle escaped before she said, "You are good for Anne; the tenderness you show her has transformed my cousin entirely. I am so proud of her, for there is no doubt that she followed her heart. Love does not care about money or rank. And certainly not about a difference in age."

And then Anne walked in the room, seeing no one but her betrothed.

Mr. Pastel had to look away, and naturally he looked to his partner, Georgiana. There it was, that look of adoration and ultimate loyalty.

It was so rare to see someone leak their true self out among those who they do not know well. He felt honored to have caught a rare glimpse of her inner beauty.

Returning to the dimly lit room, he tried to refocus his mind. With another exerted effort to calm his mind and body, he removed the papers from his satchel.

He sighed, looking up at the family portrait hanging on the wall. It was still so dark, that Georgiana's golden hair was the only clue that the proper, stiff, distant-looking girl was Miss Georgiana. The artist did not know how to paint the soul. For Georgiana's soul was . . .

He was beginning to wonder if coming to Darcy House was a good idea. He had admired Miss Darcy before his arrival, but now she seemed flawless. She was in her element here, surrounded by those she loved, and she took his breath away. Anyone who listened to her play the pianoforte could not help but be impressed. She had a way of demanding the attention of those around her. She was, admittedly, a bit shy, but that made her all the more charming. It made her innocent and loveable.

Even Henry Darcy seemed to be taken by her. Benjamin did not think there was any serious regard at the moment, but Georgiana seemed to watch him a great deal.

Georgiana. He played around with her name in his head. It was a delightfully feminine name, a unique one, too. It had a tantalizingly delicious nature to it, one that lingered on the lips, like the aftertaste of a perfectly aged wine.

He had never called her Georgiana before. He had never asked permission to—such a request would have been completely inappropriate. Part of him wished he had a playful nature like Henry did, or could claim a similar kinship, just so he could let the name fall from his lips. He reminded himself that it was entirely improper for him to call her by her Christian name.

It did not stop him from trying it out here in the pre-dawn hours while alone in the library.

A small smile crossed his lips, and he sat back and closed his eyes and imagined bowing over her hand. He would kiss her gloved hand ever so slightly, nothing improper, and then before fully rising from the bow, he would look up at her. She would give him that look, the look of adoration, that he hungered for, and he would say, "You look lovely, Georgiana." His whisper broke the silence. Hearing her name roll off his tongue was just as delicious as he had hoped.

He heard a rustling in the corner of the room, and he opened his eyes. "Who is there?"

"Mr. Pastel? Is that you? It is Georgiana. Did you address me?"

He stood and carried the candle over to where he heard her, his racing heart beating wildly in his chest. She heard him use her name? What must she think of him? He should never have let his imaginations get the best of him.

He was a stickler for the rules of propriety. He was no Henry Darcy. Henry could get away with things like that with all his charm and good grace, but Benjamin only felt safe when the rules were followed. That was what made him such an excellent solicitor. It was why people all over the country sought him out.

"Miss Darcy? What are you doing in the library in the wee hours of the morning? The sun is not even up." She had just begun to stand, and she was brushing her fingers along her skirts to smooth out the wrinkles, which were plentiful.

"I must have fallen asleep. I wanted so badly to see the sunrise that I kept waking myself up and looking at the clock. By five o'clock, I finally decided to come down here and read."

Her hair was still in a plait but the typical curls on each side of her face had been flattened.

She saw where he was looking and put a hand to her hair and said, "I must look affright."

Actually, you have never looked so beautiful. With the candlelight reflected in your glossy eyes and the subtle crease on your cheek from sleeping . . . He certainly could not say what he was thinking. "Here, let me . . ." he reached to her cheek and gently rubbed the impression left on her cheek from sleeping. "You must have been sleeping a while. It is nearly six-thirty."

Even in the candlelight, he could see he had embarrassed her. She looked down at her hands, and her shoulders rose, indicating she took a deep breath. "I am glad you woke me. It looks like I have not missed the sunrise. Would you like to watch it with me?"

He smiled at her. "I would be delighted." Any time with her would be welcomed.

They both turned toward the large bay window that faced east. He now understood why she had come to the library. There was a large grassy area across the street, directly outside of the window. It meant the view was not hindered by another house or building.

They both took a seat on the window seat. The sky had a golden hue to its horizon, and it was beginning to clear exactly where the sun would rise over the trees. Benjamin took turns alternating looking at the sunrise and examining Georgiana. She had a serene look, as if she were literally drinking in the light. Her blonde hair began to be more clearly defined, and he couldn't help but notice that her nightdress was a pale-ivory muslin which hugged her curves charmingly.

He looked away and refocused his attention on the glowing light. It was clear it would be a dramatic presentation. There were hints of red and orange now in the east, and with the scattered clouds, it took on a surreal nature. After a few minutes of watching it unfold, a full spectrum of colors presented itself. The reds and oranges bled into the blues and purples, chasing them to the west.

It was clear that Georgiana—and he knew he was helpless to call her anything else in his mind now—had a certain amount of reverence this morning as she drank in the emerging keeper of the day. It was even more obvious than the growing light in the room. Why she wanted to watch the sunrise so badly was beyond him, but he would stand by and support her in this quest, no matter how out of character it was.

Her body was turned as much as possible without actually taking her feet off the ground, but he could see she hoped to turn further. He wanted her to feel comfortable around him. He hesitated, but then picked up a knee and turned his body more fully toward the window and the celestial display in front of them. It was a more casual position, but he told himself that he did not always have to be formal in his behavior, even though that was what made him most comfortable. His movement had its intended effect on Georgiana. She too bent one knee and was able to turn more without the ache of a twisted back.

He could tell out of the corner of his eye that she had glanced his direction. He met her eyes briefly and smiled at her but said nothing. She turned back toward the growing light that was now lighting up the sky so brightly that his candle was no longer needed, and so he blew it out.

Tiny objects outside began to take shape. He could hear the birds singing their merry tunes. He could see the colors of the cobblestone changing from dark gray to the varying shades of pink and green. Everything took on life. It was a cherished moment in the day for him as well. It was rare that he did not wake before dawn, so he had seen many sunrises over the years.

He rarely had problems sleeping and simply felt rested far earlier in the morning than most people. Rising early meant he could get more done. One of the things he enjoyed the most during these morning hours is seeing how easily solutions to his problems arose in a sharp, rested mind. His mind was unusually clear and unburdened with concerns in the early morning.

He hoped this morning would be no different. For at this moment, his mind was burdened, even overwhelmed, with thoughts of Georgiana. He had been at Darcy House for only a few days, but it was enough to put his admiration for Georgiana in sore need of assessment. If he wasn't careful, he wouldn't be the only one painfully aware of his growing attachment. Admiring her from afar was all fine and good. However, he doubted that Mr. Darcy would be as hospitable if he knew Benjamin was beginning to stare at her like this.

He turned his attention forcibly toward the sunrise again. It was nearly completely risen now. The sun's glow brought a certain vivacity and animation to the world. Outside on the street, a street sweeper was pushing a broom, whistling a cheerful tune. The world had awoken with the sun, and so had his admiration for Georgiana. He wasn't sure if that was entirely appropriate. Her brother, he was sure, would never let her marry a solicitor. Not when true, titled English gentlemen were hovering, waiting for the season to begin like horses at the starting line anticipating the starting gun.

He suddenly felt heavy-hearted. The show was over, and he turned away from the window. Was it really as hopeless as that? Did he simply want something he could never have?

Were there dozens of men lined up, waiting to have stolen moments like these with her? Men like Henry Darcy who would never appreciate the peaceful moment that he just spent with

Georgiana watching the sunrise? Henry would not recognize the reverence that was in her eyes, or the way her breath caught in her throat when the first evidence of the actual sun peeked over the horizon. He would not recognize that, this morning, more than any other, was special to her for some reason. Henry would not know that what Georgiana needed was to drink in the moment until she was satisfied. He would never understand this sunrise had been important enough that she had been restless in her sleep for fear she would miss it.

No, Henry Darcy was a pleasant man, but his jovial attitude would have made an entirely different experience. Benjamin understood Georgiana in a way that Henry did not. Perhaps he still had a chance to win her heart.

He stood and retrieved the shawl she had been sleeping with and draped it over her shoulders.

She glanced up at him with round, moist eyes and said, "Thank you." Her profile highlighted from the sun made a spectacular sight.

She turned around again toward the brightened day. Benjamin quietly said, "It is picturesque." She need not know he was talking about her personal beauty. He cleared his throat. "You should paint it."

"I was just thinking the same thing. How did you know?"

"I was just appreciating the moment. It seemed important to you. It is only natural that you would want to capture it. You seemed to be watching it with a certain amount of reverence."

"Reverence?"

"It is the only way I can describe it. It was like you were thirsty and could not be satisfied with simply observing the sunrise. You wanted to permanently etch it into your memory."

He turned away from the window now that the show was over.

Georgiana replied wistfully, "I suppose you are correct. I think I shall begin to paint it tomorrow. Do you always get up this early?"

"Yes, I enjoy the quiet hours. My body is quite attuned to waking before the sun." He paused, considering whether he should say the thing he was thinking. "Would you like me to knock on your door tomorrow morning so you can watch the sunrise again?"

Her face lit up with enthusiasm. "Would you? It would mean so much if I knew that I would not miss the sunrise. Perhaps I will sleep more deeply tonight. I shall have all my painting supplies set up here. Wake me at six o'clock. That will allow me to dress and mix the paint before the riot of color begins."

"Of course. You will not mind if I work while you paint, do you?"

"Of course not. What are you working on?"

"I am trying to find a new office building. Do you want to see?"

She nodded and stood and followed him to the desk. "Is there anything I can help you with?"

"Perhaps. I am looking for an office that is located just off the main road of a shopping district. A building that is regal and well made. I feel that the building needs to be respectable, because it says a great deal about the tenants that occupy it. I want enough space, perhaps fifteen hundred square feet, so I can have three offices, a reception area, as well as some storage. These papers were sent over by Mr. Darcy's agent." He picked the papers up and showed her.

He continued, "I am not even considering this one. It is too big and the price is beyond prudent. But this one looks big enough. I am unfamiliar with Silverthorn Court."

"Oh, it is a fine area! There is a wonderful café on the corner. Let me see." She took the paper and pointed at the map the agent had drawn. "Right there. It looks like you are actually in the same building as the café. It is one of my favorite places to dine. They serve a custard laced with cinnamon and baked apples. I would do anything for the recipe! Nothing makes me happier than eating that apple custard."

Even though she had said it in jest, he made note of it. "I intend to see it today. I will make sure to sample the custard. Thank you."

"You are welcome. I should probably get ready for the day. Elizabeth's cousins, the Gardiners, are taking me to the circus."

"Say hello to Miss Gardner for me."

"Yes, of course. I had forgotten you had met Avelina last year at Pemberley."

"Delightful girl. What is she now, sixteen?"

"Yes, she turned sixteen this summer. I am sorry you will not be able to go with us. Henry and Lady Jane are coming. I hear there will be a live tiger, and," she whispered, "for a half-penny, I could have a real gypsy tell my fortune! It makes me wonder if she will tell me about my future prince . . ."

He smiled at her enthusiasm. "You will have to tell me all about it. I do have quite a bit of business to attend to. I will be meeting with my brother, Clyde, and presenting a proposal for transferring offices. I intend to buy him out of the London office completely in exchange for the Liverpool office."

"Why is that? You do not wish to be his partner anymore?"

Henry frowned. "It is complicated," he replied. "Let us just say that Clyde has different priorities. He tends to focus his attention in areas that may not be respectable and therefore attracts people like—"

"—Mr. Collins. You need not explain. I have never doubted your honesty. It is obvious to those who meet you. When you executed Mr. Collins's will, I feared that you were just like him. But it was not long before I could tell you were only duty bound to perform what you had been hired to do. I could see the pain it brought you to investigate the stipulations of the will, which I understand were extensive. But you are simply driven to always do what is right. It is who you are."

His chest rose with pride in her very admirable assessment of him. "That is the nicest thing anyone has ever said to me. Thank you." She curtsied and a bright flush appeared on her cheeks. With that, she turned and walked out the door.

Maybe he had a chance to win her after all. Maybe she would be enlightened further to his character if he just gave her enough time. She certainly didn't have an unfavorable opinion of him.

He may not have the birthright of a gentleman, but he had earned her respect so far with little effort on his part. It was a start. One thing he felt strongly about in business was, if you are ever going to see something to the finish, one must start, then persevere. Today was a very good beginning. And he had an abundance of perseverance.

CHAPTER 7

Georgiana was just finishing her breakfast when her brother addressed her. "Georgiana, could you come to my study before you leave for the circus?"

"Is there something wrong?"

"No, of course not. I just have something I would like to address with you privately."

"Of course, William. The Gardiners are dropping their children off in about a half an hour. I just have to gather my things. Would you like to talk now?"

He folded his paper and said, "Now will work. Are you sure I am not rushing you?"

"Not at all." She put her napkin down and glanced to Elizabeth, who had leaned toward her husband and was whispering something Georgiana could not hear.

William stood and said just loud enough to make out, "I will keep that in mind." Then turning toward Georgiana, he motioned for her to lead the way.

As they entered the study, William did not sit at his desk, but rather sat on the chaise, and he patted the seat next to him.

She sat down. "Is there something amiss?"

"No. Nothing has to be wrong for me to want to spend a little time with you. I know I have been a bit distracted lately. I never understood the kind of pressure I would be under with your coming out," he marveled. "But that is not what I wanted to talk to you about. Elizabeth is worried that I am putting undue pressure on *you*."

"I know you mean well."

He leaned forward onto his elbows and clasped his hands tightly. It was clear he had more to say. "I take that to mean you *have* felt pressured." He sighed heavily. "It really is overwhelming. My baby sister's life is entirely in my hands." He sat up, but looked past her, as if his mind were miles away. "What if I choose wrong? Every time I see you sad, I will be haunted in knowing that it was all my fault."

"William, you take too much on yourself."

But he continued as if she had not said anything. "I tell myself that there is nothing to fear so long as I choose wisely. He needs to be a man who is honest and loyal and financially secure enough to take care of you for the rest of your life. You are ten years my junior, and I most likely will die before you. I need to know that you will be taken care of. Even if I were to die next year, I need to know that you will always have the luxuries you grew up with. Now that I have David as an heir, Pemberley's assets belong to him. The weight of it all is indeed very heavy. All you will have is your thirty-thousand pound dowry. I might be able to put another ten-thousand aside but—"

"You do not need to do that. Thirty-thousand is plenty."

"But what if it is not? I cannot go through life without knowing you will be well cared for. You were all I had until two years ago. Perhaps I could gift you the estate in Scotland." He was talking to himself, and so Georgiana let him go on. "But what good would an estate in Scotland be if you lived so far away and I never saw you? Then I thought about finding you a house here in London. You like London, right?"

"Yes."

"But what if your future husband already has a house in London? If that is the case, a second townhouse would not benefit you in the slightest. It is really rather difficult to puzzle out. Part of me hopes you do not find a match so you can always live with me. I hate to lose you. It has all crept up on me so fast. The season will probably begin in a few short weeks. It is the end of August, and people usually start flooding the city just before October. I have already seen more people than usual. It might be a full season." Darcy paused and finally looked directly at her. "I am rambling a little, am I not?"

She smiled at him and put her hand on his fists, which he was unconsciously rolling around like a baker kneading bread. "I have to admit I am quite nervous myself, but, Brother, can we not just take it day by day? Must you worry today what will happen six months from now?"

"But I am a planner. The more I prepare for something, the

more likely it will be successful. I think I would like to host a ball when Charlotte and Richard come back. Perhaps the Saturday afterwards. What do you think?"

"I have always loved Pemberley's balls in the past. I have never attended one at Darcy House but I imagine it would be splendid."

"I think if I talk to Henry, he would open the ball with you."

"Oh, do not talk to Henry. Please, I beg of you. If he offers, I would be happy to dance a set with him. But I do not wish him to feel obligated."

"He seems to enjoy your company. If it is not him, it should be me, but Elizabeth is my—"

"Of course you should open with your wife. Brother, please do not put any pressure on Henry to court me."

William seemed surprised. "Do you not like him?" he asked. "I thought you two would be perfect."

"I like him very much. But I most definitely do not want him to think you are arranging a match with him."

"You do not think you would be happy with him?"

Georgiana sighed and removed her hand. "Please, William. You said you did not wish to pressure me. I met Henry only a few days ago. I hardly know him. I know he seems like a fine fellow, and perhaps a wise match, being a wealthy landowner in the county next to us, but I truly hope to find my own match, just as you and Richard did. You did not choose Elizabeth because it was a wise decision—you fell in *love* with her. Just as Richard could not help but love Charlotte, despite the difficulties. I hope I do not disappoint you, but is it too much to ask to let go of the reigns a little? Maybe you could simply stand on the side and guide me away from the Wickhams and Mr. Collinses."

He leaned back and took a deep breath. "Elizabeth warned me about this. She said I was going about this with too much intellect and not enough heart."

"Elizabeth is very wise," Georgiana giggled. "Especially when she takes my side."

He shook his head, not in rebuttal but in self-castigation. "But what if you choose wrong, Georgie? What if your heart becomes engaged before I can see that the man is unworthy?"

Georgiana put her hand on his shoulder, and waited until he looked directly into her eyes. "I think that if my heart becomes engaged to a man, I will be wise enough to determine for myself if he indeed is worthy." As soon as she said it, she felt a surge of rare confidence. "You must trust me a little."

"What exactly are you saying?" her brother asked.

"I would like to marry for love. I only ask that you help me to recognize love when it comes around. I worry that . . ."

"What?" William asked.

"I worry that I may be blind to what is right in front of me. I know that when you first met Elizabeth, you did not realize how much you loved her—"

"That is an understatement if I ever heard one," William chuckled. After a silent pause, he continued, "And you wish to avoid a similar fate?"

"Indeed," Georgiana admitted. "What would you advise?"

Her brother considered the question carefully. "When I first met Elizabeth, I thought I knew what love was," he began. "I thought I saw her true feelings. But in truth, I saw love only as a mirror. All I saw was my *own* feelings. It is human nature, I suppose. We are all acutely aware of our own thoughts and feelings and experiences, but it is much harder to see what those around us may be feeling. Elizabeth detested me for months and thought I looked at her with disgust, yet I was sure she saw my admiration and my herculean efforts to avoid falling in love with her because that is what I saw."

"Then what is to be done?" Georgiana asked.

"You must find a way to look past the mirror. If you sincerely want to marry for love, you must focus on others and see past your own feelings and thoughts. Make the mirror a window. Then a whole new perspective will open up."

"I have the best brother," Georgiana said through tears.

"I see Elizabeth is not the only wise woman in this house."

She leaned over and kissed his cheek. "Thank you."

"Can you at least be open-minded toward Henry? He truly would be perfect."

"William . . . " she warned.

He put his hands up in surrender. "I know, I know. I will trust you. You may have to remind me a few times, but I shall try very hard to not pressure you with Henry. He is just so lovable! Even I love him already."

She stood up. William was not likely to let it drop in the near future. She worried this conversation would never end. "If he is right for me, then I shall have no problem falling in love with him." She patted his head and said, "True love never needs to be pushed. And if you push me, I might just push back. We have had a good run, William, you and I. Let us not ruin it over an Americanized cousin."

She walked toward the door then turned around. His head was hung low, and his shoulders were slumped. Her heart reached out for him. For so many years, he had been the only family she had. It hurt to see him so worried. "William?" she added. He looked up. "I do like him."

He grinned wider than she had seen in months. "Thanks, Pumpkin. I will try to be better."

*****

As Georgiana left the study, she saw the Gardiners being ushered in through the front door. Avelina skipped a step or two and then demurely walked the rest of the way to meet her.

"Georgiana, I am so glad you can come with us!" Avelina exclaimed.

Georgiana kissed her cheeks on each side and replied, "As am I! I would not miss it! And it looks like it will be a beautiful August day!"

Henry waltzed into the foyer and with false gloominess—for truly, how could he ever sound gloomy?—declared, "I do hope it will not be too hot. Hot days are such a bore here in England. It is entirely unacceptable to strip oneself of clothing if one so desires!" Everyone laughed.

Henry bowed to Avelina, but eyes Georgiana curiously.

"Forgive me, Avelina, this is my cousin, Mr. Henry Darcy."

"It is a pleasure to meet your acquaintance, Avelina. You have the most beautiful light-brown hair. Such dramatic highlights in it!"

"That is because she is outside so much," Georgiana replied

to spare her blushing cousin from forming a response. "Have you brought your drawings with you, Avelina?"

"Of course! Would you like to see them?"

Henry interjected, "You draw? What do you draw?"

"Mostly flowers and insects, like butterflies. It is the perfect time of year to capture them. I hope to find more specimens today at the circus."

They all followed Avelina over to the table where she emptied her satchel of several drawings. Henry was most complimentary of her skill and asked several questions, which only made Avelina blush even more.

The knocker on the front door banged, and Henry stopped in midsentence. "Is that Lady Jane?"

"I hope so. She is the last person we need before we can head out." The butler opened the door, and both Lady Jane and her companion entered.

Georgiana embraced Jane, and they all started putting on their outerwear. The party was rather large. There was Mrs. Gardiner; her daughter, Avelina; her sons, Edward, Nathan, and Wesley; Georgiana; Jane; Jane's companion; and Henry. Their group of nine would require two carriages. Mrs. Gardiner suggested that she and the three boys ride in her carriage and the remaining five ride in the Darcy carriage.

Henry handed Avelina, Jane, and her companion in and then reached for Georgiana. As Georgiana entered, she realized that the three of them were all along the front of the carriage, which required her to sit next to Henry.

She suspected Jane's companion had insisted on the seating arrangement. Mrs. Smyth was hired not because of her father's great foresight into what Jane might need in a companion, but rather to ensure that Jane adhered to the strict rules her father insisted upon.

Georgiana suddenly wished she had warned Henry beforehand so that he might be more circumspect when Mrs. Smyth was around. But it was too late now. He climbed in and sat down. To Georgiana's surprise and relief, very little was said along the ten miles to the outskirts of London where the circus had set up camp. Perhaps Henry sensed the need to behave without any warning. He seemed to be on his best behavior.

Georgiana had brought along her sewing, knowing that it would be almost an hour's journey. Eventually the houses disappeared and the road got bumpier, at which point she was forced to put her sewing away. They soon turned off the main road and headed down into a valley. The whole glen was filled with the circus encampment. Colorful flags waved in the gentle summer wind. There were men walking on stilts near the makeshift entrance, their rainbow-colored, oversized costume pantaloons waving in the breeze. The stilt-walkers had to lean down to peek into the carriage.

Avelina giggled a bit at their hearty welcome. "Oh my!" she squealed. "How on earth do they walk like that?"

Henry replied, "It is not too hard once you get the hang of it. I used to own a pair when I was a child. My father's steward showed us how to use them to pick the fruit in our orchard. Quite practical."

Jane asked, "You helped in the orchards?"

"My father prides himself that he could fire his steward at a moments notice, without a single hiccup in the running of Kryton Park. So, yes, I helped in the orchards. I learned everything I could about the estate. Does that surprise you, my lady?"

Jane looked pensive for a moment. "Now that I think about it, I suppose it is entirely fitting."

"I shall take that as a compliment." Henry put his hand to his hat and made the slightest tip.

The carriage stopped, and Henry handed everyone out. He tucked his right arm behind his back and made his way to the other carriage and handed Mrs. Gardiner out.

The boys were chomping at the bit to see the tiger and were nearly shouting their plea to run on ahead. Mrs. Gardiner turned to Henry and asked, "Would you mind so terribly if our groups met back up for luncheon? I fear the boys will ruin the morning for you with their unbridled energy."

Henry turned to Georgiana and asked the group, "You don't mind, do you?"

The group murmured their agreement.

"Then it is settled," Henry announced. "Shall we meet up under the giant maypole around twelve-thirty?"

Mrs. Gardner agreed and headed off, calling out threats to

leash the boys if they did not wait for her.

Avelina shook her head. "My brothers will be hard to manage until they have seem that tiger," she explained. "Edward has heard that the trainer puts his entire head *in the tiger's mouth* during the show!"

"That is something I wish to see as well!" Henry said with a chuckle.

They began walking around, gazing at all the different exhibits. It was all very captivating to Georgiana. Avelina kept grasping her hand and pulling her to the next showcase and pointing out all the wonders. It wasn't long before Georgiana realized that she had lost Henry, Jane, and Mrs. Smyth. She certainly wasn't worried about them, but she feared that Jane would feel uncomfortable. She did not know Henry like Georgiana did, and may not fully understand his humorous ploys and desires for attention. She knew Jane could handle the flirting just fine. But with Mrs. Smyth pinned to her hip, it might be slightly more difficult. Georgiana hoped that Henry was behaving himself.

Over an hour passed before she saw them again. This time Georgiana was determined to save Jane from Henry. She laced her hand through Avelina's arm and guided her toward the trio, who had stopped at a game of darts. Henry was closing one eye and taking care to aim. His tongue was sticking out adorably. Georgiana giggled at just precisely the wrong moment, just as the dart was leaving his hand, sending it far off the intended red center of the target.

"Drat!" Henry cursed. He turned to Georgiana. "Now see here, Cousin, I was quite close to winning that toy tiger for Lady Jane. I should call you out for such a distraction. What say you to a duel? I am good with my fives, but something tells me that you could hold your own with fisticuffs. But it seems all we have at our disposal for weapons are these blasted darts!" The ladies giggled at his charade. "You now laugh at my disgrace? Well, then I am afraid you have no choice in the matter. Darts it is."

Georgiana giggled again. He was pretending to be truly affronted, but the seriousness only made her see the silliness of it all. "How dare you change the rules of a duel! If you call me out, it is I who chooses the weapons, and I am quite skilled with my needle. Those are the rules. I pick Avelina as my second. Will Jane do for your second or will you chose the ever-steady Mrs. Smyth? She is a wickedly good seamstress."

"Is she really?" He rubbed his chin contemplatively. "I will take wicked anytime. What say you, Mrs. Smyth? Will you be my second? It appears we are dueling with two-inch needles."

Mrs. Smyth's displeasure was evident. "No, sir, Mr. Darcy. I do not make sport of dueling. It is illegal."

Henry was having a hard time holding back his chuckle. "I shall take my chances with the law. I am honor bound, you know. I have no choice. Lady Jane, I am in need of a second. Will you be my partner?"

Jane smiled at him and said, "I shall. You can count on me."

"Splendid! Georgiana, name the place."

In keeping with the spirit of the duel, she lowered her voice and raised her fist. "Right here, right now. I have the needles in my reticule. I shall not be intimidated by your overconfidence." She put on her fiercest frown and fished out her sewing she had been working on. She unthreaded the needles and handed one to him.

Then she took the fencing stance with one arm up and the other one behind her. "On guard!"

Henry dramatically swiped at his brow. "I shall not be intimidated," he said to himself as if he were trying to give himself a pep talk. He put the needle in his mouth temporarily, then took off his coat and handed it to Jane. He removed the needle from his mouth and explained, "If Georgiana were a man, she would know that a real man does not fence with such dangerous weapons while dressed in his coat. For with my coat removed, I have the freedom to do this—" In one quick motion he lunged, and Georgiana had to jump back from his needle.

Everyone chuckled at Henry's mock seriousness. He was very good at role-playing. Georgiana schooled her features, and they began the fight. Each of their fingers were holding very tightly to the needle as they fought back and forth. His posture and footwork were impressive to Georgiana, who really had no training at all. Even still, she couldn't help but be proud at how well she was holding her own in the charade.

Georgiana was getting a bit short of breath at retreating from all his lunges. She paused momentarily to swipe her hair from out of her face, and he lunged, lightly grazing her shoulder with the tip of the needle. It was not enough to pierce the skin but enough to make her jump. "Not fair! I was taking a break!"

"I give no mercy."

"I do not even know how to fence!"

Avelina replied, "That much is clear. Georgiana, you have to lunge at him like this." She took a giant step forward and thrust her imaginary weapon into Henry's abdomen.

"And you also must feint," Jane added. "It means to attack so that you get a certain reaction. If you want him to block to the right, lunge at him at the right. It will leave his left side open for a new attack."

Henry stopped, turned toward Jane, put his hand on his hip, and said, "You are supposed to be helping *me*!"

"Oh, sorry," Jane said, trying not to smirk.

Under his breath he muttered, "You are a sorry second, that is what you are." He then winked at Jane, which made her giggle into her glove. "Georgiana, it is a series of those things. You lunge, you feint, you disengage, you attack, and you lunge again. The faster you attack, all the while defending the opponent's attacks, the more likely you are to make a hit. Like this." He then came at her so fast that she had to take three or four steps back.

With a flick of her wrists, she blocked his needle, then lunged toward him, accidently stabbing him in the thumb.

"Ouch!" he shrieked.

She lowered her weapon and stammered, "I am so sorry!"

He raised his needle menacingly. "I warned you, I give no mercy," he threatened.

"Are you all right? It is bleeding!" Jane cried.

He flicked his head nonchalantly. "Minor flesh wound. I shall have her fingers sewn onto my lapel faster than she can identify her shadow! On guard!"

Georgiana brought up her weapon once again, and they battled with miniature fencing moves swatting sewing needles back and forth. She tried to be as serious as Henry, but his false seriousness only made the situation even more humorous, and she began to giggle. His thumb had a small trickle of blood that shook every time the needles collided. His brows were furrowed, but his lips curled up in such a way that no one could deny that he was enjoying himself.

Jane cheered him on, yelling, "That is the way! Kill her!"

He took his eye off the needles for a moment to look at Jane while he winked at her. "I believe I shall," he said.

Georgiana saw her chance. She took her left hand and grasped his needle-wielding hand, then stepped forward and put her needle directly under his chin. With her fiercest look possible, she growled, "You lose." She pressed her needle against his stubble with just enough pressure to remind him of its sharpness.

He flinched dramatically and then flung his left hand to his forehead and moaned. She let go of him as he threw himself to the grass. He continued to moan and writhe as if in pain.

She had not noticed that a small group had formed while they were playing. She suddenly felt an intense self-consciousness rise from her navel to her ears. Most of the people gathered were guests there to see the circus, but there were a few gypsies standing in a group to the side. The oldest of them was looking directly at Georgiana. For the briefest of moments, the woman locked eyes with her and then smiled and waved her over to her.

Georgiana put her hand to her chest and lipped the words, "Me?", silently, as if by making no sound, it would get the message through the boisterous crowd.

The woman motioned again for her to come toward her. She seemed urgent in her request. Georgiana was happy for an excuse to leave the mass of observers that had formed and left the group to walk toward the tent that the woman was entering. She could hear everyone cheering and laughing at what a spectacle they had made.

The woman was holding open the tent door and waving more frantically to her. When she got within range, Georgiana heard the older gypsy say, "Come. Fortune. Pretty lady needs. Come, fortune, now."

CHAPTER 8

"Oh, no thank you," Georgiana told the old gypsy lady, pronouncing each word plainly since it seemed she did not speak English well. "I do not want my fortune told."

The old woman looked to her companion, a husky lady in her late twenties. The younger gypsy spoke in a foreign language. Whatever she said obviously shocked the older lady. The woman hobbled over to Georgiana and grabbed her hand firmly. "Must! It written! How you say?" She turned to the younger gypsy and spoke in rushed tones in the foreign language.

The younger lady translated. "There is an important fork in the road. You must know how to proceed."

"Yes! Fork. Decision! Big decision," the older lady insisted. She squeezed Georgiana's hand harder, and Georgiana tried to pull away. "No. Must stay. Sit. Only a minute. Big decision."

Georgina took her other hand and removed the lady's grip. "I must go. Thank you though. Perhaps another time."

The lady let her go and then folded her arms. She muttered several sentences and then motioned to the younger gypsy to tell it to Georgiana.

"She says that there will come a time when you will have no choice. You must listen to what she has to say. It is vital."

"Tell her thank you. Perhaps we will stop by before we leave today." Of course Georgiana was only trying to be polite.

"No. No today. Next week." She pointed to her eyes. "I see. Stormy weather. You come." The lady appeared to understand English better than she spoke it, because none of it made any sense.

Georgiana backed out of the tent. All the lightness of her mood from the needle fencing had dissipated. There was a part of her that had wanted to hear her fortune before they came. Even though the idea seemed sensational, even exotic, she had never put any power behind it. But seeing the intensity of the woman's conviction knocked her off kilter. It didn't seem like some innocent pastime anymore.

Georgiana could hardly set one foot in front of the other, but she forced herself to put space between the disturbing woman and herself. As she reunited with her friends, she found she could not shake the gray cloud that lingered. It was time to head to the maypole and have luncheon.

Henry kept Jane occupied, and in the short time Georgiana had been in the tent with the gypsies, Avelina had caught a butterfly in a glass jar from her satchel. The specimen was occupying everyone's conversation.

This allowed Georgiana to trail behind the group in silence. But being alone in her thoughts did not help. Her mood had plummeted, and no one seemed to notice.

Not even Henry, who was always so quick to lighten the mood, observed her despondent state.

Not even her dearest friend, Jane.

She wasn't sure she would have been able to put words to her thoughts even if they had asked her.

Which they didn't.

*****

Benjamin only had time to see three of the real estate properties before he was due to meet with his brother. He walked toward Clyde's office at Pastel & Sons. He drew up his courage. Clyde was known to cheat his customers and occasionally his friends, but he had never cheated Benjamin. He hoped today would not be the first.

He took the stairs two at a time to the second floor and let himself in. He greeted the secretary. "Good morning, Harold. How have the races treated you?"

"Mighty fine. I won three out of the last five. Lost it all the last time, but I'll make up for it tomorrow."

"I am sure you will. Is he in?"

"Yes, sir. Go on back. He's waiting for you. Would you like something to drink?"

"Some of your special coffee, please."

"Coming right up."

Benjamin knocked on the open door and waved. "Hello, Clyde."

Clyde was the younger brother, but he didn't look it. Life had been much harsher to him than to Benjamin—all by his own choosing, however. Benjamin was still thin and well built, but Clyde had indulged in both drink and delicacies. He had a sweet tooth for French pastries. It looked like he had put on quite a bit more weight from even a few months ago. He looked a hefty twenty stones now, possibly more. The pipe that always hung from his lips had caused premature wrinkles that made him look like he was permanently frowning. Clyde smiled widely, revealing several newly-missing teeth.

"What happened to your front teeth?"

Clyde chuckled, "Nothing to worry about, Brother. Call it a misunderstanding that went south in a hurry. Come in, come in. Did Harold offer you something to drink? He knows I keep the good stuff under lock and key. Can I offer you some French brandy?"

"No thank you. He is bringing coffee."

"So, it will be one of *those* meetings. All work and no play?"

"I am afraid so. Did you get a chance to look over the proposal I sent you before I came to town?"

Clyde rubbed the stubble on his jaw. "I did. Yes. Seems pretty straight forward."

"And? Does it meet your expectations?"

"Come on, Ben. At least say hello before we get down to business."

Benjamin nodded and took the last few steps between them and embraced his brother awkwardly, ending with a few firm pats on the back. He took his seat and they chatted for a few minutes until the coffee came in.

He sipped it, cherishing the brew Harold was so good at making. Harold stood to the side waiting for Benjamin's praise. "It is as good as it ever was. What exactly do you do to it to capture all my senses?"

"You won't believe me when I tell you. Salt."

Benjamin raised his eyebrow.

"Yup, salt. There is a pinch of salt in each cup. Everyone thinks coffee needs sugar and cream, but what really takes away the bitterness is salt. Mark my words. But don't go telling everyone my secret. I hope to open a café someday, and coffee will be my specialty."

"It certainly will. Thank you."

"There is more in the kettle. I'll let you get to work. I know you have a lot to talk about." With that, Harold turned and closed the door behind him.

The silence in the air was palpable. Benjamin could almost hear his unanswered questions being shouted. His brother seemed to feel it too. Clyde sat down, put on his spectacles, which were also a new addition, shuffled a few papers, and then looked at Benjamin.

"To tell you the truth, Ben, I like what you have proposed except for one minor detail."

Benjamin drained the last of his coffee and sat forward. "Let us start with what we agree upon. Then we will see what needs to be negotiated."

Clyde nervously shuffled the papers again, but Ben doubted he was actually reading them or looking for information. Clyde had a knack for numbers and facts like no other. Finally he looked back at Ben and started to disclose his thoughts. "I think you estimated the worth of the London office fairly, and I am satisfied with the difference you calculated between the two offices. Liverpool has a much smaller clientele and has less varied resources, but it is a growing metropolis. I think you were very fair in how much I might require to sell out of the London office, which you know is far better established."

"But . . ."

"But I don't see why you have to change the name. I know it sounds petty, but this was our father's dream. His name should be on it forever."

Clyde's sentimentality surprised him. Benjamin would never have guessed that the boy who drowned kittens on a dare would feel a kinship to a father he had loathed. It didn't add up. But being this close to a deal made him tread carefully. "You do not want me to change the name of the office? This is the only snag that is holding up the deal?"

"I know it sounds like I grew a heart or something, and maybe I have, but the last few years have been hard on me. A part of me wants things to go back to the way they were when Father was alive. Splitting up the company is one thing, but changing the name is a different thing altogether. Do you see what I am getting at?"

Benjamin stood and poured more coffee. This might take a while. He took the time to drink half the cup before answering. He chose to be direct. "You never quite got along with Father. You were constantly at odds. He did not approve of the lifestyle you lived—still live, if I am not mistaken."

"Ah, don't go judging me now. I made my bed, and I can sleep in it without you taking my covers."

"Clyde, we do not value the same things anymore. I will be honest with you. I am a bit afraid of whom you have become."

"You are not the only one. I scare myself every time I look at this toothless grin." He chuckled wholeheartedly. "Nah, I am serious though. A man can change. Not me, however, not really. I'm still going to gamble and drink and visit the brothels, but the older I get, the more I realize that what really matters is slipping through my fingers."

Benjamin was a little more intrigued than he had been a moment ago. "What is it that really matters?"

"You know, the people in your life. Ever hear the story of the prodigal son?"

"The Bible story?"

"Hell, is it in the Bible too?"

Benjamin laughed. "Yes, Clyde, it is in the Bible. That is where it came from."

"The one where the son goes and spends his inheritance and then begs to be a servant in his father's house again, even willing to sleep with the pigs?"

"Yes, that is the one."

"Well, I'll be a monkey's uncle. I have been thinking on that story ever since I heard it. Wouldn't Mama be proud? I've been contemplating God! Lord have mercy!" Clyde grinned. "But you know what I get hung up on in that story?"

"What?" Ben asked.

"The boy did it all wrong. Everything. He made every

wrong choice, but deep in his heart, he knew that what his father taught was the right way. And he eventually made it home and made his father proud."

Benjamin did not answer right away. "So are you saying you are like the prodigal son? And that I should kill the fatted calf?"

"The what?"

"Never mind. Are you saying you are going to change?"

Clyde laughed and his protuberant abdomen shook. "Ah, Ben, you have always been the hopeful one! I won't be returning to ask for another inheritance. This proposal is mighty fair, if you ask me. I just wish that you would keep the family name. You know, just so that I can say I was a part of it. We built it together, under Father's guidance, and I just want my name to carry on the legacy. I just want people, generations from now, to know that I did something great. I haven't done a lot of great things in my life, but this company is one of them. If you say you will keep the name, I'll sign the proposal right now in front of you."

"I do not know, Clyde. I made it clear in my cover letter all the reasons why I need to separate the new business from your previous clients. You have a reputation that I do not wish to carry over. You know you do."

Clyde ran his fingers through his hair nervously. "You have been very fair with me. I can't deny that. I am not doing a very good job at putting words to my concerns. Could you just think on it for a while? What if you called it Pastel's London Services or something along that nature."

"It is really that important that I keep Pastel in the name?"

"It is. Could you do it for me? I may play hard, but you can't deny that I work damn hard too. I want my name—our name, Father's name—to carry on our legacy. It will be hard enough to move across country, say goodbye forever to clients that I have served for almost ten years, some even longer. You and I have both been working since we were lads, before we could even officially practice law. But you changing the name erases all the work I've put into it, and all because my brother was more loyal to his conscience than his own flesh and blood."

"That is not fair, Clyde. I love you and always will. You know I would send you business at the drop of a hat. You are the best solicitor I know. You have a knack for numbers that far outshines me. I had to study hours to each of your minutes to get where I am today."

Clyde smiled. "You always were too hard on yourself. I am not wanting to debate with you on who is the better man. I know that the man sitting across from me has made something of himself through blood, sweat, and tears. We each have been quite successful. But we both know the truth, too. You worked harder than me; I used—what can I say?—less-honorable methods than your hundred-hour weeks. You always were the loyal one in the family. You know you were. I am just asking for a bit of that loyalty now."

It took him all of three seconds to debate it in his heart. Benjamin stood and put his hand out. "You will always have my loyalty. I will keep Pastel in the name."

Clyde looked like a weight had been lifted, and he nodded his head vigorously. "Splendid. I will sign the contract right now." They shook hands, and then Clyde took up his pen and signed all fourteen pages of the document.

The London office was his.

Benjamin could not believe how smoothly the morning had gone. He would even have time to see a few of the other potential business sites.

Of course he was a great deal poorer now, but some part of him felt like even though he may have paid a small fortune to his brother for his half of the family business, perhaps Benjamin was the one who ended up with something far more valuable.

He felt like he had gained a brother.

CHAPTER 9

The carriage ride home was filled with conversation of the circus and its numerous attractions. Yet Georgiana said nothing. She made only the briefest of replies to direct questions. Perhaps to the others, she seemed to be merely enjoying the view from the carriage. But Georgiana could not shake the unease she felt.

What had been so urgent? Could a gypsy really see someone's future?

After bidding, what seemed to Georgiana, a very drawn-out farewell to Henry and the Gardiners, Jane put on her pelisse and Georgiana gave her one more kiss on the cheek. Henry escorted Jane to her carriage, which was waiting by the front door of Darcy House. The Gardiners headed up to their guest suite. And Georgiana, alone at last with her troubled thoughts, headed to the music room.

She hadn't played since the wedding. And as that had been a performance in front of almost a hundred people, it had not exactly been relaxing. She sat down and chose a piece by Mozart. It was a long piece, one she knew by heart, which would allow her to think on the day a bit more.

She was about halfway through when she realized that Mr. Pastel was standing in the doorway. He nodded his head in greeting and then walked in and sat down. He was carrying some business files in his hand, but he set it aside on the side table next to the sofa. She continued to play, letting her fingers dance across the keys. Part of the music was slow and brought out her deepest emotions. As the song progressed, it brought about a tinkling that reminded her of something simmering on the stove. The music jumped and hissed, and parts of it came alive. Her thoughts were most certainly simmering right now.

She allowed her fingers to travel up and down the keyboard. It relaxed her, but the unease did not fully abate. Mr. Pastel had his head tilted to the side as if he were straining to hear something. Finally the piece ended. He had closed his eyes during the last portion, only opening them again when the music stopped.

Standing up, he walked over to her and raised his eyebrow quizzically. "Miss Darcy, is there something wrong?"

"What do you mean?"

"Perhaps it is nothing, but I have heard you play Mozart's Rondo in A before, at Rosings, but tonight was different. It was like you were chasing something and could not quite catch it. Did everything go as hoped today?"

He got all that from hearing me play the pianoforte?

A wave of emotion bubbled up, nearly choking her. She dropped her head to hide the tears, but all that did was help the tears escape.

She heard a scraping sound and looked up to see that Mr. Pastel was moving a chair toward the bench. He sat down next to her. She looked at his kind, tender eyes, eyes that were the color of toasted almonds, and she was overcome again. Why was she so despondent? Why had she broken down so quickly?

"Forgive me, Mr. Pastel. I did not know I was so readable when I played. You are very observant."

He took her hand and held it softly in his. He was not big and brawny like Henry or Richard, but her hand looked tiny in his strong, masculine hands. It gave her a sense of security.

"It was not just the way you played the music that clued me in," Benjamin noted. "It was what danced across your face as you went through the movements. When the lightness of the notes should have brought joy, your brows furrowed as if it was abrasive to your current mood. Anyone could have seen it."

"No, not everyone. I have been in a melancholy mood for several hours. You picked up on it in a matter of minutes, yet no one else has."

"Then I am sorry to hear that." He squeezed her hand and said, "What happened? You had such a pleasant time watching the sunrise this morning. I did not think anything could dampen your mood."

She sniffled a bit and looked at his brown eyes. They were darker than Henry's, and did not have gold specks in them, but she noticed that there was a warmer brown ring around the pupil that faded into the darker brown. There was kindness in their depths.

She knew he would not judge her and her foolishness.

"Can I ask you a question?" she asked.

"Of course." His fingers started caressing her hand gently, and she had a hard time concentrating for a moment and looked down at their hands. He looked down as well and then pulled his hands away.

She reached over to his and took it again. "I do not mind. It was rather nice to hold your hand."

He resumed his gentle touch and said softly, "If I overstep my bounds, you will tell me?"

"Of course." After all, Mr. Pastel was practically family.

"What transpired?" he repeated.

She took a deep breath and told him all that had happened with the older gypsy. She told him of the fire in the old lady's eyes and the desperation in her voice. "When I was finally able to leave, I told her that I might be able to come back later that day before we left. But she shook her head and argued with me. 'No. Not today. Next week. I see,' she insisted. I was a little afraid of her. Do you think people can know what will happen in the future? Can a stranger really see my fortune?"

It was clear that Mr. Pastel had listened with full attention. He patted her hand, not dismissively, like a father would to a child, but compassionately. "I think that those are two different questions. Do I think that people can know what will happen in the future? Yes. And I will explain. But, do I think that a stranger can see your future? No.

"I do not believe in destiny," Pastel continued, "but I believe each of us has a birthright, or a potential, if you will. Take me for example. I am not talented at playing music, but I still enjoy hearing well-trained musicians, like you, perform. And I know good music when I hear it, which allowed me to read your mood tonight. This gift of mine, to hear what is between the notes, will not direct me in my decisions, but it has brought us to this moment where I can hold your hand like I this. Perhaps I would have noticed your mood at dinner, but we would not have had this chance to talk to each other so intimately. I would have never known the depth of your sorrow."

He continued, "But I am digressing. My point is that each of us is given gifts and talents which are like paddles in a boat. If we use the talents and gifts, our course is steady and sure. We will not be tossed to and fro with every wave or obstacle. Do you see what I am saying?"

"I think so. You are saying that we have innate, God-given gifts that lead us to a certain path, a destiny of sorts."

"Exactly!" He squeezed her hand again. Her heart picked up speed when he smiled at her. "You are so intelligent, Miss Darcy."

"Mr. Pastel, you can call me Georgiana." His smile froze in place. "Unless you feel uncomfortable." She bowed her head and then looked back up at him when he didn't say anything. Had she been too bold? Maybe he didn't think of her as family.

His eyes softened, and he whispered her name as if it were a caress. "Georgiana, it would be my pleasure." The way he said it stirred her. No one had ever used her name like that. It seemed to mean something to him. It confused her as to why this was though.

She thought she would explode with the flush of heat that infused her entire torso. "You were saying?"

"Pardon? Oh, yes. Back to the gypsy. I think if we know our gifts and talents well enough, we can be inspired in the course our life will take. I have always been good with numbers and have a knack for detecting falsehoods. This has led me to be a solicitor. Even if my father had not trained me in his profession, I would have probably found my way into the field. I am really quite good at it. Now, does that mean that my father could have predicted my profession? Perhaps. But could a complete stranger have made the same prediction? I do not think so."

"I suppose you are right," Georgiana admitted. "But you should have seen the way she looked at me though. It was like she was desperate for me to know something." Georgian hesitated, afraid to reveal the depth of her worries. "You do not think she actually *saw* something, do you? Like a vision?"

"I suppose that is another possibility. A part of me wants to believe that visions do still occur. Numerous people in the Bible had heavenly visitors. Many prophesied what was to come. I believe that Moses really did see the face of God. I believe that Mary Magdalene really was visited by the resurrected Lord. Just because no one today shouts about their visions from the rooftops, does not mean it does not happen in our day."

"But I cannot imagine anyone having such a vision today, not in our modern world," Georgiana argued.

"Perhaps. But nor can I imagine that the same God who communicated to his children back in Adam and Eve's time would deny us that same gift of revelation today. I suppose it is possible that certain people have an affinity to see or hear things that others are indifferent to. Just as I could detect your mood when others could not. Maybe the gypsy gets promptings about things, maybe not. I cannot say."

Georgiana considered his words. "I suppose I was too fearful to think of it that way," she replied. "Her urgency unbalanced me. My instinct was to flinch and pull away. Now I am a little . . . curious. I suppose I was too overwhelmed by the upcoming changes in my life to see the benefit of further guidance. I have had enough guidance to last me a lifetime from William lately. Just this morning I had to remind him to back down."

Mr. Pastel laughed. "Yes, I can imagine. No doubt your brother has already made up his mind about what kind of man that you should marry."

"Quite correct. I had to remind him that the decision did not *entirely* rest with him. I think he will be better now. Speaking of decisions, how did your meeting with your brother go?"

He smiled wider and replied, "You are looking at the sole owner of the London office. Clyde surprised me."

"Congratulations!" she said with a grin. "How did that happen?"

Benjamin shrugged his shoulders. "I thought I knew who Clyde was. I thought I could predict his response. I offered a fair offer that was perhaps a bit padded. I must admit I was ready for a fight. But he accepted readily. He said as long as I did not remove Pastel from the name of the company, he would not stand in my way." Pastel paused and added, "Clyde said the name 'Pastel' is the only good thing he has to show for his life so far."

"How odd. Do you think he is feeling remorse for the things he has done? Do you think he will change?"

"A part of me wants to believe it is possible. Do you think men can change their habits? He seemed quite genuine." As Georgiana asked more questions, Pastel described the meeting and how sincere Clyde had sounded and how it had felt to sign over a small fortune.

"I felt like I gained something today far more valuable than either the business or the money," he confessed. "I saw a glimpse of the brother I grew up with. For the first time in at least fifteen years, I detected stirrings of something other than greed."

Georgiana sighed. Sitting next to Mr. Pastel relaxed her, but hearing him speak about his brother made her think of George Wickham. "I once knew a man who was motivated by greed, so much so that he did not care whom he hurt in his quest for money. He was very talented and charming and knew it too. You said I am intelligent, but there was a time, in Ramsgate, when I was nothing but a fool. This man, Mr. Wickham, waltzed into my life like a tornado, but just like a tornado, he left only destruction in his path. He convinced me that I should marry him; that we were in love. I thought I knew what love was.

"All my life I had looked up to him, for he was the son of my father's steward. I trusted him. But he was not a good man. He preyed on my like a wolf hunts in a pack. My brother saved me from myself." Georgiana suddenly realized the enormity of what she had just confessed, but for some reason, she knew there was nothing to fear from Mr. Pastel. "I trust you more than I ever thought I could trust a man. I probably should not have told you all that, but I know you will be discreet with this revealing story of mine."

"Of course. You will always be able to trust me."

Georgiana smiled. "When you first told me about your brother, I thought of this man," she replied. "He would have done anything for my dowry."

The pressure he placed on her hands increased, and she looked down at their hands. Mr. Pastel's voice filtered into her heart as he reassured her. "Knowing that there are men out there who will not see the loving loyalty in your blue eyes, or savor the music you play, or feel their soul uplifted by your smile, but instead see only your thirty-thousand pound dowry makes me so very angry. But it should not make you afraid. There are many good people in the world. Look at your brother and Mrs. Darcy, even Mr. and Mrs. Fitzwilliam. All these people are proof of the world's wholesomeness. You should not be afraid because of one man."

"Thank you, Mr. Pastel. You are so easy to talk to. I do not feel like I have to perform a certain role or strain to say the right thing. I think even if I said the most average, dull thing that you would still listen."

"You can count on it," Mr. Pastel promised. "If you speak, I will listen. Which reminds me, I have something for you."

"For me?" Georgiana asked in surprise. "I cannot take a gift from you."

"I suppose I can give it directly to the cook if you prefer." He laughed at the look of confusion on her face. "It is hardly significant. Do not worry so, Georgiana." He stood and walked to his satchel and took out a small folded piece of paper. He handed it to her.

She stood and hesitated for a brief moment but then decided it could not be anything of real value since it was simply a piece of paper. She opened it and read the words scribbled on it.

She was wrong.

It *was* valuable. It was the recipe for the apple cinnamon custard from the café she loved on Silverthorn Court.

Mr. Pastel had been wrong too.

It *was* significant—all folded up into a nice, neat paper.

*****

The morning after the circus brought gray, stormy skies, so the sunrise was not nearly as dramatic. Georgiana got the horizon sketched, but she was unable to capture the riot of colors she had seen the day before.

The next day, Mr. Pastel woke her again—just as he had done the previous two mornings. And although he said he was going to work while she painted, he stood behind her the entire time, watching her paint. But she found his presence did not make her uncomfortable in the slightest. She finished her work with the yellows, but would have to wait until the oils dried before she could begin bleeding in red and orange hues.

So, on the fourth day, she eagerly dressed. But she was met with dark skies again. The clouds were inspirational all the same, and she added a few to the painting.

Each day Mr. Pastel worked quietly behind her at the desk

or watched the sunrise beside her. It was another two days before the colors made as a dramatic display as that first sunrise. She worked furiously trying to capture the rainbow of hues. Mr. Pastel remarked that, "The reds and oranges are chasing the blues away." It felt poetic, and she worked even harder to express the idea through her brushstrokes.

A full week had passed, and she put the finishing touches on the tree. She simply had to show how the sun highlighted each clear and distinct leaf, despite the lingering shadows in the foreground. She dabbed what she thought was the last bit of layer on the green leaves and sat back arching her spine to stretch.

Mr. Pastel appeared at her side. "It is perfect," he whispered. "It truly speaks to me. Somehow you have not only drawn the peace a sunrise brings, but you have breathed life into the painting, just as the sun breathes life into the world each morning. Anyone can see that the moment you just captured is a cherished, sacred moment."

"Do you really think so?" She had been gazing at the picture, tilting her head to look at it from different angles. When he didn't respond right away, she turned toward him and caught him looking at her.

He quickly looked back to the painting. "Yes," he stammered. "The painting is quite beautiful. I am grateful to have been able to spend this time with you this last week. You shall be sorely missed tomorrow morning." He let his voice trail off, an unspoken question hanging in the air.

Georgiana felt a bit heavy in this realization too. She had truly enjoyed having his company every morning. There was something special about their pre-dawn hours, something that was missing from the rest of the day.

"Actually, I was thinking of beginning work on another painting. These early hours have been so productive for me. I have rarely been able to devote such a large chunk of time to painting, and I found it most enjoyable. I often feel guilty trying to paint when there are other people around. I feel like I must be social and interact or risk offending them."

"Georgiana, you should never feel afraid to be who you are. Mrs. Darcy and your brother know you well; they do not expect you to entertain them."

She bowed her head. "I suppose I was not speaking of them." She was ashamed she had said anything at all.

"I see. I do not think that Henry expects you to spend every waking minute with him either."

"But my brother . . . well, he wants me to get to know Henry. In case . . . in case, Henry might be interested in something more."

Pastel turned and walked toward the window. "And would that be acceptable to you? A match with Henry?" He seemed genuinely interested.

She considered it a bit. "I suppose he is a good man. He certainly makes me laugh. It is too early to know. Do you think he is a good man?"

Mr. Pastel stood straighter for a minute before subtly nodding. He looked away from her frowning and, with a hoarse voice, he said, "He is a good man. I think if you fell in love with him, then you would not be unhappy. If you will excuse me, I must . . . I must go."

Mr. Pastel left her staring at her painting and wondering why he had left so abruptly. Was it something she said?

CHAPTER 10

The same day she finished the painting, Henry suggested that he, Jane, Mr. Pastel, Avelina, and Georgiana all go rowing. He had heard of the new Grand Union Canal in Brentford, west of London, and he wanted to see the man-made water system for himself.

Just after luncheon, they all got into a carriage and traveled the ten miles. Everyone had fun, especially since Henry was in rare form. He was throwing puns and jokes around every five minutes. The hour it took to travel was over fairly quickly. Georgiana was relieved by their arrival as her sides were beginning to ache from laughter.

At one point she thought she recognized the scenery, but she was sure she had never seen the Grand Union Canal. As they rolled to a stop, she was hit with another wave of familiarity.

The gentlemen exited first, and Mr. Pastel handed the ladies out while Henry got the picnic basket down from the back of the carriage.

"I was told our rowboat will be over that hill by a bridge," Henry announced. "It shouldn't be hard to find. Follow me this way."

Henry started up the hill with the picnic basket of food. Mr. Pastel was the only gentleman left, and yet there were three ladies. He looked to be uncomfortable for a moment, as if he were debating which lady to exclude from his offer of escort.

"Do not worry, Mr. Pastel," Georgiana laughed, "you may offer your arm to Lady Jane and Avelina. That hill is no match for me, considering the terrain I grew up on at Pemberley. It will be like childhood again." With that, she picked up her skirts and headed off in Henry's direction. It was an overcast day but still quite warm. Usually when it was this close to September, the days cooled off in the afternoons, but as she walked, she felt her neck moisten with the exertion. There was something therapeutic about exercise. William rarely let her exert herself, except when riding. And it was hard to find a good time and place to ride in London. In fact, it had been several weeks since she had been on her horse.

Henry pressed on, and when he reached the top of the hill, he called back to his followers, "I see it! It isn't much to look at, but it will do."

When Georgiana reached the top of the hill she sucked in a breath. The canal was not very wide, but the greenery that grew along the side was plentiful.

Are those blackberry bushes?

She rushed down the hill to find out. Sure enough the berries were perfect for picking. She plucked one and savored the perfectly sweet tartness that only wild blackberries held. London hothouses could never supply berries like these.

Soon Avelina was right beside her, eating her fair share and making all sorts of pleasurable noises. Georgiana giggled at her and raised her eyebrows playfully. "They are mine! I saw them first!"

"Oh, these are heavenly! Mr. Pastel, come partake of this perfection!" Avelina shouted.

"I should probably make sure Henry does not need help with the boat," he called back.

Georgiana quickly picked a few and skipped over to him. "No, Mr. Pastel. You will not be 'all work and no play' today. Today you will taste wild blackberries. Now, if you please, open your mouth."

His eyes lit up, and he cautiously opened his mouth while she put two berries in and then waited. He closed his eyes, and his mouth moved reverently over the berries. He opened his eyes and nodded. "They are definitely worth letting Henry sweat it out a moment longer."

"Would you like more?" Being confident in his reply, she took his hand and put the remaining few in it.

"You are not going to feed them to me? I am entirely sure they will not be nearly as sweet," he said playfully.

Georgiana giggled and said, "You have been around Henry too much."

"At least I made you laugh."

"Yes, you did. I am going to eat some more."

*****

Benjamin Pastel watched Georgiana walk away from him. The blackberries' intense flavor could not be denied, yet it was not strong enough to distract him from watching her tall form walk away. If it were possible to have control over his heart rate, he would have enlisted that talent by now. He had just endured an hour of listening to her laugh at Henry's jokes while he sat in the carriage like a fool with nothing to add. Georgiana's playful mood was a direct response to Henry's gaiety. Her hips swayed gently as she walked away, unaware that he was watching her feminine curves.

Lord! I have to control these thoughts somehow, or it will be the death of me! Surely I have some heart ailment.

She had no idea of the effect she had on him. From the small sighs she would make while she painted, to the way she looked at him from across the room every time he spoke. She gave him her full attention in every conversation. And she left him with a hollow ache inside whenever she departed.

He had relished holding her hand a week ago in the music room and had often relived the moment, with memories of caressing her soft skin. If he tried hard enough, he could still smell her jasmine-oil fragrance. He had been close enough that their knees were a mere inch apart. He imagined that he could feel the heat coming from her body. If he had had more courage, he would have tried to sit on the pianoforte bench with her.

He was a stickler for rules. But at moments like this—with her feeding him delicious wild blackberries—he wanted to curse the rules, and let his lips take hers with all the pent-up passion he felt.

Rules. They had their uses, but they would kill him as surely as the alcohol and gambling would kill his brother.

He guffawed to himself. It came out more like a snarl.

Just yesterday, his brother Clyde had helped him look over the offer he was making on the office space over the café on Silverthorn Court, and when Benjamin declined brandy again, Clyde asked him if he had any vices at all.

Benjamin denied it then, but at this moment, he became

acutely aware that it was a lie.

Apparently he did have a vice.

Rules.

Curse the rules! His heart picked up speed again, this time due to a bit of defiant anger.

Curse the rule that Georgiana had to marry a titled landed gentleman. Curse the rule that he could not touch those golden locks. Curse the rule that he could not lock her in a room until she looked at him, really looked at him, for surely she would see his admiration. Curse the rule that said he could not properly court her while he was a guest in her brother's house. Curse the rule that he could not melt into her arms at the end of a hard day. Curse the rule that he could not give her everything he had. Curse the rule that said a woman was not allowed to voice her feelings for a man, because any indication of her feelings for him would be quite welcome. Curse the rule that he could not sit next to her in the carriage. Curse the rule that said she couldn't call him by his Christian name. Curse the rule that dictated a chaperone be present at all times.

And curse the rule that said he had to answer Georgiana honestly when she asked if Henry Darcy was a good man!

Curse them all!

He kicked the pebbles under his feet, but all that did was scuff his boot and garner the attention of Henry, earning him a raised eyebrow and a smirk.

Curse him too.

He looked away. He did not know why he was so worked up.

Think positive. He was in good company today. Things were progressing as he had hoped with the business.

Usually he did not struggle with his gratitude or positive attitude. But today, he was having a hard time. He very well could have been trying to decide which tooth he wasted pulled.

He pushed himself, and continued listing his gratitude.

Henry did not necessarily pay special attention to Georgiana, or at least no more than he paid Lady Jane. This thought redirected his attitude more than the others. Either Henry did not especially admire Georgiana, or he admired Lady Jane just as much.

That last thought surprised him. *Did Henry admire Lady Jane?* Was it possible? Jane was charming, for sure, and Henry often made her laugh. But had Henry made any special efforts to earn her praise or attention? Pastel would have to keep an eye out for clues.

He tossed the last two blackberries in his mouth and closed the distance to the shore, where Henry looked like he was signing his life away with a contract several pages long.

"What do you have there?" Pastel asked.

Henry frowned while attempting to read the document. "A boat rental contract that is longer than the United States Constitution. Good heavens, man! Must I sign my life away to have a few hours on the river?"

The dock worker shifted his position. "Yes, sir. I ain't never lost a boat yet with me methods. Them there boats is me lively'ood. Its 'ow I pay for a roof over me 'ead and clothe me lil' ones. You'd not risk it neither, I reckon."

Henry flipped to the last page and reached a hand out. The man handed him a pencil immediately.

Henry looked at the writing utensil. "A pencil? No one signs a contract in pencil! Give me a quill and ink."

"Can't afford no ink. Pencil is jus' fine. Won't bleed if it gets wet."

Henry harrumphed. But then he signed the document. "Let's go," he said curtly.

Apparently Benjamin was not the only one in a sour mood. This lifted Benjamin's spirits a little more. Henry was never in a sour mood. In fact, Benjamin had begun to wonder if Henry even *could* be angry. It made Pastel feel a little better about his own tantrum just a few minutes ago.

The ladies had their fill of blackberries, and the gentlemen met up with them at the dock. Benjamin helped the worker nudge the bow of the boat into the current.

Henry's countenance brightened at the arrival of the ladies. "We are ready to depart!" he announced. "Pastel, you climb in first to help me keep the boat balanced, and then, ladies, I will hand you in one at a time."

Benjamin carefully stepped in. Holding the sides of the boat, he made his way to the bow. Once he was in place,

Georgiana was handed in, then Avelina, then Lady Jane.

Clue number one. Henry had seated Lady Jane next to him.

Henry and Benjamin took up oars and the boat glided away from the dock. "Four o'clock Mr. 'Arcy!" the boat owner hollered after them. "I gotta have ya back by four!"

"*Darcy*, man! *Darcy*! With a **D**! Not 'Arcy!" Henry called over his shoulder. "Good heavens! He speaks my last name as if it resembles the back side of a donkey." His comment earned a giggle from Lady Jane and Avelina. His returning acknowledgement was to look directly at Lady Jane and smile— clue number two.

They rowed for a good fifteen minutes before Lady Jane asked Henry, "How far west are we from London?"

"About ten miles. We are just outside of Brentford."

Avelina asked, "What part of the Grand Union Canal are we in?"

"The Thames connects with the River Brent about a mile back, and the canal stems off of that river. This part has been built for several years, but they plan to extend it to Birmingham one day. It will be one hundred thirty-seven miles, all in all."

Henry continued to expound on the canal and how it was the hope of big businesses to improve trade and commerce. Benjamin tuned him out for a while and watched Georgiana instead. She was facing him, but was twisted so that she could hear what Henry was saying.

Benjamin admitted it would be very healthy for businesses if they could transport goods up and down the canal, but at the moment, Benjamin was not entirely interested in a history lesson.

While Henry prattled on, he took the opportunity to address Georgiana. "I wish we had sunny weather today." He started to chide himself for his pathetic attempt at conversation.

She turned to face him and looked up at the sky. "Indeed. I do not mind the clouds, but I hope that dark horizon is not coming our way."

Benjamin looked over his shoulder and saw what she was talking about. It was quite distant, but there was no doubt that they were rain clouds. "It might be lingering from the rain we had the hour after the sunrise."

"That was spectacular, was it not? Just as I finished the

painting, the clouds darkened, and we had a downpour like no other. It has been such a wet autumn. Would you not say so, Mr. Pastel?"

Curse the rules.

"Georgiana, I would like it very much if you would call me Benjamin."

"Are you sure you do not mind? Even Henry and William still call you Mr. Pastel. I assumed that you preferred it."

"No, I do not, not with my friends. I think Mr. Darcy still calls me Mr. Pastel for *his* comfort, not mine. I am not as stiff as I may appear."

"I have a hard time feeling comfortable with new people too. We are similar in that way. And I do not think you appear stiff. I think you merely enjoy order and predictability."

He laughed. *Oh, the irony.* "Rules. Yes, I *usually* like my rules." But his sarcasm was lost to her. *Oh well. It is probably for the best.*

"I am impressed that you tolerate Henry so well, as he is one of the most unpredictable gentlemen I know. Why is that?"

"Henry is good for me. He keeps me fighting for what I want." Georgiana furrowed her eyebrows and looked down in embarrassment. "Never mind. It would not make sense even if I could explain what I meant."

She smiled and they sat in silence for a moment, listening to the boat glide across the water. "By the way," she added, "I never got a chance to thank you for the recipe of the cinnamon apple custard. I was too overcome to form words before you bowed and left. It was the most thoughtful thing anyone has done for me."

"I seriously doubt that. Mr. Darcy dotes on you. Mrs. Darcy is the sister you never had. And Charlotte Fitzwilliam cannot look at you without deep admiration. All I did was exchange goods."

"What do you mean, exchange goods?"

He hadn't meant to disclose that piece of information. But in for a penny, in for a pound, he supposed. "I had to barter services for Mrs. Heathrow, the owner of the café, to reveal her secret recipe," he admitted.

"What services exactly did you offer her?"

"I told her I would help her find her son who left for the

war last year. She hasn't heard from him since he left. She does not read all that well and did not even know which documents to ask for at the war office. I have put in several requests, which should be ready to review next week."

"My goodness! So she practically sold her firstborn child to you for that recipe?"

"You might say that. Although in this case she is hoping to get him back. So perhaps we can consider it a loan."

Georgiana tilted her head at him and smiled, looking pensive at the same time. "I like that about you."

"What?" The question hung in the air with the ever-increasing humidity.

"I like that you took a simple comment that I said in passing and were willing to do whatever it took to gift that recipe to me. It was very sweet of you. I hope you find Mrs. Heathrow's son." She smiled at him and then glanced away, as if she were embarrassed.

His heart hurdled out of control. She had just praised him. Genuine praise. And if he wasn't mistaken, he just saw a bit of that adoration in her eyes before she collected herself.

He looked at Henry, who was having no problem making Lady Jane laugh.

The game was on.

Curse the rule that he had to play nice.

Curse the rule that he shouldn't fight for Georgiana.

*****

Georgiana knew they were nearly out of time. The clouds on the horizon were not just threatening; they were coming at full speed toward them. Both Henry and Benjamin were rowing as fast as they could, but they were fighting the current as well as choppy water. They had only rowed downstream for an hour before Georgiana pointed out the clouds. The consensus of the group had been to turn back immediately.

Georgiana was trying not to notice that Benjamin's muscles were fighting his coat for attention. She once thought he was not particularly well built, but she could see now that was entirely false. Although he strained to row the boat and its passengers upstream, he kept his breathing slow and steady.

She assured herself that it was entirely natural to watch what was right in front of her; Benjamin just happened to be in her line of sight. But he kept smiling at her in a way that made her think he could read her mind.

If he could, she would die of mortification.

He is quite handsome. She had never noticed before how much his cheekbones looked like Michelangelo's *David*. His jaw wasn't overwhelming, but it spoke of strength and masculinity. He smiled again at her scrutiny, and she looked away. She vowed she would not look at him again until they reached the dock.

But then he spoke. "Henry, I think that sandbank there is low enough to row up to. Perhaps we should disembark and find shelter. The storm will be here in a few minutes."

Henry looked to where Benjamin had pointed out, then said, "By golly, good fellow, I think you are right!"

They rowed the boat to the bank. Benjamin stepped out and pulled the boat partway up the shore. The ladies made their way onto the bank, and the men pulled the boat the rest of the way onto land.

Avelina was the first up the steep bank. She gasped. "There are several tents in the valley," she whispered. "I think it might be a gypsy camp."

Georgiana wondered how likely it was that there were two gypsy camps near London.

Benjamin put his hand on her elbow and said, "Let me help you, Georgiana. The hill is quite steep."

She looked toward him. "Thank you, Benjamin."

He smiled widely at her. "That is the first time you called me Benjamin."

"You did say I could call you that, did you not?"

"I did. Although I was a little unprepared for how it might affect me. Come. We had better hurry."

She couldn't help but wonder what he had meant. How did it affect him? Did it make him uncomfortable? It didn't seem like it. He had smiled at her. With her free hand, she lifted her skirt and hiked up the steep bank. She was quite thankful for his supporting arm, because there was a time or two when she nearly lost her footing. His steady support made her feel more confident.

Suddenly she was reminded of when she performed the musical number at the wedding breakfast. He had lifted the lid of the instrument that morning, just as he had the night before, and had stood by her, giving her strength and confidence that she sorely needed. Using him to walk up the bank felt the same as it did then. He made her feel sure of herself. Part of her knew that there was no way she could fall on her face if he was beside her. He brought a steadiness to her that she rarely felt around others.

All the Darcys were a bit shy—well, all but Henry Darcy—but Georgiana must have asked for a second helping in heaven when they were dishing out anxiety. And she sometimes worried she had declined any serving at all of social grace. She was never quite comfortable in groups. No, that was not entirely true. She simply preferred *small* groups.

She especially enjoyed one-on-one time with those she cared about. Like the mornings she spent painting in the library. Benjamin rarely disturbed the quiet solitude they shared in those early morning hours. When he did speak, it was not unnecessary prattle. He did not feel the need to fill silence with lighthearted banter. It was as if he knew how important it was for her to paint the sunrise. How did he describe it? He had said she had a certain amount of reverence when watching it. She decided that Benjamin Pastel was quite good at reading her. She did not know how she felt about that.

Once she was at the top of the hill, she could see that Avelina was right. There were a good twenty tents, and her heart dropped for a moment when she recognized the colorful flags. It was not just any gypsy camp; it was the same gypsy camp from the circus. They were in the same valley they had visited a week ago. No wonder the ride to Brentford had looked familiar.

"Oh, dear. The rain is starting!" Jane said.

Georgiana felt the first scattered drops moisten her cheeks. No one needed to remind her to pick up the pace as thunder cracked the skies, one right after the other. The storm had arrived.

As they neared the encampment, Henry raised his voice a bit and called out for help. "Ho there! Can we get some assistance?"

A man with dark shadows under his eyes was whittling a stick. He stood and wordlessly walked toward them.

Benjamin asked, "Is there any way we could find shelter in your tents? We seem to be trapped in the rain."

A woman ventured out of a tent, looked the new visitors up and down, and whispered something to the man. He looked up at the sky and waved for them to come over.

As they entered the tent, Georgiana saw that that the interior was already crowded. There were several gypsies, both men and women, huddled inside. Adding five more bodies made the area quite cramped.

Their host, who introduced himself as Marcus, gently kicked a man who must have been sleeping on the ground and muttered something to him in a foreign language. The sleeping man grumbled, sat up, and rolled up his blanket, thus freeing up a bit more space. There was a small table to the side that looked to be held together with a few rickety screws and some rope. Other than that, the tent held no possessions of any kind.

Marcus motioned for the boat party to occupy the space that the sleeping man had evacuated. Even with the man gone, it was still quite crowded. They were nearly shoulder to shoulder with their neighbors. The unfamiliar faces seemed to be watching them distrustfully. Georgiana repressed the desire to shudder. She told herself there was nothing to fear.

The storm fully hit moments later. As the tent shook, she heard a steady clack of thunder, and the light in the tent dimmed to the point that someone decided to light a candle. Its small flame didn't make much of a difference in the semi-darkness. Every now and then lightning illuminated the small tent, giving an eerie glow to the strangers' faces.

Thunder cracked again, and she jumped. Benjamin put his arm around her and rubbed her shoulder. She instantly let out the breath she had been holding.

"Are you cold?" he asked her quietly.

She looked up at him and felt the closeness of his person. Propriety told her to step away, but there was nowhere to move to. Besides, it was comforting to have someone to hold while so many strangers looked her up and down. The noise from the storm and the scattered murmurs throughout the tent made it difficult to hear the rest of the group.

Rubbing her forearms, she replied, "I am fine. It is only that the temperature has dropped quite suddenly."

Benjamin dropped the arm that was around her shoulders and started removing his coat. The motion was a bit awkward since they were huddled so tightly in the tent. "Here, if you will forgive the impropriety of me wearing only my waistcoat and shirtsleeves, you can have my coat."

"Thank you." He placed it around her shoulders, and she put her arms through the sleeves. She had to push the cuffs up as her arms were not nearly as long as his. "It smells like you."

He chuckled. "I imagine so. But it will probably smell like jasmine oil here shortly."

She looked up at him curiously. "And how did you know I wear jasmine oil? Have you been in my chambers, inspecting the contents of my dressing table?" she teased. "I quite like the scent, and I will not be persuaded to wear rose oil or gardenias."

A flash of lightning brightened the room, and she could see he was rather flushed. She had embarrassed him!

"No, of course not!" he stuttered. "I have never been in your chambers! And, ah, I would n-n-never want you to wear rose oil or gardenias. I rather like the way you smell."

She giggled a little and leaned into him a bit, nudging him with her shoulder. "You are always so serious, Benjamin. I am afraid it makes it easy to tease you."

He put his arm around her shoulders again and leaned toward her ear. "I can take it," he whispered. "Do your worst."

They stood there for another fifteen minutes listening to the storm. It had been a very good thing to take shelter. She could not imagine being out there right now.

There were two children in the corner, huddled together with a woman who was presumably their mother. They appeared to be scared of the storm. Georgiana empathized and wondered if she looked scared too.

As her eyes searched the semi-darkness, she found the face she knew she had been looking for. The older woman who had been so adamant about reading her fortune a week ago, was staring at her with the grin of a Cheshire cat. The woman caught Georgiana's eye, and she flicked her head backwards, waving her hand, motioning Georgiana to come over.

Georgiana started walking toward her. Benjamin put his

hand on her elbow. "Where are you going?" he asked.

"Do you remember the gypsy I told you about?" He nodded and looked to where Georgiana was looking. "That is her. Somehow she knew I would be back in a week when it was stormy. I have to see her."

"May I come with you?"

"I would like that."

As they made their way, he asked, "You do not seem nervous this time."

As they weaved through the crowded tent, she glanced back at Benjamin and said, "I have thought a lot about what you said. God has always talked to his people, from Adam and Eve down to Peter, James, and John. Why would he deny us revelation now? Somehow that woman knew I would be back in a week. Maybe she has a gift that is not understood. Or maybe she is a fraud. But there is no way to know unless I talk to her."

They passed Henry and Jane who both asked where they were going.

"To have my fortune told," Georgiana announced.

Henry smirked. "This I *must* see. Come, my lady. Avelina, come get your fortune told."

Avelina exclaimed, "Truly? How intriguing! That should occupy us until the storm blows over."

Marcus was standing next to the old gypsy lady. Georgiana stopped in front of them. "You knew," she said to the old lady. "You knew we would get stuck in the storm. How?"

Marcus translated it, and the woman responded. Marcus replied, "She saw it in her mind."

In her broken English she asked, "You believe? Now you believe?"

Georgiana nodded and held out her hand, her fingers barely peeking out of the end of the jacket. Isn't that how they read fortunes? The woman shook her head and said, "Friends first." Georgiana looked confused. The lady spoke to Marcus.

Marcus said, "She wants to read your friends' fortunes first."

The woman pointed to Avelina, who eagerly stepped forward and offered her palm. The lady looked at it and shook her head. "No. I see. Not I read."

Marcus explained. "She has the ability to see without reading the palm."

Avelina said, "Oh. Very well."

Marcus translated the strange language as the woman spoke, "You have the gift of vision. Where those around you are blind, you will see. Many will come to you for their answers. You must never lose your tender heart when interacting with your fellowmen." The woman stopped talking and so did Marcus.

Then the lady pointed to Henry. He stepped forward. She began talking and Marcus translated as before. "You traveled far to find a great treasure. But you should look for that which will keep your soul light and unburdened." The woman stopped talking.

Henry looked between the lady and Marcus. "Is that all?"

The lady understood his question and said. "All is more."

"What is that supposed to mean?" he asked.

She and Marcus argued back and forth for a few minutes in their foreign tongue. Marcus finally turned back toward Henry and said, "The more you study her words, the more your future will hold. What she said is of great worth. She thinks you do not believe."

He chuckled a little. "She is right about that. This is hogwash."

The gypsy then pointed to Jane. Jane shook her head and said, "No, thank you."

The woman then shrugged and pointed to Benjamin, who nodded his consent. Marcus resumed translating. Her words came out with a great deal of passion. "You are a man who has a valuable birthright. It will be the very thing that sets you free. There is more patience in your heart than there are drops in the ocean. Your brother was dead, yet he will rise and bring you much joy—but you must believe. And if you desire an answer, you must first ask. Hold onto those you value, for they will be the very vessel of your happiness. You are one that need not be told to love the heart."

Benjamin smiled and bowed respectfully. "Thank you."

The lady looked more serious and spoke to Georgiana. "You now."

Georgiana nodded. She was ready.

The old lady's words were slower now, as if she did not

wish Marcus to miss any of the translation. "A time will soon come when you must take a stand and face your biggest fear, but it will not be as dangerous as you might think. You have a big decision in your future. One decision will be bring you temporary happiness while the other one will be the destiny of your soul.

"You will need to prepare your loved ones. There will be much fear for them, but the stronger you are, the more they will trust in your judgment. Never will it be more important to follow your heart. For your heart is pure and kind, unblemished from the ways of the world. But beware, the world will attempt to thrust its shadows on your happiness. If you stay strong, unfettered bliss will be yours to claim. Choose wisely. You can choose gaiety, bringing with it a little temporary joy, or you can choose to listen to the language of your heart and be filled with genuine, unabashed happiness for the rest of time."

The woman kept talking, but Marcus had stopped. The lady turned to Marcus, pointing to Georgiana. "You tell!"

"No, it isn't right to tell her that."

The woman started shouting at Marcus, but he just shook his head. "Some things should not be told." Marcus turned back to Georgiana and apologized. "Forgive my grandmother. She is fatigued. Pay her no mind. The fortune is finished, just as the storm is. You may all go now."

Georgiana suddenly realized the rain and thunder had stopped. She had been enthralled that she had not noticed the change.

Georgiana took the lady's hand and kissed it. The woman took her other hand and caressed Georgiana's face. "You must believe."

"I do."

"No. In not me. Believe in you."

Georgiana smiled back at her and said. "I will, I will."

CHAPTER 11

The party managed to return the boat on time, despite the storm, but they were forced to forgo their picnic luncheon. Everyone was quite tired and famished by the time they reached the bridge where they had started.

Benjamin silently pondered the fortunes the old gypsy woman had told. They seemed different from the typical fortunes offered by gypsies for a shilling or two. They were not truly fortunes at all, but rather like a blessing or guidance or good advice.

As Henry Darcy finished returning the boat rental, Miss Gardner began handing out the picnic foods. Lady Jane was helping her. Benjamin noticed that Georgiana appeared to have a great deal on her mind.

He took a few steps until he was beside Georgiana. Just being next to her brought him peace. She still had his jacket on, and even though her petite fingers only came out at the very tips, he took her hand and wordlessly guided her toward the fallen tree a few paces away.

"Your mind is weighed down again, Georgiana."

"There is so much to think about."

"I agree. The gypsy seemed to be just vague enough to let each thing she said be mysteriously accurate. It was common sense, said poetically."

She looked up at him and then patted the fallen tree by her. He sat down.

"At first, when she said that Avelina had the gift of vision, I doubted the truth of it. But the more I think about it, Avelina is more observant than any other girl I know. Where others do not notice the bird or the butterfly, she captures each note they sing or the very shade of the underside of the wing with her chalk. Have you ever heard her talk about butterflies?"

"Yes, I have."

Georgiana nodded. "The gypsy said it perfectly. She said Avelina was tenderhearted. And I would never want her to lose that. It is her best quality. The gypsy woman seemed to know her better than I did. Which made what she said about everyone else all the more interesting. I suppose Henry really did travel all the way to England to make money. And I hope he finds a treasure that keeps him light and carefree. I would hate to see him lose his natural cheer."

"As would I. But you need not worry. Henry is more likely to follow his heart than a trail of money."

"Do you really think so? I mean, I told you about how my brother hopes for a match with him. Sometimes I fear he might be showing me kindness only because of my dowry."

"Oh no. He and I were discussing finances a few days ago, as a matter of fact. And he has hundreds of thousands of pounds at his disposal to invest. It is one of the reasons he wanted to see this canal. He hopes to help build the rest of it and set up a business shipping goods up and down it."

"Truly? No wonder he was so well informed," Georgiana replied. After a moment, she continued, "The canal would be very good for him. I imagine he would enjoy managing shipping goods. He would be able to rub shoulders with all sorts of people. He seems to be relaxed with anyone and everyone, so he would be a very approachable employer. It is reassuring that he does not need my dowry."

Benjamin considered how best to respond. He did not want to encourage her toward Henry Darcy any more than necessary. A part of him knew that she was just working things out in her mind, and he told himself not to worry about it. After all, she had not once described how Henry made her feel. Whereas on their way to find shelter, she had thanked Benjamin again for the custard recipe, saying he was "so thoughtful and sweet". It was encouraging to know that she admired him, however slightly. Not only that, but she had praised him for "not filling silence with useless prattle" like so many others.

Benjamin knew that Henry was not the right person for her. Somehow he had to help her see that. It was going to be tricky. Perhaps even arduous. But it was possible.

He would worry about winning her brother's blessing later.

He and Georgiana were just so compatible. Benjamin had seen it from the very beginning, although it wasn't until he actually lived under the same roof with her for a week that he realized the depth of his feelings. He could not let her go without a fight. Her heart was too precious a commodity. He would sacrifice all he had to win it.

He looked over at Henry, who was now openly flirting with Lady Jane. He was bowing to her and taking her hands in his and twirling her around in circles. Lady Jane was literally glowing with delight. They seemed to bring out the best in each other. She was a bit shy as well, but she had a young heart and seemed to enjoy his carefree, happy attitude. There had been plenty of clues today now that Benjamin had begun to watch for them.

Plus, Henry hadn't had a single private moment with Georgiana all afternoon, whereas Benjamin had several with her. Perhaps there was not much competition after all.

He had even been lucky enough to put his arm around Georgiana protectively when she looked nervous in the gypsy tent—a precious moment he was sure to treasure. The whole ride back to the dock had been spent in quiet companionship, but there had been a few moments when their eyes locked.

Benjamin was hopeful that the deep blushes that infused her cheeks each time meant perhaps that she was not entirely immune to him. And even this moment now, as he sat quietly next to her on the fallen tree—was an easy investment, that would eventually reap rewards.

Georgiana was a rare commodity. She was someone who had the ability to be still. Some people always had to be doing something productive, or at the very least, must be entertained. They felt compelled to be social and fill the silence. But Georgiana was comfortable in stillness. She did not feel the unsettled agitation and boredom that plagued others in a quiet room. Being still was a valuable skill that many did not occupy or employ easily.

Benjamin had that skill. Henry did not.

That is why Henry was all wrong for her. She needed someone who she could sit and watch the grass grow, like him, because he knew that it was the quiet moments that put Georgiana at ease. She enjoyed getting lost in her own thoughts.

She sighed next to him, and he took her hand and squeezed it gently, leaving his hand resting on hers. She looked up at him with her blue eyes and smiled sweetly. "Thank you, Benjamin. You always know what I need."

"Do you want to talk more about what is weighing on you?"

She sighed again. "I just keep thinking about my fortune," she admitted. "The gypsy said I was about to come face-to-face with my biggest fear, and that there will be a big decision to make."

"What is your biggest fear?" he asked quickly, without thinking. "I am sorry to pry," he added. "You do not have to tell me if you do not want to."

She smiled at him. "I think you could probably guess if you put your mind to it."

"You want to marry someone you love and who loves and adores you. You want your husband to cherish you and to see your great worth. Your biggest fear is missing out on that."

Georgiana nodded. "I knew you would understand. You seem to always know just the right thing to say. I suppose her words could mean that I will find people who will make me happy. One of them will be bring me 'temporary happiness while the other one . . .'"

". . . will be the destiny of your soul." Benjamin remembered it clearly.

"Yes! Those were her exact words! Her words brought me comfort to some degree. At least I know that there is someone out there that will make me truly happy. But it sounded like it was going to be up to me to make an important choice. As if there might be two men in my future."

"And part of what she said was a warning," Georgiana continued. "Or at least I took it that way. She said I had to be strong and prepare my family. She said the stronger I was, the more they will trust my judgment. I could not help but think of my conversation with William this morning. I was strong and held my ground—I even asked him not to pressure me with Henry. It seemed to work."

"It will ultimately be your choice whom you marry," Benjamin reassured. "I am very confident that even though Mr.

Darcy seems to be preoccupied and focused on finding you a match, he will ultimately defer the decision to you. I think he would be understanding if you fell in love. He trusts your judgment."

"Do you really think so? I mean, I hope so."

"There is hope for you, Georgiana. May I ask you a question?"

"Of course, Benjamin."

He couldn't help but smile at how lovely it sounded for her to use his Christian name. "What makes you happy?"

"Wh wha what do you mean?"

"I mean, if you could describe the perfect day, what would you do? Would you read? Paint? Draw? Go to a ball? Who would you chose to converse with and in what manner?"

She tilted her head in that way that indicated she was truly contemplating something. It was adorable. He interlaced their fingers and just patiently waited for her to answer.

"I suppose, if I could chose, I would be at home with a small group of close friends and family. We would all be quietly enjoying each other's company. We would not necessarily be doing anything in particular. Just being together. I enjoy time with people, but I do not like feeling pressured to entertain them. Oh, dear, I sound so dull!"

He squeezed her hand a bit again and said, "It sounds like a perfect day if you ask me."

"That is just because you do so much that any time when you can just sit, sounds like heaven. You work too hard, Mr. Pastel."

"Benjamin."

"You work too hard, *Benjamin*."

"I admit that I work hard, but that makes moments like these where we can smell the fresh rain and I can sit and enjoy time with a beautiful lady all the more special."

"It is nice, is it not?"

"Very nice. Come, let us be social. My stomach is threatening to riot against me if I do not provide it sustenance soon. Even in this peaceful moment, I find I am having a hard time hearing your sweet voice over its rumblings."

"You could not have said it better. Let us eat! I am starved.

Besides, it looks like I need to save Lady Jane from Henry or he might eat her! The man looks ravenous."

Benjamin stifled a laugh. "True. That is probably a very accurate description."

*****

When they finally returned to Darcy House, Georgiana went in search of Elizabeth. She wanted to tell her all about the gypsy woman and the mysterious fortunes. She was told that Mrs. Darcy had gone to the Fitzwilliam townhouse to see the General. Georgiana felt a little guilty because she had only visited the child twice in the last week.

It was only a mile down the road, and the day had turned out so beautiful. She surely had a good hour before dusk, and if she left quickly, she could catch Elizabeth and get a ride home in the carriage. Georgiana put her pelisse on, and Benjamin happened to walk by just as she was about to leave.

"Where are you going Miss Darcy?"

"Please, Benjamin, you may call me Georgiana."

He looked to the butler briefly. "I assumed you meant when we were alone."

"I suppose it would be inappropriate in society, but this is my home. Yours too!"

"Very well, Georgiana. Where are you going?"

"I am going to check in on the General. Elizabeth is there now, and I am hoping to connect with her."

"May I come with you? There is a townhouse along the way that I would like to see."

"I thought you made an offer for the building on Silverthorn Court?"

"I did. But that is for my offices. The townhouse is for the future. If I marry someday, I will need a larger home. I cannot stay at Darcy House forever."

Georgiana felt a surge of sadness for some reason. It had become so natural to see the sunrise every morning in the library with Benjamin that the thought of him living somewhere else was rather distressing. He had fit so well in the family that she had forgot he was only a temporary guest.

He smiled at her in his reassuring way. "Do not worry, it will be a few weeks yet before I move to Silverthorn Court. Will you be starting a new painting tomorrow? Or shall you sleep in for the first time in a week?"

He always seemed to know the right thing to say. It was like he sensed what she was feeling. "Knock at six o'clock sharp. I will be ready. I would not miss it."

He nodded, and suddenly her sadness was gone. At least for now she could still see him every morning, and that made her heart so light she had to concentrate on not skipping to the Fitzwilliam townhouse. She completely forgot that she intended to tell Elizabeth about the gypsy.

*****

Two nights later at dinner, Elizabeth noticed something interesting: Mr. Pastel accidentally called Georgiana by her Christian name. Upon realizing his error, Mr. Pastel had glanced quickly at Will, as if to see if he had noticed. Will had not. He was deep in conversation with Henry at the time regarding his ideas on investing in the Grand Union Canal. They were so consumed with each other that Will had to be asked twice if he was ready for the third course.

"Oh, yes, bring it in" was all he muttered, and then his attention was again directed to Henry.

Elizabeth took the opportunity to ask Mr. Pastel about his business ventures.

"And was your offer approved, Mr. Pastel?" she asked.

Mr. Pastel wiped his mouth and happily said, "Yes, I heard back from the agent just before dinner. The offices will be mine as soon as my funds are transferred."

Georgiana squealed excitedly. "That is wonderful news! When will you move in?"

"It will take a few weeks to get ready and move all the files. Clyde has been packing them up the last few days. And I still need to buy sitting room furniture fit for the grand opening of Pastel Accounting Services."

Elizabeth was happy to see how proud he was, but she was a bit surprised by Georgiana's enthusiasm. Georgiana praised the choice of name profusely and gushed over how regal it sounded. She very nearly glowed when she talked to Mr. Pastel.

William must have heard the level of the energy in her voice as well, because he paused in his conversation with Henry. "What have I missed?"

Georgiana turned to William and said, "Everything is working out just right for Benjamin!"

Elizabeth noticed a slight flinch in her husband. He had definitely noticed Georgiana's use of Mr. Pastel's Christian name *this* time.

"Georgiana," he said with authority, "I do not think it appropriate—"

"Will, dear," Elizabeth interrupted, "I believe I will delay the date of the ball until Richard and Charlotte for the following Monday. I would hate to rush them into things. What do you think?" It was a gamble, but the distraction seemed to have worked.

"I do not see a problem with that. It will give them a chance to go to the theatre with us. I hear they are playing the Italian number, what was it called again?"

Elizabeth answered, "*L'Orfeo* composed by Claudio Monteverdi. I believe it is over two hundred years old."

It was clear that Georgiana remained oblivious to the near scolding that her brother had just about delivered. "Oh, I would love to see it!" she replied eagerly.

Mr. Pastel cleared his throat and nervously said, "When shall we go?" Elizabeth took the opportunity to look in wonder at Mr. Pastel, who was red to the tips of his ears. But to his credit, the young man did not waver from looking William straight in the eye.

William's protective streak seemed to have been deflected for now. In a perfectly amiable voice, he replied, "I was hoping to go the Wednesday after Charlotte and Fitzwilliam return. Would that work for everyone?" He looked pointedly toward Henry.

Henry smiled and responded, "I would like that very much. I admit I am a bit of a softy for sopranos, and the *Times* said that Signora Paulina is highly rated. Italian is her native language." He looked to Georgiana, "Should we make a party of it? And extend an invitation to Lady Jane? Then we would have equal numbers of ladies and gentlemen."

Georgiana smiled and nodded. "I think she would like that very much. I will make sure she is available. Will we all fit in the Darcy box?"

William leaned back. "Yes, the box seats eight," he acknowledged. "Shall we do a dinner that night too?"

As conversation waxed and waned, Elizabeth continued to observe Georgiana and Mr. Pastel. Both spoke little to any other person at the table. Perhaps that was partly because they were seated next to each other at the end. But Georgiana rarely even looked at anyone else. What was the most surprising was the soft, happy glow in her eyes. Her very countenance was bright and relaxed.

Only once did Henry look in Georgiana's direction. He seemed just as content to converse with William.

Elizabeth started detailing in her head how often Georgiana and Mr. Pastel were together versus how often Henry was with Georgiana.

The scales were tipped heavily in Mr. Pastel's favor. She had not realized that Mr. Pastel might actually harbor a tender for her. The most interesting realization was that Georgiana seemed oblivious to her Americanized cousin sitting next to her because her entire attention was directed at the solicitor to her right.

Well, Henry Darcy may have some competition.

CHAPTER 12

The rest of the week flew by. The whole house was a buzz of activity awaiting Charlotte and Richard's return. They were due to arrive any minute. Georgiana had instructed the cook to fill the pantry for them. Elizabeth and Georgiana were both at the Fitzwilliam townhouse directing the last-minute details. All the bed linens were freshly laundered. The General had been bathed and was in a brand-new gown. He was walking around quite well now; even still, the nursery maid had a devil of a time keeping him off the floor so he would not soil his gown.

When he fell for a third time, Georgiana took it upon herself to pick Isaac up and carry him to the rocking chair. "Come, General, we only have a wee bit more time to wait before they arrive. I know you are just as excited as I am to see Mamma and Papa again!"

The General looked at her so seriously with eyes that were big and quickly filled with tears. "Oh, do not cry, Isaac Byron Fitzwilliam. I should not have mentioned your parents. How unthinking that was!"

Elizabeth smiled and put her hand on Georgiana's shoulder. "Do not worry. He is really quite tired. I thought that Charlotte and Richard would be here an hour ago and told the nursery maid not to put him down for his morning nap. It was probably unwise of me."

Georgiana rocked the General a bit, and he seemed to gain control of himself. Georgiana's necklace soon provided adequate distraction.

Elizabeth took a seat on the other chair and looked at Georgiana for a moment. "May I ask you a question?"

Georgiana nodded. "Of course."

"You seem at ease lately regarding your upcoming season. Even when we went to the dressmaker, you seemed more confident than usual about what your preferences are."

"I suppose you are right. I am less worried about my season. In fact, I am getting excited for it."

"You have never enjoyed society much. What has changed?"

Georgiana pondered the question a bit. "Benjamin thinks it will be fairly easy to tell if someone is after my dowry or not. If they come on too strong too quickly and start talking marriage right away, then I should take that as a warning sign. He says that there will be many who pass me over without a second glance, and only a few who will take the time to really see me—how did he put it?—'as the priceless commodity' I truly am! Is that not sweet?"

"It is very sweet," Elizabeth agreed with a smile.

"Benjamin also says that if I am looking too hard, I might miss the man who admires me the most. So I have decided he is probably right. Just like you said, love comes on so slowly, like a sunrise, until one day you suddenly are able to see things clearly. Benjamin says that love should always start with friendship. That is not so scary. I know how to be friends. I am friends with Benjamin and Henry, and if my goal is to be a friend to the gentlemen I meet, then it should be easy to tell who admires me. At least that is what Benjamin says."

"It sounds like Mr. Pastel has a great deal to say. You spend quite a bit of time with him."

"I cannot help it. I try not to be a nuisance, because he is always so busy with his business. And he spends a good deal of time arranging his new offices. But I cannot help but ask him about his day every evening when he comes home. Sometimes he finds me when I am playing the pianoforte and just listens to me play. Other times I find I am nearly pacing the foyer waiting for his arrival."

Elizabeth smiled at her. "He is a good man."

"He is. He showed me the new office yesterday."

Elizabeth looked a bit worried. "Do you mean to say the two of you were at the office alone? Just you and Mr. Pastel?"

"Yes, but Benjamin is practically family. I did not think you or William would mind. I was helping him pick out drapes. And then his brother, Clyde, dropped by, so we were not entirely alone."

"I do not think your brother would want you to associate

with Clyde Pastel."

"Oh, he is not so bad. Even Benjamin says he is different than he used to be. Clyde did seem a bit nervous to meet me though."

Elizabeth murmured something and nodded. She paused for a moment and asked, "How soon will Mr. Pastel be able to move his files into the office? It is officially his now, correct?"

"I believe in two days. He is at the old office right now with Clyde Pastel. Clyde said there was some urgent business to discuss, otherwise Benjamin would have loved to be here with us to welcome Charlotte and Richard."

Elizabeth nodded again. "I see."

"Oh! Did I tell you that I had my fortune read? So did Benjamin."

"No," Elizabeth replied. "When was this?"

"Last week when we went rowing on the canal. We had to take shelter from a storm in a gypsy tent. Do you wish to hear about it?"

"I would be delighted."

Georgiana told her as much as she could remember—about how she would someday be forced to face her greatest fear and make a big decision, one between a moment of joy or lasting happiness. Until that moment, she had forgotten that the gypsy had said how it would never be more important to follow her heart.

She related the gypsy's words to Elizabeth: "She specifically said that I should listen to the language of my heart and then I would be filled with genuine, unabashed happiness for the rest of time. Truly! That is exactly what she said! I cannot explain how much peace I felt when she said it. I have no doubt she spoke of me finding a love match. Just knowing that I could find 'unfettered bliss' was so comforting!"

Elizabeth looked doubtful. "You know that I do not put much faith in fortune-telling. None of what she said was very specific. These people tend to avoid details so that their customers can interpret things in hindsight to fit the circumstances."

"I thought so too, but she *knew* things. She knew that Avelina was tenderhearted and observant. She knew that Henry had come from far away to earn his fortune. She said that Benjamin had more patience in his heart than there were drops in the ocean. And you know all of those things are true! But if you want specifics that are not vague, listen to what she said about Benjamin's brother, Clyde—she said that his brother was dead but will rise again and bring him joy if Benjamin believes. Clyde is already showing signs of reformation. Benjamin even said it is like he was getting the old Clyde back."

Elizabeth frowned. "That is all fine and good, Georgiana, but remember, your future is not written on ancient tombs. It is yours to decide."

A bit of the excitement drained from Georgiana's heart. She had hoped that Elizabeth and William would understand, but it seemed that Benjamin was the only one who did. She reminded herself that she had to be strong so her loved ones would trust her judgment. "Elizabeth, do you believe the Bible to be the word of God?"

"Of course. What an odd question!"

"Then you believe that a voice spoke to Saul? And that Joseph was told to marry Mary even though she was with child? Because I do. Perhaps Saul was destined to be a servant of the Lord and change his name to Paul, thus becoming one of the greatest apostles. Perhaps not. But on the road to Damascus, Saul heard a voice asking him why he persecuted Jesus. Saul only asked two clarification questions. First he asked 'Who art thou?' Do you remember what he asked next?"

"I do. Saul asked, 'What wilt thou have me to do?'"

"Exactly. Can you imagine the faith that took? Saul was a fierce persecutor of Christians, but upon hearing that voice, he did an about face and even changed his name to Paul to prove he was a different person. His life was redirected because of revelation. I feel like that to some extent. Benjamin says that—"

Elizabeth put her hand up and stopped Georgiana in mid-sentence. "Please, do not tell me one more thing that Benjamin says. Mr. Pastel is a wonderful man, but I want to know what Georgiana thinks."

"Well, I think that maybe this gypsy woman has a special gift. A gift of seeing into someone's heart. I think that God will use every available opportunity to guide us in our lives if we just believe. I think that God loves me and knows that this woman could offer a sense of hope for little old me. I was in need of hope for Georgiana. I believe that the gypsy knew things about me that could not be seen with earthly eyes. I do not think she is a prophet, but she might be blessed with a touch of vision, and she uses that gift to provide hope to those who desperately need to know that God has not abandoned them. That is what I believe."

Elizabeth smiled and relaxed into her chair. "I am pleased to hear you found hope. We all held out hope for you, my dear. It is thrilling to see you grasp onto your future with confidence."

They heard a ruckus down the hall, and Georgiana sat up straighter. "They are here!"

She leaned down to the General, who had fallen asleep during her discussion with Elizabeth. She lowered her voice and gave him a kiss. "Sweet one, you held on as long as you could. You fought valiantly, but fatigue took you at last."

Charlotte and Richard came in, and both their eyes searched for the General. Their faces lit up with adoration in seeing their son. Richard may not have been Isaac's biological father, but there was no doubt that the General was his son.

Charlotte came and scooped up the boy in her arms. Joyful tears dropped while she kissed him tenderly. "I missed you, little one."

"What a sight for sore eyes! We shall never be gone from him so long again," Richard promised.

Elizabeth smirked, "I certainly hope not! I will be quite disappointed if there is ever another wedding trip for either of you. I was under the impression that you were both in it for the long haul!"

Charlotte smiled and blushed but continued to kiss her sleeping son. She knew Elizabeth was only teasing. "It is good to be home."

Richard echoed, "You can say that again."

Georgiana sighed. Everyone she loved was an arm's length or back at Darcy House. She felt such a serene peace. She knew she had everything she could ever want. The homecoming was so sweet. She just wished Benjamin was here to see it. She couldn't wait to tell him all about the adoration in the parents' eyes. He would appreciate that.

It did not occur to her to share the experience with Henry Darcy.

*****

Benjamin didn't knock this time on the Pastel and Sons office door. It was halfway open, and he heard grunting and groaning on the other side of the door. As he pushed it open, he saw his brother straining to move an entire filing cabinet. It looked like the cabinet was winning.

"Clyde, what are you doing? Let me help you."

Clyde was red in the face and sweating profusely. His cravat was stained with a ring of dirt around the collar, and the knot was in disarray.

Part of Benjamin was disappointed. Clyde had shown signs of reformation over the last two weeks. He was always in the office—a rarity in recent years—and the separating of the reputable clients' files from those that Benjamin did not wish to bring to the new office of Pastel Accounting Services was progressing much quicker than he anticipated. All because Clyde was working so hard.

Clyde relented and stood up to lean against the wall and wipe his brow with a handkerchief. He was panting, and it took some time to catch his breath. "Moving is for the birds," he moaned.

Benjamin went across the room to the locked bureau on the other wall and traced his hand along the underside feeling for the key.

His brother scowled. "What ya doing? I have never known you to drink this early in the day. It isn't even the noon luncheon."

"It isn't for me. You look thirsty."

"You can say that again, but you won't find any liquor in there no more. I tossed it out."

Benjamin froze. He could hardly find the words. "You threw out brandy from the seventeenth century?"

"I'll be the first to admit I do stupid stuff. It wasn't the first time. Doubt it will be the last," he grumbled. "Oh, don't look so shocked. It was going to be the death of me and you know it."

"But . . ." Again, Benjamin was struck dumb.

"Hey, don't get the idea in your head that I'm ready for you to kill the fatted calf."

Ben stared at his brother in confusion for a moment or two. "Clyde, have you been reading the Bible?"

"I'm full of surprises, Ben. 'Sides, a good lawyer always reads the original documents. So I read about the prodigal son right from the source. I imagine the fatted calf was some sort of sacrifice. So I made my own offering and threw out my drink. I can't say it has been a fun few days."

"A few days? You have not drank *any* alcohol in a few *days*?"

"Nope. I gotta tell you, I'm all jittery. Every little thing makes me jump out of my skin. Couldn't hold a quill if my life depended on it. Look at these hands."

He held out his hands—they had a significant tremor running along his entire arm from fingertip to the shoulder. His face was blotchy, and even though he'd had several minutes to catch his breath, the breathing was still a bit labored. He truly looked miserable.

"But why?" Benjamin asked. "I thought you said you would never change, not really, at least."

"I'll tell you. Come on, let's have Harold make coffee. I haven't given up that vice yet."

Clyde hollered out to Harold that Benjamin was here. "Hurry up with it too! Make it damn strong! I don't want no cream neither. Black as midnight. You hear?"

From the other room, Harold called out. "You got it, boss!"

There were boxes and boxes everywhere. Clyde's desk looked as if a tornado had deposited the entirety of the Church of England's records for the last thousand years. Benjamin imagined there was some order to the chaos, but he was unwilling to decipher the code. Clyde may be odd and more than a bit shady, but he was meticulously organized. Their father had drilled it into them since they were young.

"What is the urgent business, Clyde?"

"Needed your help with that file cabinet, but you were late. Where it's at is good enough," Clyde joked. Benjamin pursed his lips together. "Oh, don't be mad. I really do have something to show you. Do you know we had an uncle?"

"Of course, Uncle George."

"No, not mother's brother. Father had an older brother,

Christian Lucas Pastel. Ever heard of him?"

"Father never spoke of his family. I thought he always said he had no family, they were dead."

"Close but not quite. His exact words were 'My family is dead *to me*.'"

For the fourth time today, Benjamin was struck dumb momentarily by his brother's words. He swallowed, afraid to let the hope emerge. Finally he asked, "We still have family alive? We are not alone?"

"Not sure whether they're *alive* or not, but I found this file in my searching. Have to admit the name Pastel caught my eye, and I dug a little deeper. Take a look," Clyde said, offering his brother a file of papers.

Benjamin flipped through the contents. There was a birth record, a few newspaper clippings, a miniature of two boys, and several legal documents. As he read through them, Harold brought in the coffee.

Christian Lucas Pastel had been born four years before their father. A newspaper article detailed a carriage accident where both their parents were killed. It looked like his uncle had been severely injured and not expected to make it through the night. He quickly thumbed through the articles looking for a death record but did not find it. He did find a legal document that looked like a crudely drawn-up will. Perhaps drawn-up in haste.

Benjamin scanned the will, and in it, he found that Benjamin's grandfather had left Christian a property called Rolling Farms in Kent—along with a staggering sum of one hundred twelve thousand pounds. It was an enormous amount to be associated with a farm. He couldn't remember what his grandfather had done for a living. He only remembered that Benjamin's father had often reminded his sons that "Happiness comes from hard work, not money."

Had his grandfather been the owner of Rolling Farms? And what kind of farmer had access to one hundred twelve thousand pounds? The idea of a country farmer's wealth eclipsing his own to such a degree was almost incredible.

Benjamin looked up. "Clyde, where did you say this was?"

"I was going through the files of old clients, weeding out the ones you may not appreciate, and found one titled 'Pastel' and couldn't help but be curious. Did you read about the part where Christian survived the accident?"

"No. The file is extensive. I could study it all night. Just tell me what it all means."

"Well, I think it means we have an uncle who lives in Kent. I wrote to a chum who lives there to see if he ever heard of Christian Pastel or Rolling Farms. I expect I'll hear back in the next week or so. I do not know why Father would say his family was dead to him. But with a bloody inheritance like that, I imagine Rolling Farms could be a midsize, perhaps fairly large, estate. Further in the back, there are documents that indicate that Christian may have been the local magistrate. So I sent my best guy who knows how to extract information—probably should not have told you that. Oh, what the hell; it's out, and I can't take back the words. Anyway, he is currently on his way to look at the court records to verify this." Clyde wiped his brow again. His face was still quite red and blotchy even though he was not exerting himself.

"Are you quite sure you are well? Maybe going off liquor cold turkey was not the wisest idea."

"Ha! I felt worse than this that morning I lost my front teeth. At least I can see clearly today. Felt like I was floating up in the sky all day yesterday. Don't worry about me. But do you see the significance of this?"

"No. Nothing except that we have a very wealthy uncle."

"Ah, Ben, always the innocent lamb, you are! Didn't you see the article indicating that his wife was barren?"

Benjamin furrowed his brows, and at the same time, he blurted out, "You think we are his heir?" He chastised himself for not politely hesitating, but then he remembered whom he was talking to.

Clyde smirked. "Not me . . ." His brother politely paused, and repeated himself, "Not me. I'm the younger son. You. You are the next of kin. If he has no children, and he hasn't squandered away all that money, it may be in your best interest to make contact with our uncle."

CHAPTER 13

As Clyde stared at him intensely, Benjamin experienced a whirlwind of swirling emotions, and inadvertently looked at his hands. "I do not care about the money, Clyde. I have proven that I know how to make a living on my own. I only care about . . ."

"The heritage," Clyde finished for him.

Benjamin looked up briskly. "How did you know?"

"What kind of lawyer would I be if I couldn't detect something so obvious?" Clyde snorted. "You have always cared about title and the family honor and whatnot. But do you know how I really knew?"

"How?"

"Miss Darcy. I saw the way you looked at her the other day when you were picking out drapes. You look at her the way Father looked at Mother. And this particular *heritage* gives you a real chance to court her; so of course you're thrilled."

Clyde shook his head and sighed. "Better you than me, Ben. I would sooner be horsewhipped than become a bridegroom. Or a member the House of Lords."

Benjamin was surprised and curious. "Really?"

"Yes. Well, maybe I wouldn't mind the money," Clyde admitted. "Or a pretty face. But I couldn't stand that kind of fancy life. Whereas you actually *care* about all that pedigreed mumbo-jumbo. You already dress and talk like those in the finest circles. You love all those rules. I'm perfectly content with my lot in life, but I'd wager you secretly yearn to be a gentleman. Am I close?"

Benjamin stood and walked to the window. Even though Clyde's voice was still shaky from the lack of alcohol, his words were solid and held intense power. "You are entirely correct. But it is not because of the money or the title. I only wish for it because of Georgiana. I want to be what she deserves, and she deserves a gentleman. I have allowed myself to steal moments with her, but the idea of actually making her an offer has never been a real possibility. For the first time, I am allowing myself to hope for Georgiana."

"I'm glad. But is she really so prideful that she will not consider your suit if you are just a solicitor?"

"It is not that. I see subtle signs that she considers me her friend. And there is *some* evidence that I mean more to her than that, but . . ."

"But what? Look, Ben, regardless of how this thing with our uncle plays out, you shouldn't hesitate. You're clearly moony-loony for this girl. So go after her!"

"But she has not given me any indication that she admires me! I do not know how to win her heart."

"Have you told her how you feel?"

Benjamin sighed and shook his head. "If she were only to open her eyes and really see the way I look at her, then I would not have to say anything. It would be obvious."

"You can say that again. How does her family feel about you?"

Benjamin groaned and turned back toward Clyde. "That may be a detour to a happily-ever-after. Not necessarily a roadblock, but something that might take some time to work around. Her brother has been fairly vocal about finding her a titled wealthy Englishman."

Clyde frowned. "Is your admiration for his sister as clear to him as it is to me?"

"I am not sure. Georgiana once called me Benjamin at the dinner table, and he looked quite upset. I thought he was going to rebuke her right there in front of everyone, but his wife changed the subject. I believe Mr. Darcy respects me as a solicitor, but he would never allow his sister to marry anyone less than a true gentleman. The man has a great deal of pride. He almost passed up on true love because he could not wrap his head around the fact that Mrs. Darcy did not come from the finest circles. Apparently he told her he loved her *in spite* of her shortcomings in that area."

"Lord have mercy!" Clyde blustered. "You're teasing me, aren't you?"

"Oh no. To hear Elizabeth tell it, he said he 'liked her against his will, against his reason and even against his character.'"

Clyde whistled. "And he still calls himself a gentleman?"

Benjamin was quick to say "He is one of the finest gentlemen I have ever met."

Clyde held up his hands. "Don't jump down my throat. But I think I see what you mean by a 'roadblock'."

"Just a small one. It may take a bit of persistence, but now, now there is hope."

Clyde lifted his coffee cup, "For Georgiana."

Benjamin tried not to smile, but lifted his cup as well to the toast.

*****

Benjamin and Georgiana continued to meet every morning to see the sunrise. Georgiana was pleased with the progress she was making on the current painting. She had chosen to do another sunrise, but this time, instead of a landscape setting with trees and hills, she chose a busy city street.

Benjamin stood behind her, watching her paint. Normally, Georgiana would feel self-conscious with a spectator, but she didn't ever feel that way with Benjamin. The aroma of his coffee mixed with his unique clean smell was soothing and helped her relax. Today was overcast, and the sunrise was not as impressive as it had been the previous days, so she worked on the buildings instead.

The painting was going to be a present for Benjamin. She had gotten the idea from Charlotte on the day the Fitzwilliams returned from their wedding trip. Charlotte and Georgiana had spent a few hours catching up while she unpacked, giving Georgiana a chance to tell Charlotte all about her last two weeks. Georgina had not realized how much time she had spent with Benjamin until Charlotte pointed it out. Georgiana remembered the conversation well.

"Georgiana," Charlotte had asked, "You seem to bring up Mr. Pastel, or Benjamin, quite frequently."

"He is a dear friend."

"How dear exactly? It seems that he is involved with everything you have told me about. You have hardly mentioned anyone else. Do you admire him?"

At first Georgiana was shocked at the implications of her

comment. She even dropped her jaw in surprise, but slowly, as Charlotte patiently waited for her reply, Georgiana began to see that it was all said with an element of hope. Somehow she knew that Charlotte would not judge her. More importantly, the shock of the comment did not come from the actual question, but the unknown answer.

"I am not sure," Georgiana admitted. "I have never considered the issue before." She reflected on the last two weeks. Her days seemed to be entirely made up with moments of enjoying his presence and moments spent looking forward to seeing him again. "I admit that I think a great deal about him. I seem to have an insatiable need to talk to him. At times, when my friend Jane has been distracted and less observant, Benjamin has stepped in and filled that void. I would say he is my closest friend right now."

"So, you cannot wait to talk to him every evening, and you cannot wait to watch the sunrise with him every morning. It certainly sounds like he is your best friend. What are you painting now?"

"Another sunrise. This time I want a city skyline to be in the forefront."

"What part of the city? Buildings like Darcy House?"

"I suppose. I was thinking more along the lines of the shopping district."

"Did you not say that Mr. Pastel just bought an apartment downtown?"

"Yes."

"And did you not say he is overwhelmed with finding the furniture and decorations for the office?"

"He is. Why?"

"What if you painted the front of his office building for his waiting room?"

Georgiana was overwhelmed with the idea. "Of course! What a thoughtful gift! He would love that. But how will I explain it to him? What if he asks about the setting before I am finished? I know I do not have a great deal of skill, but he is sure to recognize a building he enters every day."

"Did you not say that your favorite café is there too?"

"Yes! In the same building! I can say that is the setting!" Georgiana envisioned it in her mind's eyes—little tables out front with two people enjoying a cinnamon apple custard. "Perfect! You are so wise, Charlotte."

The next morning she was very glad for Charlotte's wise suggestion. As she painted the outline of the buildings, she felt Benjamin step closer to her. With each brush stroke, she knew he would find awareness at any moment. She had purposely painted other buildings first and left out the gargoyle—as that would have given it away immediately. Adding the Roman pillars at the entrance was finally what made him suck in a breath.

She turned to look up at him. He looked down at her and placed his hand on the crook of her neck, sending tingles down her spine.

"That is my office building . . . It is beautiful, Georgiana," he whispered. His eyes were kind, and if it were possible to actually see admiration pouring out of those toasted almond orbs, she did. It was the first time she had noticed it. Her heart was already beating furiously, but she had never detected anything like that before.

Their eyes locked. She couldn't look away if she tried.

His eyes communicated a deep intensity that he rarely showed other people. She saw it when she played the piano . . . but he had always loved music.

But this wasn't about music, and she was confident it was not about her painting; it was about *her*.

He loved her.

No man could look at a woman that way and not feel love. She soaked up his admiration, surprised that she felt no need to look away in embarrassment. For some reason, it felt right to come to this realization. It wasn't terrifying at all. It all felt so natural.

His eyes softened even further, creating an intimacy that they had never shared. She knew without a doubt that he could read her very thoughts at the moment.

What *was* she thinking? She could feel each of her senses come to life. As she gazed at him, she could see how the sunrise had highlighted his brown hair to the point that it almost had a bronze tone to it. The clock ticked methodically, and at a far different tempo than her heart. She felt the softness of his fingers at the base of her bare neck, putting the gentlest of pressure on her exposed skin. As he softly pressed his palm a bit, she felt his fingers caress in a way that she was left with no doubt of his tender expression of love. She could smell his coffee, as well as the clean lemon and sandalwood musk.

It was all there. Everything she had wanted to find was looking right back at her; kindness, tenderness, respect, admiration, and devotion. She knew it had happened.

She had found a man who saw her for who she was.

It wasn't because she was a Darcy, or had a thirty-thousand pound dowry. It wasn't because she was young and beautiful. It was because he saw who she was inside. He had once told her she was a priceless commodity. She felt every bit of that statement now as he looked at her.

It had come on so slowly, for he had become such a fixture in her life, that she had not had a chance to evaluate how important he was to her. She craved each and every moment, no matter how slight, spent with him. She ached to tell him about what made her happy and what troubled her. She wanted to share her best and worst days with him and felt confident that he would not judge. He understood her just as she understood him.

There was no one she hoped to see more in the morning, than him. He was the last one she thought of when she went to bed.

She knew it now. She loved him too.

CHAPTER 14

Benjamin felt it was too good to be true. *She sees me! Really sees me!* There was awareness in Georgiana's eyes as she looked at him. His heart picked up speed at an alarming rate, its pulse protesting the tightness of his cravat. The sun, or something, was making the room unbearably hot. He saw the admiration in her eyes that he had begged to see all these weeks.

His love was not unrequited! The joy in knowing this filled his breast with confidence, but he dared not let himself think on all those hopes he had silently caressed in his mind in the quiet hours when he was alone, for he would most definitely act on them.

The thoughts came unbidden anyway. How would it feel to embrace her? To touch his lips to her sweet mouth? To run his fingers through her hair? To place his lips at her collarbone and smell the jasmine and taste her porcelain skin?

But he dared not make a move in case the moment was just a figment of his imagination. He tried to convince himself that just seeing the admiration in her eyes was enough, for he was entirely content with seeing the longing—longing that was for no one else but him. He had thirsted and hungered for this moment; nothing could break his eyes away from hers.

Just then a very unwelcome voice shouted irritably outside of the library door, "Elizabeth, I cannot find it!"

Except that.

He removed his hand from Georgiana's shoulder and stepped away, sick that they were being forced to break eye contact. He only hoped that he had looked away in time. Darcy's determined stride brought him three paces into the room before he realized the library was occupied.

"Oh, forgive me. We have misplaced David's blanket, the one with the blue silk stitched on the edges, and he is inconsolable this morning. It was a miserable night."

Georgiana stood. "I will help you look for it," she offered.

"Give me a minute to clean my brushes."

Darcy looked confused for a moment. He looked at the painting and then looked at Benjamin and back at the painting. "What are you doing painting this early? It is hardly the best light for such activities." Darcy looked at Benjamin for another prolonged second, as if Benjamin should explain, but Benjamin only stood straighter and allowed Georgiana to do so.

"I am painting the sunrise, William. I have been waking early to paint for the last several weeks. Have you not noticed?"

"Apparently not." He again looked at Benjamin. "Have you been painting the sunrise *alone*?" There was a hint of emphasis on the last word, yet also leaving the word hanging on his lips, leaving one unsure if the question was finished.

"Benjamin usually works on his business while I paint. It was I who has been trespassing on *his* space. The library has a very good view of the eastern horizon."

Darcy's eyebrows rose significantly. "Benjamin? You call him *Benjamin*? I hardly think it appropriate that you call him by his Christian name."

Georgiana looked down at her hands.

Benjamin felt it was time to say something. "I do not mind it, sir," he replied. "I gave her permission."

"Is that so?" Darcy muttered.

Benjamin couldn't help but notice the ice in his voice and how Darcy's arms had stiffened at his sides.

Without looking in Georgiana's direction, Darcy barked, "Georgiana, would you please look in the music room for the blanket? *Benjamin*," he said sarcastically, "and I, will wash your brushes out."

"Yes, Brother." Georgiana walked past her brother toward the door and then looked back over her shoulder at Benjamin and gave him a sweet, but nervous, smile. He knew Darcy was watching him very closely, so he just nodded to Georgiana and resisted the urge to smile back.

He started gathering the brushes and putting the caps on the paints.

When Darcy didn't say anything, Benjamin chanced a glance in his direction. Darcy had his arms folded and was stretched to his full height.

Benjamin took a deep breath and put the brushes down. "I suppose it will not hurt them to soak in the water for a prolonged moment."

"Indeed," He said with no more feeling than if he was asked whether or not the winter would end at the expected time. But his next words held suppressed feeling. "Would you like to explain why you have been alone with Georgiana every morning for the last few weeks without even letting me know? Under my own roof! You might as well be courting my innocent sister without my permission!"

Benjamin knew he had to play it cool. It wasn't the first time a gentleman had yelled at him—not by any means. Many gentlemen had sought his advice on investments, chose to not follow it, lost their fortunes, and then, inexplicably, returned to his office to confront him with blame. But the stakes were even higher this time. Darcy was unexpectedly facing the real possibility of losing his lifelong treasure—his only sister. The situation would take some finesse.

Benjamin began, "I know she means a great deal to you."

"Of course she does!" Darcy nearly shouted. He then collected himself and lowered his voice. "I like you, Mr. Pastel, I do. I trust you and respect you. But Georgiana . . . well, she is a Darcy, and you are—"

"Just a solicitor who wholly adores her." He knew honesty was very important, but he also knew that it could either make the situation hotter or defuse it. He prayed it was the latter.

Darcy's eyebrows rose in both fear and disbelief. "Adores?"

"Yes, sir. I cannot imagine loving a woman more."

Darcy unfolded his arms and turned his back to Benjamin. He propped his arm on the mantle above the fire and hung his head. The heat in his words and stature had lost its initial shock and awe, as he said, "I cannot allow this."

Benjamin heard the pain in Darcy's voice, which gave him hope. Darcy was surprised, no doubt about that, but he wasn't one hundred percent set against the idea.

Mr. Pastel carefully inched forward, asking, "What can I say, what can I do, to help you know I would treat her as the priceless commodity that she is, for all of time?"

With no measurable pause, Darcy responded. "Nothing, Mr. Pastel. There is nothing you can do. Georgiana cannot marry you. I will not allow it. She will fall in love with a gentleman this season, and I will give her away at the altar, and she will never think of you again."

Benjamin felt the pain from his words, but did not give up hope. There was something Darcy said that he could use. "Then you admit she thinks about me *now*. Because you are correct. I believe her heart is already engaged."

Darcy startled and turned around. "Has she told you such? Have you declared yourself to her?"

"Very nearly so. I was just about to when you walked in."

"Then you have no confirmation that she loves you."

It was clear he was trying to convince himself and not Benjamin.

"Perhaps we could talk to her."

"*We* will do nothing. *I* will talk to her. And in *my* own time. In the interim, how close are you to moving into your townhouse? It would be an excellent idea if you left on your own accord as soon as possible."

Benjamin's heart dropped. There was conviction behind Darcy's voice. His decision had been made. But Benjamin had to try one more time. "And when you talk to her, and find out she loves me too, what will you do then? Ask her to marry Henry Darcy instead?"

"He would be an excellent match, and she has told me she likes him. So, yes, I think I shall discuss an arrangement with Henry today."

"I recommend having your discussion with Georgiana first. It might save you some time, not to mention a sticky conversation with Henry."

"And what makes you so confident?" Darcy demanded. "If she has not told you how she felt, how do you know she loves you?"

"Mr. Darcy, I have lived under your roof for nearly three weeks. I was there when Anne married Captain Jersey. I saw the glow on the Fitzwilliams' faces before they came to an understanding. I see the perceptible current of passion that passes between you and your wife every time you come back from watching the sunset. I know what love looks like, sir. And until this very morning, I could not have been half as confident that she returned my feelings. But today, Georgiana looked at me with the same adoration that Elizabeth looks at you. I have never felt so confident about anything as I did at that moment."

Darcy peered back at him silently. "I said I would talk to her," he replied dryly. "I understand you signed on your townhouse yesterday?" Darcy was reinforcing his decision.

"I did. I will devote my time today to finding the barest of furniture. I imagine I can rummage together enough basics to move out next week after the ball."

"Next week? How much does a bachelor need?" Darcy blustered. "I can lend you a bed. And I can lend you a servant or two to carry it there if needs be."

Benjamin heart sank further. Darcy was trying to be polite, but there was no mistaking his opinion on the matter. "I understand. I will be out by the end of the week. I only ask one thing."

"I am not particularly in the mood to grant favors, Mr. Pastel," Darcy warned.

"I can see that. All I ask is that you keep an open mind. I may not be Henry Darcy, but I am wise with my money. I can provide for her. I trust you will eventually see that her happiness is the important thing. And I have no greater priority in life than her happiness. What more can you ask of a husband? What more did Elizabeth ask of you?"

"Leave my wife out of this."

"On the contrary, I hope that you *do* involve her. In fact, I suggest talking to her even before you talk to Georgiana."

Darcy turned away from him and looked at Georgiana's painting. It was clear he was struggling with the decision.

Darcy finally said in a monotone voice, "Clean the brushes yourself." He then turned sharply and left the room. Apparently the conversation was over.

Benjamin watched Darcy leave, and sighed.

It could have gone worse . . .

And then after a moments pause, he finished his thought.

Perhaps not, he did well-nigh throw me out . . .

The morning had been beyond brutal for Darcy. He hadn't slept a wink with David crying all night. The baby had a mild fever, and the only thing that calmed him was being suckled by Elizabeth, but even that seemed to provide only momentary relief. It was far too early for teething. There was no real explanation for why David was so fussy.

With these thoughts occupying him, Darcy entered the breakfast room. In doing so, he ran into the footman carrying the coffee tray, staining his cravat and favorite waistcoat. He let out a swear word and snapped correction angrily at the servant, which Elizabeth chided him soundly for. That did not help his mood either.

To top it off, Richard had sent over a hastily scribbled note warning him that their aunt Catherine was coming to town. That was all he needed!

He plopped his coffee-stained, swearing self down and tried to hide behind the newspaper. And right on the front page was a notice that the award-winning soprano at the opera had taken ill and the understudy would be performing tonight. Henry had gone on and on about the soprano's skill, and now it looked like none of them would get to experience it. Preliminary reviews of the understudy's performance were reported as "painful and exhausting to endure".

He felt his head throb. He turned the page and read about King George's worsening condition. It seemed the British Empire was dependent on a man who was mad, and his son, who was entirely devoid of morals!

The footman stepped in and reported that the cook's new assistant had dropped the eggs. Would he like to wait while they dispatched a maid to the market, or make do without eggs?

"Good God! Can this day get any worse?" Darcy grumbled.

Elizabeth placed her hand on his and answered the footman for him. "No need for more eggs, Lionel. We can eat something else today."

Darcy stood and folded his newspaper. "No! If I want eggs, I shall have eggs! I will wait. I cannot promise I will wait *patiently*, but I will wait. Good Lord!"

Darcy continued, "Go, man, go! We do not need your presence *here*. Go tell the cook!" He snatched the newspaper up again and plopped himself down.

They sat in silence as Lionel hurriedly finished serving the breakfast trays and excused himself. Darcy knew that as soon as the door closed behind Lionel, Elizabeth would have something to say.

Three. Two. One.

"Heavens, William! What is wrong with you?"

Darcy scoffed. "With me? With *me*?" he repeated.

Elizabeth raised her eyebrow and softly said, "Yes, I have not seen you this worked up for some time. You never speak to the servants that way. You never curse, but you have done so several times this morning. And you have not even looked in my direction since you entered the breakfast room. I know you. I know something is troubling you. What is it?"

"I do not want to divulge it right now. Georgiana will be joining us at any time. Not to mention 'Benjamin'!" he replied sarcastically.

"Mr. Pastel already left for his office, and Georgiana asked for a tray to be sent to her room. It will just be us."

Darcy looked over at the remaining footman, and with as much patience as he could muster, he grumbled, "You may go."

He then turned toward Elizabeth and began. "Mr. Pastel and Georgiana have become close. At least Mr. Pastel thinks so. She calls him *Benjamin*!"

"Yes, I noticed. I am surprised you have not noticed before."

"Do you mean to tell me you were aware of this?"

"I know that she spends a great deal of time with him. I know that she brings him up a lot when he is not around. She seems to respect him and his opinion. But I do not know how engaged her feelings are. Do you think she loves him?"

"I do not know."

"Have you talked to her?"

"I thought I would talk to Henry first."

"What does Henry have to do with Georgiana and Mr. Pastel?"

Darcy fidgeted a bit. Pinpricks began at the base of his

neck, but he thrust that unease down.

It is the right thing to do, he said to himself.

"I think it is about time we arrange a marriage between Henry and Georgiana. I could not pick a better candidate."

Elizabeth laughed, then seemed to catch her reaction and drew it in. "Forgive me. I did not realize you possessed such complete control over whom Georgiana is in love with."

"She is not in love with anyone!"

Elizabeth put her hand on his, and the tenderness calmed him some, as her touch always did. "I did not mean to laugh, Will. I was just surprised that you had not seen how little time Henry and Georgiana spend together. I suspect Henry has no more tender feelings toward her than you have toward Lady Catherine's cat. If you have not noticed, Henry is perhaps a bit spirited for Georgiana. She is not at ease with him."

Darcy frowned, but made no reply.

"Whereas, I cannot say she is ill at ease with Mr. Pastel," Elizabeth continued. "I see a part of Georgiana that she rarely shows when he is around. It took her several months to show her true self to me and only a little less time for Charlotte. I need not say it, but your sister is very reserved. Mr. Pastel seems to have restored the self-assurance you say she lost in the incident with Wickham. And I suspect he gives her a bit more than confidence too."

Darcy considered Elizabeth. Her eyes were tired from the long restless night with David, but they were kind and compassionate. Darcy may not want to hear what she was saying, but there was truth in her look. He wasn't ready to admit that she was correct, but it was clear that she was sincere.

"So, you think Georgiana loves Mr. Pastel?"

Elizabeth sat back in her chair. "I have no idea. I think she admires him. I think she feels closer to him than any other person in her life. You and I both have left her to her own devices since David was born. I did not realize how much time and effort it would take to care for a baby. Did Mr. Pastel say he admired her?"

Darcy groaned. "He said he 'adored' her. Said he 'loved' her. But how could he have developed such tender feelings and left me so unaware? A real gentleman would have told me he wished to court my sister."

"Ah, I see it now. I see why this is bothering you so much. Mr. Pastel is not a gentleman, or at least not the land-owning kind. I have guessed your hand, have I not?"

Darcy's voice rose a bit higher than usual. "What? Of course not!" His voice returned to normal and he added sincerely, "I like Mr. Pastel very well. I am very impressed that he has made his fortune by being frugal and working hard. I cannot discount that I admire that he wishes to disentangle himself from that immoral brother of his. Or that he is so vocal about always maintaining propriety. But actions speak louder than words! What exactly was proper about spending every sunrise alone with a lady he admires? Answer me that! If he is so moral and proper, why did he omit that bit of intelligence from those of us who might have stopped it?"

Elizabeth smiled, the grin widening with each passing second. Her silence meant that the answer should be obvious.

He thought long and hard for a few seconds before the answer came to him. "Because I would have stopped it."

Pastel probably didn't say anything because he knew I would have made sure they were never alone. He knew I wouldn't let him openly court her.

"Are you saying all this secrecy is my fault?"

"I did not say anything, dear. But you have always impressed me with your wisdom. I will leave you to think on that a bit," she chuckled. "I am going to check on David again," she said, standing up and kissing the top of Darcy's head.

"Just one more thing before I go," Elizabeth added. "It would disappoint a great number of people if Georgiana were to be unhappily married, but no one more so than the lady in question. I think it is time you ask her how *she* feels."

"I cannot, not yet. I am far too emotional to address her sensitively."

"I have a very wise husband. And that is why I love you so much."

CHAPTER 15

"Brother?" Georgiana asked as he passed her by without a glance for the third time that morning.

"I am busy right now, Georgiana."

She watched with trepidation as he walked away. She would have to find a way to talk with him.

She was no simpleton. She recognized when her brother was upset. She knew he was burrowed deep inside his mind right now, letting two conflicting foes battle it out without so much as a flinch.

Back when he thought Elizabeth would not have him, he had adamantly denied that anything was wrong, but she saw more than he meant to show. His eyes grew distant. The creases around them were more pronounced. His shoulders drooped under the heavy load. His brow had a slight sheen to it. But the conclusive evidence was his refusal to look anyone in the eye.

It was nearly noon luncheon; she had watched him pacing the halls as if he couldn't sit down if his life depended on it. The doctor had come and gone, prescribing an elixir for baby David's fever. The few times when William did sit down, he quickly got up and left again as soon as Georgiana entered. It seemed he suddenly needed to check on David, or report some important piece of information to the housekeeper. Once he randomly asked if there were any roses still in bloom before anxiously heading toward the garden.

There was no denying it. Her brother was avoiding her.

Perhaps tonight, before the theatre, she could pull him aside and talk with him. Until then, she had to come up with some distraction. Her first thought was to go see Benjamin at his office. But something told her that was a bad idea.

Her next option was to go see Charlotte, but then she remembered that Charlotte had an appointment with the dressmaker for the final fitting on her new gown for tonight. She was going to go in a deep-burgundy velvet dress that Colonel Fitzwilliam had encouraged her to buy. Charlotte was nervous about the boldness of the color, but she dearly wanted to look good for her first public appearance as Mrs. Charlotte Fitzwilliam. Besides, the happy couple had only been home a few days. No doubt the house was flooded with visitors and well-wishers. Charlotte would be far too nervous to visit with Georgiana today.

Georgiana suddenly thought about how she hadn't had a good heart-to-heart talk with her friend, Jane Andrews, for some time. In less than a minute, she found Elizabeth and told her of her plans. Since Elizabeth was busy nursing David, Georgiana agreed to take a maid with her.

She ordered the carriage and impatiently waited by the front door. She didn't realize she was tapping her foot until Henry came up from behind and startled her.

"Dear me!" she gasped. "You should not sneak up on someone like that, Henry!"

He chuckled and then stopped in mid-laugh and his eyebrows pulled together. "Is there something amiss? It is a beautiful day and you look as if you can't wait for it to be over! Here, let me help you." He took her hands and pulled off the gloves and removed her bonnet.

"What are you doing?"

"I can't rightly dance with you when I can't feel your hands or see your eyes."

"Dance with me? Henry, there is no music. And, I hate to burst your bubble, but in England, we all dance with gloves."

"Pity. American customs are preferred in this case. They must come off."

Georgiana looked around, and a maid reached for the gloves and bonnet and stepped to the edge of the foyer.

"I must say I am not in the mood to dance," she admitted.

"Which is precisely why you should. Allow me." He reached one hand around her waist and the other took her right hand. He winked at her and authoritatively said, to no one in particular as if the conductor was waiting for the instruction, "A waltz, if you will."

"Henry, I have only had one lesson in the waltz! I did not know they danced it in America."

"They don't. But Colonel Fitzwilliam showed me how just yesterday. Fascinating little three-step thing; it definitely has its benefits. Like this," His grip around her waist held her close, and he spun her around and around.

She couldn't help but giggle.

"Or this," he dropped her waist and rolled her out and then pulled her back in and caught her with a jolt, looking deep into her eyes. He had such a serious look on his face, almost forced sternness, that she laughed outright.

She was perfectly content letting her mind drift and she imagined Benjamin's hands, and Benjamin's warm breath, and . . .

"What a beautiful smile." he said genuinely.

She startled a bit when it was Henry's voice, and not Benjamin's, saying it. It caused her to miss a step.

"It appears I am sweeping you off your feet!" Then he winked in a teasing way.

"Oh, Henry, you are such a tease! You always know how to make me laugh."

He gave her one of his charming smiles, and he continued to dance around the foyer, nearly bumping her into the table with flowers on it.

"Oh dear!" he grimaced. "Please keep the tale of my sub-par performance between us, Georgiana. If Richard finds out, I will never hear the end of it."

"Of course," Georgiana giggled. "I fear my performance is equally poor."

"As a gentleman, I must protest any ungenerous characterization of your skills," Henry insisted. "But it is of no consequence. All I wanted was to do it well enough to bring a smile to a lady's face. And I see that I have succeeded."

"You certainly have. Thank you, Henry. I was not in the best mood." She bowed her head a bit remembering the frustrating morning she had.

Henry stopped dancing and tipped her chin up. "Georgiana, I was wondering . . ."

With his one hand around her waist and the other gently raising her chin, she could do nothing but look into his brown eyes. She had never been this close to him before, and could smell a musky smell that was very different from Benjamin's lemon and sandalwood.

Suddenly the look in Benjamin's eyes from this morning, the one where she saw his love for her, came to mind, and she knew she had to step away.

She did so and turned around to the maid for her things, but caught sight of her brother on the stairs looking down at them with a small knowing smile on his face.

Her heart dropped.

She knew how that moment must have looked. There was no doubt in her mind that Henry was just trying to cheer her up, but from William's perspective, it probably looked like he had interrupted a near kiss. She looked back at Henry one last time.

He had just noticed her brother too. Henry bowed slightly to him in acknowledgement and then said in low tones that even the maid a few feet away from them could not understand, "I must talk with you. It is very important. Can you find me before we leave for the theatre?"

Fear flooded her heart. Henry had always been a friend; was he implying a private conversation? A conversation of *that* kind? The kind that meant *more* than friends? A conversation about their future? Together?

She looked up at William one more time and saw his expectant eyes. She knew he had not heard what Henry had said, but she felt exposed nonetheless. It would be better to have the private conversation with Henry, where she could refuse him in a kind and sensitive way, than leave him with the impression that she desired a future with him as his wife.

She knew she could never marry anyone other than Benjamin. Her heart had made that decision for her and she had always been one who stood by her heart. It had never led her astray before and knew that it would not now.

"Of course, Henry," she agreed. "But I am on my way to Lady Jane's townhouse for several hours. Perhaps after the theatre?"

"Oh, is that where you are going? To Lady Jane's?"

"Yes, I thought I had told you that."

"No, you didn't. From the look that was on your face, I thought you were delivering a message from the undertaker. Would you like me to accompany you?"

"No, thank you. It will just be us ladies this time."

William had descended down the stairs by this time and must have heard the last few comments. "Georgiana, pumpkin," her brother said, "why not let Henry escort you to Lady Jane's?"

"No, really, I shall be fine with Mary Ann."

"You wound me, Georgiana. Surely I am a better escort than a maid," Henry teased.

"Henry," she eyed him meaningfully, "I would rather see her myself. We have things to discuss."

Henry smiled and winked, "Well, I do have some paperwork to look over. Please send Lady Jane my most sincere regards."

She didn't know why he winked at her, but she was grateful he had yielded. William, however, looked a little defeated—no doubt disappointed Henry and Georgiana had missed out on another private moment. But she wasn't ready for that yet. She would have to be strong.

*****

As soon as she got to Jane's house, she was shown into the parlor. She waited for several minutes before anyone came and saw her. When the door finally opened, it was not her friend who met her, but Jane's father.

Georgiana stood and curtsied. "My Lord! I did not expect you! I thought Jane, er, Lady Jane would be here."

"And so she shall. May I interest you in tea? Or something stronger? I am in the mood for port myself, even if it is a little early yet."

She was always a bit nervous around Lord Porterhouse and was surprised that she did not stutter when she spoke. "Tea. Tea would be nice. Thank you."

He motioned with his head to the servant, and the unspoken command was ushered into motion. "How are you, Miss Darcy? Are you prepared for your coming season?"

Lord Porterhouse always reminded Georgiana of a fat steak—in both his body shape and his ruddy, scar-marbled complexion. His title was humorously well-suited. So well-suited in fact that it was sometimes difficult for her to take him seriously.

Especially now that he had a bit of gray mixed with red in his beard, which only added to the marbled effect. He had a robust belly and frequently placed his hand on it as if to hide its gross size, but that only accentuated it more. Today he kept his hands busy with a pocket fob that was too ornate for the middle of the day.

She realized she had not answered him and said, "As ready as Jane probably is. I fear I have only had one lesson, well, two, I suppose, in the waltz. I hear it is becoming very popular."

"It is disgusting, that is what it is! I do not care if it is popular, Lady Jane will not dance it, ever!" Georgiana tried not to laugh when he referred to his own daughter as Lady Jane, instead of simply Jane. Jane Andrews's father was entirely enamored with propriety and status. Hawthorn Hall was already an architectural masterpiece, but he was remodeling most of the second wing to make it the most coveted estate in all of Derbyshire. It would eclipse even Pemberley by the time Lord Porterhouse was finished. She suddenly had an idea that would avoid the discussion on the waltz.

"How is the remodeling coming along?" she inquired.

"We really are just in the planning stages right now. I have a few legal loopholes that I need to work around."

"My friend, Mr. Pastel, is a solicitor and was very interested to hear of your plans. Have you considered consulting him?"

Lord Porterhouse pondered it a bit and said, "How do you know Mr. Pastel? He is not exactly the kind of man that I imagine Darcy wants you to associate with."

"Oh, I did not mean Clyde Pastel," Georgiana explained, "although I hear he is mending his ways. I was referring to Benjamin Pastel, his brother."

"I do not take my business as far as Liverpool when London can meet my needs."

"But did you not know? Benjamin Pastel has entirely bought out the London office. He just purchased an office on Silverthorn Street. He is a very good solicitor and would appreciate the business of a man as well connected as yourself."

Lord Porterhouse's chest puffed up slightly at the complimentary reference to his status. "Perhaps I will stop by this afternoon and call on Mr. Benjamin Pastel. What did you say Clyde Pastel was doing?"

"He will take over the Liverpool office. He is much changed these last three weeks. Benjamin Pastel says he is like the prodigal son come home. He has even given up alcohol."

Lord Porterhouse's eyebrow rose disapprovingly, and he took another sip of his port. "Then the man is just as crazy as he ever was. No man should give up drink entirely. It is ungentlemanly. What would he drink at dinner?" he guffawed. "Warm milk?"

Lady Jane came in and curtsied deeply to her father and then to Georgiana. "Father, I hope you kept Miss Darcy company and did not bore her with stories of Parliament."

"Certainly not," Lord Porterhouse replied. "I have had endured enough discussion of reformation for one day," he announced. "I will leave you ladies to visit by yourselves. Do say goodbye before you travel to Darcy House. Where is Mrs. Smyth?"

"I dismissed her for the afternoon when I heard that Miss Darcy would be here. She has a nephew who just came home injured from the war. She begged of me to let her visit him."

He guffawed again, but this time it came out more of a snort. "She should have asked me, not you. I pay her wages."

"Yes, Father. I shall remember that."

He stood and kissed Jane on both cheeks. "Good girl," he whispered before strutting out the door.

The atmosphere in the room relaxed immediately. Jane sat down next to Georgiana and tucked her feet under her skirts and rested her chin on the hand that was on the back of the sofa.

"How is Darcy House? Is everyone well? Henry? Mr. Pastel? Mr. and Mrs. Darcy? How is little David?"

"Little David had a rough night," Georgiana sighed. "And it took a toll on the entire household. Everyone seems to be off-kilter, irritable, and unusual."

Jane tucked her chin and her brows furrowed. "I cannot imagine Henry being in an irritable mood."

"Oh, he was not irritable, he was the unusual one. I was referring to my brother and even Elizabeth. This morning—"

Jane interrupted her, "Henry was unusual? How?"

Georgiana considered telling her about Henry's strange

request for a private conversation, but there was urgency in Jane's eyes. She looked as if she were an African child who had lived on rice for the last ten years and was now being introduced to a buffet of foods.

It was so apparent that it made Georgiana pause. How strange it was to see Jane so animated. She was usually shy and deliberate in her action and words—a symptom of being raised by an extremely stiff father—but today she seemed ready to inhale Georgiana's very words.

Although it gave Georgiana pause, it was also nice to feel like the distance that seemed to have formed between them had lessened. The light in Jane's eyes, coupled with finally being able to have a private moment with her best friend, put Georgiana at enough ease to be able to discuss what she so desperately wanted to discuss with someone.

"Never mind about Henry. I have big news."

Jane looked disappointed for the briefest of moments, but then giggled and said, "How big?"

"Potentially, the biggest!"

"Mr. Pastel proposed!" Jane guessed.

"What?" Georgiana shrieked in reply. "No!"

Jane smirked and turned her head to the side as if to evaluate what Georgiana was hiding. "Do not lie to me, Georgiana. I see how he looks at you."

Georgiana looked down at her hands and felt her face flush crimson. She tried to speak, but nothing came out.

She looked up through her eyelashes at Jane and saw how her best friend was smiling, and all that came out was an entirely girlish giggle. Then both ladies erupted into fits of laughter.

The next hour and a half was spent discussing Mr. Pastel. Georgiana tried to explain to Jane what had changed. She found herself describing things that she never had been able to put into words before.

"Elizabeth once tried to tell me what love felt like. She asked if someone had never seen the color green, how would I describe it to them? I have thought a long time about that. All my initial efforts would be to say it is the color of a frog, or a leaf, or grass, or eyes of someone they might know, but none of that would help because they have never seen any of those things. I would have to describe it with emotion or feelings. This is why Elizabeth is so wise. Love is not something you see, but something you feel."

Jane sighed, "So practice on me. How would you describe the color green, or love, to me?"

"Let me see if I can." Georgiana thought for a minute. She thought of all that she felt when she was with Benjamin. She closed her eyes as if it would help recreate the feelings right there in Jane's sitting room.

"I would have to say that the color green is a warm summer day; it is a picnic of your favorite foods, followed by fresh lemonade. It is that strange feeling you get when your insides are all mixed up and you are nervous, but the feeling urges you forward, confidently, through the unknown.

"Green, or love, has a selfish nature to it; always wanting more, but yet never quite denying its total satisfaction with what it already has. It is a hungry color, devouring all that it comes across, especially all your thoughts and dreams, both waking and sleeping. It is all around you, but rarely noticed until it is right in front of you. Love is warm and gooey but with a distinct impression you can never recreate without the other person. Love is . . . love is what life is made of. Yes, Jane, love is the color of green."

CHAPTER 16

Benjamin was torn. "Say it again, Clyde." He wasn't sure if he heard him the first time.

Clyde lifted the piece of paper back up to his face and read with a monotone voice, seemingly irritated at being forced to repeat himself, "'At your earliest convenience, please call on me at Rolling Farms. I have not long to live and am eager to hear how I could have not just one, but two, nephews to carry on my legacy. My wife and I had such hopes for a family of our own, but were never blessed with that opportunity. I look forward to meeting my nephew and heir. I shall expect you on Thursday. Sincerely, Christian Pastel.'"

"So our Uncle Christian is alive? And he wants to see us?"

"Not quite. The letter is addressed to *you*. It specifically says, 'Mr. Benjamin Pastel'."

"What did your man find out about this Rolling Farms in Kent?"

"All I know is that it is a gated estate on the east side of Kent. There is a gatehouse and a gatekeeper, who is under strict instructions not to admit anyone without his master's consent. My man couldn't do much more than leave a note, but he did include the office's address for correspondence. Damn good thing he did too. The farm is nearly ten miles outside of Kent. The roads have not been properly kept up. There was nothing but farmhouses along the road, none of whom were loose with their tongue about the Master of Rolling Farms."

"Was it a large estate?"

Clyde shrugged. "My man couldn't tell. The gate was too far from the estate to see."

The agitation was building. "Well, surely someone knows *something* about Rolling Hills or our Uncle Christian Pastel!"

Clyde creased his eyebrow together suspiciously. "I don't understand you, Ben. This is good news. Go see the estate for yourself. You can have all your questions answered in two days."

Benjamin looked away from Clyde's prying eyes. He had not been in the best of moods since speaking with Mr. Darcy this morning. He was trying to do exactly what Darcy had asked of him—readying his townhouse so he could leave Darcy House.

There were still a hundred things that needed to be done, but he couldn't focus on anything but one pair of adoring blue eyes. Lovely eyes, which made him want to stay at Darcy House for as long as possible.

Although Benjamin was not looking at Clyde, he knew his gaze was on him. It was rather irritating.

"All right, spill it. What happened?" Clyde said flatly. "I just told you *fabulous* news that will help you win the heart of your fair lady, and you look like someone just fed you cod liver oil. Did something happen with Miss Darcy? Did she refuse you?"

Benjamin looked down at his hands and brushed the imaginary wrinkles from his breeches. He cleared his throat. "How is it avoiding alcohol?"

"Honestly? It makes me miserable. But at least the shaking and flushing is over. Don't have that nagging anxiety anymore, but the craving and the constant burn in my throat . . . Wait! Oh no you don't! You're not changing the subject that easy. Answer my questions. What's gotten into you?"

Benjamin looked at his brother and half smiled. "Well, to be honest, I feel much the same as you today—shaky, anxious, and with a nagging craving that I truly feel I may never be able to quench . . . for her."

Clyde smiled and nodded. "That bad, huh?"

"That bad."

"Well, shouldn't be long now. When will you propose and quench that thirst?"

"I do not know if I can."

"Why the hell not?" Clyde yelled. His assistant poked his head into the room, and Clyde motioned him away. "You just got confirmation that you are part of a legacy. Your dream of being a true gentleman is coming to fruition. You will finally have that fancy status you have always wanted. What's stopping you now? And don't tell me it is your insecurities, because you have a quiet strength about you that I never did. I always looked for my self-worth in objects or things; and like your money, you always reinvested your self-worth and it has grown exponentially."

"That was quite philosophical, Clyde."

Benjamin sighed. There was no point hiding it any longer. "Mr. Darcy knows that I love Georgiana. And it took him less than thirty seconds to decide I was not good enough for her. He is determined to arrange a match with her cousin, Henry Darcy. I cannot go to Kent right now. What if I went to Kent as a solicitor, and came home a gentleman, only to find out that Georgiana has been promised to Henry?"

"Then propose before you go! Secure her hand. Has she given you any indication of her affection?"

Benjamin couldn't help but smile. "She has."

Clyde smacked the table with his hand. "Ah ha! You see? It is not so dark as you think! What did she say?"

"Nothing really. But she loves me too. I just know it."

Clyde's jaw dropped. "Good God, man! You just '*know it*'? You're risking your whole future on that! I don't care if angels from heaven started singing the wedding march, you have to close the deal!—Now, Ben! Heavens! Why didn't you propose? You do *nothing* in business without getting it written down. Verbal agreements are meaningless; you have to get a contract. Didn't Father teach you anything?"

Benjamin chuckled, "You know? I am not sure which brother I like more, the drunk who was ill-mannered but distastefully predictable, or the one who suddenly is pushing me to risk it all and follow my heart."

Clyde scoffed. "Leave the heart out of this, Ben. Think of it as a business deal. Present your assets to her, including your new title as a gentleman, and ask her if she wants more involvement in your future than simply picking out drapes at your office. It is as simple as that. If she loves you as much as you say, then you have a partner for life."

"And if not?" Benjamin asked.

Clyde hesitated. "Well, then you will know once and for all."

"I see the wisdom of your suggestion, I do. But I am not sure that is the right way to go about it. Really, Clyde, Georgiana does not care about money. I think she would marry me even if I do not tell her how much I am worth."

"So you say, but in my experience *everyone* cares about money, especially rich women who have always had everything they desired. She may not realize it, but being a Darcy opens doors for her. She may not want to give all that up for a little friction under a ratted quilt at night—"

"I warn you, do not be crude, Clyde. Our relationship is nothing like that, and you know it. Do not talk so ill of her. What we have is a solid friendship based on selfless companionship, kindness, tenderness, and an invaluable consideration of each other's feelings."

"Oh, don't get your knickers in a twist. If you ask me, that all sounds a bit boring. Hell! You sound as if you're still a virgin!"

The silence hung in the air as Benjamin hesitated a fraction of a second too long.

"You are! Good God, Ben! How are two inexperienced people supposed to know what to do?"

"I am sure we will figure it out. But leave my wedding night out of this. It is not the easiest topic to avoid in my own head, and I do not need any of your help with it. Back to what to do about Kent." He hoped changing the subject would work with Clyde. "Do you really think I should go? It is a very fragile time. She may not have told me she loved me, but I saw it in her eyes."

Clyde sat back and intertwined his fingers under his chin for a moment. "Hmmm. I still think the best thing would be to present your assets and show her you can provide for her. You see, if her heart is already engaged, then her only reservations must be about the money. So, clear the air, and communicate how good a provider you will be. It may be the only thing standing between you and a kiss."

Benjamin wasn't so sure, but Clyde had a better instinct for reading people than Benjamin. Little wonder it had taken him several visits to see the truth between Charlotte and Colonel Fitzwilliam.

Clyde, on the other hand, could close business deals in the first sitting with little to no research beforehand. He had met Georgiana twice now, once when they did drapes, and another time when Clyde showed up at Darcy House to drop off the contract for his townhouse. Georgiana had invited him in, but Clyde declined tea at the time, graciously taking a rain check. Benjamin didn't even know about the second time until a day ago.

"Very well, Clyde. I certainly do not have nearly as much income as her brother. Maybe that worries her a bit." Benjamin's stomach felt twisted in knots at the idea of actually proposing to Georgiana, but he wouldn't put it off any longer. Not while her brother was working against him.

"Trust me," Clyde assured him. "Settle her concerns with a few numbers and details and you'll get the deal signed."

"I pray you are right. Thank you for the suggestion."

"So, you will go see her tonight and then leave for Kent to see our uncle?"

"I think I shall."

*****

Georgiana and Jane had finally quit giggling like little girls about what it felt like to be in love. Georgiana talked to her for what seemed like hours about Benjamin Pastel. They even talked about what kind of flowers they would be able to get for the wedding in the next few months. Georgiana hoped for lilies, but she knew that might be impossible this time of year.

She made it home just in time to prepare for the evening. Her lady's maid put the last of the pearl hairpins in her hair and declared her ready for the theatre. Jane was already downstairs, and Georgiana hoped that Henry and Benjamin were being good hosts to her.

After applying one more spritz of her jasmine toilette water, she gathered her skirts and her long gloves and reticule, placing a new handkerchief in it and headed down the stairs.

Benjamin seemed to be waiting for her. The sight of him made her heart skip excitedly in her chest.

Georgiana realized at that moment, that the widely unknown benefit of being newly in love, was the tantalizing anticipation of seeing him again after being separated, regardless of the length of time apart. And in doing so now, her entire being was infused with an overwhelming frenzy of energy and utter delight. It would have been impossible not to smile back down at him; but nor did she attempt to suppress it.

"You look lovely, Georgiana. You will be the most beautiful lady at the theatre, but I did not need to see you to know that." His face had colored slightly, and when he reached for her hand and bowed over it, his hands shook slightly.

"Thank you, Benjamin. You look nervous. Is there something wrong?"

Benjamin dropped her hand gently and cleared his throat. He took a deep breath and said, "I am pleased that we have a few minutes before we must leave. Can I show you a book in the library that I found which you might enjoy?"

Georgiana's heart picked up speed. This was surely a ploy to get her alone. For the briefest of moments, she was reminded of Henry asking for a private moment. Certainly, if Benjamin proposed, then refusing Henry would be less difficult. Not that she needed an excuse to refuse Henry. But it might make things easier when she had to tell William.

"Of course." She could not believe her luck. The halls were quiet, and no one passed them as they entered the library. She felt her stomach flip upside down as she realized that he was about to declare his love for her. It was everything she had always hoped to have. Even the sconces on the wall were romantically lit for the right mood. Someone, probably Elizabeth, was playing one of James Hook's concertos in the music room down the hall.

She tried to ponder how she would accept him. Should she say yes right away? Would that look too eager? Would it make her look desperate? She hoped not.

She was not the kind of lady who played games or liked drama. Women like Caroline Bingley might prefer pomp and circumstance, but all she really wanted was to hear him declare what was in his heart.

Suddenly all sorts of scenarios were playing in her head of what he would say to her.

She wondered how long he had admired her, and would he tell her when he knew?

Or would he tell her he had always admired her?

She wondered if he would get down on one knee. The image him doing just that formed too easily in her head.

She wondered if he had a prepared speech, or if he was going to speak unrehearsed.

How should she accept him?

Would she get her first kiss? Tingles erupted all over her body.

She was relieved that she would not need to endure a season after all. She had never really wanted one, but William had insisted.

That thought brought William to mind and how he had avoided her all day. It would be a very big relief to him to have her engaged and married off, and although it wasn't Henry Darcy, she knew that William would be happy to have her marry for love, for that is all she ever wanted.

She realized she had allowed herself to daydream and that he had been talking for some time.

She recommitted herself to pay attention.

" . . . and I have quite a bit of money saved up so you really need not worry about me being able to support you. I am a hard worker. I know you are not used to the man of the house having employment, but I enjoy my job and have an excellent reputation as a solicitor.

"My income alone should speak for itself. It may not be as much as Mr. Darcy makes, but I have been very wise in how I spend it, as well as how I invest it. In fact, even though I have just purchased an office, as well as a townhouse, I have no debt, and that is how I like it. I am sure that with my steady work ethic, and the interest from what is left over, it will be sufficient income to live on. When we are blessed with children, all of your dowry can be used for our son's education or our daughter's dowries . . ."

Georgiana attempted not to let her jaw drop, but she forgot to make the same demands on her heart.

He was certainly proposing, however, *none* of it was about *love*. In fact, it seemed to all be about money! The more she listened, the more ill she felt, and the more she needed to find someplace to sit.

She numbly walked to the sofa and moved the books to the table so she could sit down. She tried to be polite, but the more she listened, it seemed, the more he delved into his bank balances.

Was he actually quoting numbers to her? His voice began to tremble, and his speech became pressured, but she was too shocked to stop him. He began to detail how his father had insisted on a university education, Cambridge in fact, and he would insist on it for his sons as well. He asked her if that was pleasing to her. She nodded slightly but then shook her head.

"No? Would you prefer they go to Oxford?" Benjamin asked.

This was not going well. She rubbed her brow and shook her head further. "No, I do not care if it is Cambridge or Oxford. Mr. Pastel, are you proposing to me?"

"I thought we settled on Benjamin. And yes, I hope to show you just what kind of man I am. You can have little doubt to my ability to provide for you in every way."

"Provide for me?" Where were the declarations of love? Where was the unabashed joy? And the long-awaited kiss?

This is not how it is supposed to go! She could have sworn that Benjamin loved her, but then again, he had never actually declared his love, she just thought she saw it in his eyes that morning. Could she have been mistaken?

She searched his eyes for any evidence of that love, but all she saw was furrowed brows, an element of false bravado—he was definitely nervous. There were no words of admiration or expressions of making him the happiest of men.

"I would hope you need not ask if I was proposing." He stepped toward her and sat next to her, his hands firmly gripping his own knees. Why was he so nervous? They had always had a very casual relationship, one that was based on open communication. After that special moment this morning while she painted, she thought she knew what she wanted.

She looked over at the painting. Mindlessly, she stood and walked toward it. It was about halfway done, but the sun and the sunset she painted were not nearly as breathtaking as the original that inspired it. She let out a sigh.

Mr. Pastel followed her to the painting and stood beside her.

He had finally stopped talking about his wealth, which was a relief, but the silence that remained, was choking her.

Like the fog that eventually burns off, she knew she was going to have to answer him, but she feared that if she opened her mouth that her disappointment would show.

It seemed an impossible feat, but she drew upon the

strength of every person she had ever admired who had once had to make the choice she was moments away from making. She knew she had to be true to herself, and preserve the hope to have what all the others had.

She could not—would not—marry, except for love.

She bowed her head and whispered, "I cannot marry you."

CHAPTER 17

Benjamin couldn't believe his ears. Had he heard her right? Was she really refusing him?

Georgiana was looking at her hands. When he did not say anything, she looked up briefly, then looked away as if the sight of him was torture. Her lower lip started to quiver, and she bit it to control it.

He was most certainly confused—hurt, more than anything—but her pain somehow seemed to trump his.

"I can see my presence is unwelcome. Forgive me for having taken up so much of your time. Do not cry, Geor . . . Miss Darcy,"—*I definitely cannot call her Georgiana anymore*—"I shall forgo the theater tonight and leave Darcy House in the morning. I have an uncle who is ill in Kent, and I wish to see him before he passes. But if it is not too much to ask, I hope you finish your painting, for I desire . . . I will pay you for it, of course. I would dearly love to hang it in my office."

Georgiana made a sound that was part hiccup and part sob. He knew that agonizing sound would be seared into his ears forever.

All he wanted to do was take her into his arms and hold her. He did not know why she had said she could not marry him. Perhaps it was because of her brother, or maybe it was because she really loved Henry Darcy.

But either way, his continued presence was painful for her. It was all he could do to turn from her blue eyes, which were filled with the fattest tears that he had ever seen.

He suppressed the urge to kiss her hand one last time. A clean break was the last gift he could give her. He bowed deeply and nearly choked on the pain in his heart as he saw her tears start to fall.

"God bless you, Miss Darcy."

He hurried from the room. Unfortunately, he nearly ran

right into Mr. Darcy as he turned sharply to go up the stairs.

"Mr. Pastel, the carriage is about to leave. Did you forget something?"

Benjamin stumbled to find the right way to say it, but trying to come up with something that would stop the questions. "I decided to take your advice. I will depart tomorrow with most of my things. I will be gone a bit longer than a week and then I will return to retrieve the rest of them."

"But you will miss Georgiana's birthday ball."

Drat! But it does not matter now.

She had refused him, he reminded himself. "Indeed. I shall make an effort to return before next Saturday."

"Listen, Mr. Pastel, about this morning—"

"No need to explain. It is a moot point." He looked at his pocket watch to avoid the confused look on Darcy's face and added, "You should really hurry."

"Yes, yes, I suppose we should. I am sorry about this morning. Giving Georgiana a bit of space will settle things down. I am sure we can think this out rationally. It is my opinion that Georgiana is confused. "

She is not the only one.

*****

The opera progressed at a snail's pace. Georgiana had been looking forward to seeing it all week. Even the renowned soprano had recovered and taken center stage, much to the audience's delight. But it felt somehow wrong now without Benjamin there beside her. Each measure seemed to drag on tediously. As she looked around the box, everyone else seemed happy and smiling, truly enjoying the music. Georgiana only stared blankly down at the stage, seeing and hearing nothing. The rest of the evening passed by in a similar blur.

The next morning, she watched the sunrise from her window, its rays pushing through the giant oak. Only rays of light and hints of the color shone through the tree's thick foliage. It mirrored how she felt inside. Only yesterday she had found herself in love with Benjamin Pastel. It happened little by little, occasionally getting hints of what it was like to really care for someone and to understand what it was like to be cherished.

It had only been a few weeks together, but each moment with him was seared into her mind and heart. She had even written about it in her journal, the one that she was encouraged to start writing over a year ago. It was all documented. The kind way he smiled at her. The sincere compliments he gave when she played the pianoforte. The quiet strength she felt when he silently stood beside her, watching her paint. The way he had noticed her unease in the gypsy tent. The way he encouraged her with conversations about faith. And yet now she doubted all of it. There was no comfort to be found in reviewing their once-pleasant memories.

She had wanted to see him off last night after the horrid scene in the library, but she knew she would end up throwing herself at him, begging him to love her the way she loved him.

She was young, but she knew love did not work that way.

Love did not come on suddenly; it was like a sunrise—the warmth of its light filled the soul, little by little, without ceremony or recognition.

Except, it seemed Benjamin Pastel hadn't seen the same sunrise she had seen.

The bitter realization brought tears to her eyes again. She didn't want any more sunrises. She didn't want to fall in love again. Not with someone else. She wanted Benjamin to love her, and now that would never be.

The rest of the morning was dull and lifeless until the noon luncheon when her aunt, Lady Catherine de Bourgh, descended upon their steps.

William greeted her with a kiss. "Aunt Catherine," he said, "I was not expecting you."

"Did Lord Matlock not inform you of my arrival? He said he would tell Colonel Fitzwilliam. Surely you have my rooms prepared. The journey was long and tiring. You must write to those who maintain the roads and inform them that there were ruts and bumps along the road that would put the Lake District to shame! I have the best carriage money can buy, and even that could not hold up against those terrible conditions! I feared for my life, upon my word, I did!"

Pausing to take a breath, but without waiting for a response, her aunt continued her tirade, "Are you not going to let me in? I shall take a chill standing here, Darcy! Are you trying to see to my demise? I know we have had our troubles in the past when you refused to marry my sweet Anne, but she states she would not have been happy with you. Heaven help her! She claims she is euphoric with Captain Jersey! I say, Darcy, let me in." With that she pushed past William and nearly tossed her things on the butler.

William smiled at Georgiana and rolled his eyes. "Of course, Aunt Catherine," her brother replied. "Your rooms are always ready and you are always welcome. Come refresh yourself. Luncheon was just about to be served."

Georgiana knew that the rest of the day would be filled helping Elizabeth mollify and appease their exacting visitor. There would be no time for anyone to mope around, not with Lady Catherine around. She was a woman who demanded an entire household's time, thoughts, and actions.

Georgiana had never been more relieved to see her.

After luncheon, Lady Catherine asked if Georgiana was prepared for her coming out and curtsy before the queen. She wanted to know all the details: the number of gowns and their colors, which invitations she had already accepted and which ones she should be sure to refuse, the family jewels that Georgiana would thus inherit—of which she was never to wear the black onyx—and how Georgiana should plan to do her hair for teas and dinners versus balls. Luckily Georgiana was distracted enough with telling the details that the afternoon flew by very quickly.

Sometime in the late afternoon, Lady Catherine asked if she had the necessary hair accessories for her birthday ball. "For you must outshine every other lady in attendance, my dear, and I am quite the expert in hair accessories. Go fetch them for me. I will tell you if they are appropriate."

"Yes, Aunt Catherine." Georgiana left the sitting room and went to get the pearl combs and ribbons that she and Elizabeth had selected. Relieved by the distraction, she hardly noticed where she was going and nearly ran straight into Henry in the foyer.

"Where are you going in such a rush?" Henry asked.

"Excuse me! Henry, are you back already? I thought you were going to be gone all day."

"I *was* gone all day; it is nearly six o'clock. What has you so flustered?"

"Is it really that late? Aunt Catherine arrived and I have been so preoccupied. She is being very helpful."

"Aunt Catherine is here? Darcy mentioned she was going to be in town—Forgive me, but did you say she is being *helpful*? Goodness, I only met her a few times in my youth but 'helpful' is not a word I would have used to describe her, Georgiana."

Georgiana smiled at him, "I admit she can be officious, but she wants to help me with my season. I believe her motives are at least partially genuine this time."

He pointed to the combs in her hand and asked, "I see. Has she offered to be your lady's maid? Does she insist on personally polishing your pins and combs?" His smirk made his handsome face glow with mirth.

She giggled. "No, silly, she is going to give me advice on my accessories for my birthday ball. She says I must be the most handsome lady there, and she has promised all her talents to make it so."

"I bet she has. Come, I will accompany you. I have not seen her in many years."

Georgiana smoothed her skirts and walked back into the sitting room with Henry following behind. "Aunt Catherine, you remember Henry Darcy, our second cousin."

Her aunt did not rise, held out her hand expectantly, and Henry bowed over it. "You seem unusually tall," she declared. "And your shoulders are far too wide for that cut of coat. It looks as if your arms will split the seams. Also, your skin is too brown, Mr. Darcy. Captivating eyes and good teeth, though. You are certainly a Darcy, that is for sure."

She let out a huff of sorts, and the room awaited Henry's response.

Lady Catherine raised her eyebrow and said, "Well? What have you to say? Will you simply smile at me or shall you voice your thoughts like a proper gentleman?"

"Forgive me, Lady Catherine. I was waiting to hear how many hands tall I was. You have evaluated my flanks and my teeth and my eyes; I assumed I was a thoroughbred up for action."

"Impertinent too, I see. All you Darcys value that disgusting trait. Where is Mrs. Darcy anyway?"

Henry made a sound like he was choking and coughed to

hide the laugh that almost escaped. Lady Catherine looked at him severely. It was clear that she suspected him of duplicity.

He stood and walked to the fireplace and pretended to rearrange the figurines there.

"Aunt Catherine," Georgiana explained, "Elizabeth has an ill babe and has not had much sleep. I assume she has sought some much-needed rest."

She harrumphed in her usual way and then said, "Well, come, child, show me the adornments you have chosen."

"Yes, ma'am."

She handed the ornaments over to her aunt who scrutinized them with a critical eye. After a few disapproving looks, Lady Catherine reported, "These will not do. I can find you much more suitable hair pieces than these. Call for the carriage."

"At this moment? But it is so late!" Georgiana exclaimed.

Henry walked over to them and added, "Maybe we could all go shopping tomorrow morning. Perhaps Lady Jane would like to accompany us."

"Oh, she would love that!" Georgian squealed.

"Who is Lady Jane?" Aunt Catherine demanded. "Is she someone I know? I must meet your acquaintances and give you my opinion of them. I am a very good judge of character. I do not know anyone who understands people as I do."

"Lady Jane Andrews is Lord Porterhouse's daughter. She will have her first season with me."

"I see. Mr. Darcy,"—Georgiana turned to the door, assuming her brother had entered the room, but then realized that Lady Catherine was referring to Henry—"do you approve of Lady Jane? Do you feel she will be an asset to the shopping expedition?"

Henry looked serious for a moment, but Georgiana knew he was doing it falsely. "Lady Jane is a very refined lady. Her family comes from an ancient line of titles and money. Surely it is born and bred in her to have excellent taste in hair accessories. I'd venture to say it is one of her finest talents!"

Lady Catherine seemed appeased by his serious manner. "Well then, perhaps it *is* getting late in the day. Send word to her to come tomorrow at eleven o'clock. I will not wake early two days in a row. I have an excellent constitution, and it is because I adhere to a very strict sleeping schedule." She then proceeded to tell them about the rigors of retiring early five nights a week and allowing herself to be entertained by her associates and friends only two nights a week. Any more than that would only cause premature wrinkling around the eyes.

"Certainly, Lady Catherine," Henry replied. "The benefits of such a strict sleeping schedule can be seen in your lovely skin. No one would ever guess your age."

"Thank you, young man."

"Speaking of kindness," Henry went on, "I must beg of you to allow me to take my leave, for I believe I have some pressing business to attend to. I will see you both at dinner."

Georgiana couldn't help but smile at how Henry was always kind, even if, on the inside, he must be laughing at Aunt Catherine's haughty opinions. As her aunt dismissed him, he slyly winked at Georgiana.

Yes, Henry was a kind man.

And he certainly always lightened the situation when he was around. He seemed to find humor in the littlest things. At least she knew that if things progressed between them that she would always laugh and enjoy the joys of life.

Maybe if Benjamin did not love her, she could still find joy with Henry.

Not love. Not like she loved Benjamin, but at least joy and contentment.

*****

That night proved just as torturous as the previous one. Georgiana could not stop thinking about Benjamin.

His kind, toasted-almond eyes kept appearing in her dreams and, each time, she saw that same look she thought she had spied two days ago. How could she have misinterpreted it? She had been so *sure* that he loved her.

It was like he was drinking her in with his eyes, and his thirst could never be gratified, for one sole reason; in no way did he want it quenched.

Granted not a single word of confessed love had ever passed between them, but she blamed that entirely on her brother's intrusion.

What would have happened if William had not interrupted them? Would Benjamin have kissed her? Gooseflesh rose on her arms; she didn't realize she had closed her eyes until she felt the slightest pressure at the corner of them from her smiling, now rosy, cheeks.

She shook her head, as if to remind herself she was daydreaming, again.

But her mind paid her no heed. How could she have been so wrong? She had many examples of true love around her. William and Elizabeth were an easy read. So were Charlotte and Richard. Their eyes flashed flirtations through the walls, like some kind of superpower. The thought made her giggle.

The next morning, before readying herself for her compulsory shopping trip, she spent some time painting. Jane had sent word the night before that her father agreed to let her come as long as Lady Catherine was going to be there. It seemed her companion, Mrs. Smyth, was still away with her war-injured nephew. She was expected to be gone for some time, so Jane was trapped at her father's townhouse unless she was properly escorted by an approved chaperone.

When it appeared that eleven o'clock was fast approaching, Georgiana washed her brushes and looked at the painting. She cocked her head to the side and really studied it. She had allowed herself the privilege of thinking on Benjamin Pastel while she painted. Her original intention had been to just touch up the buildings, but time had gotten away from her, and she had worked on the sunrise as well. Georgiana had to admit that she had made some significant improvements. The sunrise colors were more vibrant now, and the blend of the deep purples at the top into the reds and yellows at the horizon was imperceptible.

It made her feel good to know that she had recognized love. She saw how much she truly loved Benjamin as she studied the painting. She had poured all her emotions into it as if she were painting from her heart. Indeed, in some ways, she was.

It was somewhat painful thinking of him this way and painting the way they used to paint together, but it also felt good to release her energy. She was proud of herself for choosing someone so well-suited to her, even if he did not love her in the same way.

He was a kind and gentle man. He had a quiet strength to

him that outgoing people, like Henry, did not possess. She felt more like herself when she was around him than any other person she knew. And he accepted who she was without the pomp and circumstance of needing to entertain.

She allowed herself to imagine rocking a little one in a nursery with him late at night. She imagined him coming up from behind and wrapping his arms around her to embrace her for no other reason but to tell her he loved her. She imagined waking up to him; his usually carefully-combed brown curls would be in disarray, and she would allow him to kiss her until her own curls were beyond repair.

It was the kind of thoughts that should have made her sad, but it brought her much comfort today.

Somehow thinking on him was her way of letting him go. The more she thought of him, the more she knew without a doubt that she loved him. All the tenderness he showed her, and the quiet strength he offered, may have meant little to him, but to her it meant the world.

Love really had been found among the people she interacted with every day. It had not required a stiff, formal introduction at a ball where their eyes met, locking gazes, as he walked toward her—instead, it happened without her truly looking for it. Love could happen anywhere.

She would just have to find another Mr. Pastel.

She could hear her name being called by Henry, so she dried her brushes and looked once more at the painting. Another hour or two and it would be finished. There was a part of her that desperately wanted to hold on to the painting; however, the greater part of her heart wanted Benjamin to have something to remember her by. He had said he would hang it in his office. Which meant Benjamin, being such a hard worker, was sure to see it every day.

She heard Henry calling out for her again, and she hurried to the door and walked toward the front entrance. "Coming. I know, I know, it is time to depart."

"Lady Jane is expecting us at any minute." He bowed to Lady Catherine and, offering his arm, he asked, "Shall we?"

Georgiana was only a step or two behind them, choosing not to wear a pelisse since the weather had turned so pleasant. She was delayed for a second or two when she realized she was attempting to put her right glove on her left hand.

It was congruent to her thoughts about Benjamin.

To say he did not love her, rankled to the point of complete distraction, but how else was she supposed to interpret that proposal? He knew better than anyone how badly she wanted to marry for love, and yet his proposal had been cool and rational. He had listed all the monetary benefits to the match as if that was all Georgina cared about. *But he knows me better than that!*

Soon they were at Jane's townhouse and Henry was helping Jane into the carriage and Georgiana was making introductions. It was a bit of a challenge to pull her thoughts from Mr. Pastel, but she forced her mind to forfeit to Lady Catherine's discussion the appropriate jewels for a debutante. This led to a discussion on combs versus feathers and ribbons, braids versus buns, and all manner of ridiculousness.

They soon exited the first shop, finding only one or two pieces that met with Lady Catherine's keen sense of fashion. As they headed out to another shop, Jane asked Henry's opinion regarding hairstyles, given he was the only gentleman in the expedition and the primary point of the endeavor was to garner the attention of a gentleman. He hesitated before replying and seemed to be giving his opinions some serious thought, which earned the approval of Lady Catherine and discreet eye rolls from Georgiana and Jane behind their chaperone's back.

Soon, Lady Catherine was pulled aside by an associate. The three of them walked on slowly.

Henry is being very solicitous this morning, Georgiana thought.

Before she could warn him, a woman, walking very quickly around the corner, was halted in her tracks because Henry was not watching where he was going. The package she was holding fell, and several papers dropped as well.

Georgiana and Henry both bent down to help her pick up her packages, apologizing the entire time.

Henry said, "I am terribly sorry, I was distracted by an enthralling conversation on silk with my cousin, Georgiana."

For some reason that startled the woman, and she looked up, which is when Georgiana recognized her.

Mrs. Younge had been her companion when George

Wickham had tried to convince her to elope. Georgiana's heart lurched, and she found it hard to breathe. Everyone but Henry had paused in their attempts to pick up the papers.

With sharpness, Mrs. Younge snatched the papers out of Georgiana's frozen grasp. Henry was the only one talking, still making apologies for running into her. He too noticed the coolness in Mrs. Younge's demeanor.

Georgiana felt as if time held still. Slowly all three of them stood up. Mrs. Younge's face could have been chiseled out of stone her hatred was so evident. The lines at her eyes were deep, and her brows were knit together as if someone had stitched them that way.

Georgiana did not know what to say. Mrs. Younge had been her companion for over four months; they had talked about everything and every situation. She had trusted her implicitly— more than any other person in the world besides William and Richard. So why was it so hard to talk now? Why couldn't she find even a simple greeting?

Was it because Elizabeth had told her how Wickham had hunted her in a pack like wolves? That Mrs. Younge had been part of his nefarious scheme to dupe Georgiana into eloping?

What does one say to someone who cares little for the heart and saw only the chance to make a penny by ruining a lady's entire future? All those months she had counted Mrs. Younge as a friend, but now Georgiana could see her cunning duplicity. Wickham would never have succeeded in winning Georgiana's heart if Mrs. Younge had not encouraged private meetings, downplaying the necessity of the societal rules meant to preserve Georgiana's reputation.

Other shoppers were stepping around them now, yet the moment stretched on in silence. For a moment, it looked as if Mrs. Younge was going to say something, but without looking away from Georgiana, she wordlessly took her things from Henry's grasp.

Henry made another weak effort to break the tension. "Do you ladies know each other?"

Mrs. Younge answered him without letting her glare drop. "I do not associate with murderers." And without warning, her former companion—who had taught her what to do in every social situation, from teas, to public excursions, to dinners—spat in Georgiana's face.

Henry immediately came to her defense and reprimanded Mrs. Younge severely. "Bad form! What kind of lady does that? Who do you think you are?"

Georgiana choked on her breath again, but she couldn't help but wonder what her words had meant. Luckily the spittle had not landed on her face, but rather on her shoulder. Lady Jane was already trying to wipe it off for her.

Georgiana brushed Jane's hands away and stepped forward. "No, it is alright, Henry. Mrs. Younge, please, what do you mean by murderer? Whom do you speak of?"

"You and your high ways! Too proud to help a man when he is down. Your proud and haughty brother knows exactly what I mean. Wickham is dead because of him and that Bennet girl. Tell me, *Miss Darcy*," the way she spoke her name sounded like a curse, "do you enjoy sleeping down the hall from the sister of a murderer?"

"What do you mean?" But Mrs. Younge was already turning away from her. "No, wait! What happened to Wickham?" But it was clear Mrs. Younge had no intention of explaining.

Lady Catherine's voice spoke from behind them. "I dare say, Georgina, was that not your old companion, Mrs. Younge? My, she did not look happy to see you! I cannot say I blame her. But Mr. Darcy did exactly what he should have done. He told me all about how she left you alone one night to drink herself into oblivion. I would have dismissed her without a reference too! How he could have hired her without asking for my recommendation— or at least checking her references—baffles me. Why, I would never—"

Georgiana attempted to listen to the rest of her aunt's diatribe, but Mrs. Younge's words weighed heavily in her mind. Did Elizabeth and William know more about Wickham than they had revealed? Was he really dead? Why had no one told her?

"Lady Catherine, I believe you are quite right," Henry declared, coming to Georgiana's rescue by filling in the silence. "I, for one, know nothing of Mrs. Younge, but I have not the slightest doubt that your wisdom could have spared Georgiana this unfortunate event. Perhaps we can continue this discussion in the carriage. I'm afraid Georgiana is not feeling well. I think we should all return to Darcy house."

Georgiana had never truly recognized Henry's ability to smooth over a difficult situation with his words, but she did now. Henry guided her toward the carriage without even waiting for the consent of Lady Catherine. His warm hand on her elbow soothed the cold sinking feeling in the pit of her stomach. It was all she could do to blink back tears of gratitude for Henry's intervention.

Yes, she was very thankful Henry was there.

CHAPTER 18

Georgiana was firm. "No, William. You will answer my questions this very minute. I am no longer a child who needs to be coddled nor protected from the evils in the world. I am going to be neck deep in society in less than a week! Does that not entitle me to a degree of respect from my own brother?"

Mr. Darcy had felt his heart drop a moment ago when she brought up Wickham and her chance meeting with Mrs. Younge. There were few things he enjoyed less than talking about the man he had once cared for, trusted, and even defended on occasion. But Wickham had abandoned the path Darcy's father had prepared for him—he had rejected the financial, educational, and societal connections that could have made a real gentleman out of a steward's son. Now Wickham did not even deserve the reflexive flinch of pity Darcy felt whenever his name came up.

Darcy would rather speak of any topic in the world. But his sister, from the look of things, had worked herself into a frenzy and obviously would not be put off.

Georgiana crossed her arms and started tapping her foot. He would have to endure it. The determined look on Georgiana's face made him think of their mother, and he had to respect her, for she was resolved to hear the truth.

"Very well," Darcy agreed. "What do you wish to know?"

"Everything. Elizabeth told me that Mrs. Younge was part of the incident in Ramsgate. I thought I had accepted that two people had duped me, but your reluctance to disclose what you know only brings new feelings of deceit again. And this time the deceit comes from by my own brother!"

"Do not say that, Pumpkin. I did not deceive you. I would have told you if I felt you needed to know."

"Well, I need to know now."

He took a deep breath and took one of her hands and led her to the sofa. "Yes, Wickham is dead, but not because someone killed him. No one is a murderer, certainly not one of Elizabeth's sisters. It was really just an accident."

He took a deep breath. "Last spring, before Elizabeth and I were married, Elizabeth's sister, Miss Lydia, nearly eloped with Wickham. She ran off to London with him. Luckily Colonel Fitzwilliam and I found the couple before anything occurred."

Georgiana bit her lip but then bravely asked, "Did she have a large dowry too? Is that why Wickham targeted Miss Lydia? I thought the Bennets did not have large dowries."

Mr. Darcy could see dread in Georgiana's eyes, and yet there was something else there as well; a maturity he had not expected.

For a moment, Mr. Darcy studied his sister. She really wasn't the same girl from two years ago who had been deceived by the son of her father's steward. She was stronger than that now. Her naïve youthfulness had faded over the years, and especially over the last six months. He had not truly recognized her transformation from child to young lady until this very moment.

His next comment would surely prove whether or not Georgiana was ready to hear the whole story. "No, Lydia did not have much of a dowry. Some men—men who are not gentlemen—are sometimes motivated by things other than money." He watched her carefully. She blushed slightly but then met his gaze with a confidence that seemed almost foreign to his shy sister.

"I see. He thought Lydia would give him favors," Georgiana replied. "The kind that should not be given until marriage."

Relief flooded Mr. Darcy. "Yes, dearest."

"But you were able to find Lydia before . . . before anything happened?"

"This is a bit of a story. Would you like some tea?"

"William, do not delay. Please just tell me."

"Very well. I ran into Wickham in the fall of 1811, the same autumn that I met Elizabeth. He was stationed there in Meryton. Lydia Bennet took a liking to him and followed the regiment to Brighton for a few weeks. Lydia had written her sister Kitty that she was going to Gretna Green to get married and become Mrs. Wickham. When Mr. Bennet found out, he was understandably livid. I had just asked for permission to marry

Elizabeth, and the whole thing almost cost me my chance.

"So, I immediately went to London, which was where I suspected they had gone, and I sought out Mrs. Younge. She was the only tie to him that I could think of. With some convincing—or to put it bluntly, with sufficient monetary incentive—Mrs. Younge revealed where Wickham and Lydia were staying. So, Richard and I adopted disguises and followed him home from the nearest pub. Our timing could not have been better. Lydia had insisted on wedding clothes and had also been firm in the fact that she would not be giving *favors* of any kind until they were married. Wickham tried to force himself on her, which is when we rushed in and stopped it all."

"How did you stop him?"

"It was actually Miss Lydia," Darcy chuckled. "She took a swing at him after he made a particularly vile comment about her. Knocked him out cold. Then Richard called the magistrate and I escorted Miss Lydia home."

"Is that the reason she stayed at Darcy House one night? I remember Elizabeth waiting up for you, but I had no idea . . ."

"Yes, Pumpkin. That was the same night."

Georgiana took a deep breath. "What happened to Wickham after that?"

"The magistrate told me he woke up shortly after, but never was quite himself again. I only saw him one time after that night. He fell ill in prison and passed away a few weeks later."

"Oh dear! How did Mrs. Younge find out?"

"I had to put a next of kin on the admission forms to the prison. Mrs. Younge was his only relative that I knew was still alive."

"She was a relative of his?"

"Yes, she was his step aunt. After Wickham's father died, his mother remarried. Mrs. Younge was the new husband's sister." Darcy paused, considering whether or not to reveal his suspicions. But Georgiana deserved to know the truth. "I think the connection between them explains a great deal. I think that is why Mrs. Younge targeted you, why she applied to be your companion. I think the two of them schemed for months before I even began seeking a companion for you."

Darcy sighed before continuing. "And that is all I know of

the case. I told the magistrate everything I knew. We spoke again after Wickham's death, and he agreed with me that it was not murder in any way. I hope you do not blame yourself, or me, or Miss Lydia. I feel sorry for Wickham and Mrs. Younge in some ways, but I admit Richard and I sleep better at night knowing he is gone."

Georgiana squeezed his hand. "Thank you for telling me," she said. "It helps to know that you trusted me enough to tell me the whole story. I did not realize how many people have protected me over the years. You and Richard have been doing it all my life. And Henry saved me today too. This morning he whisked me away and brought me home before I melted into a puddle of tears on Market Street."

"Can I ask you about that?" Darcy didn't want to intrude, but he could not help himself. His curiosity over seeing Henry and Georgiana dancing together was ready to burst.

His sister raised one eyebrow and smiled at him mischievously. "You have held your tongue for some time about Henry and me. I am very grateful. I know it must have been hard for you not to intervene these past few weeks."

That's not exactly an answer to my question. But Darcy said nothing for fear of appearing overly eager. He knew Georgiana would clam up if she felt he was pressuring her again.

"I like Henry," Georgiana admitted. "I really do, and lately I think that I could find real happiness with him. He is funny, and he always has something to contribute to the conversation. I know I would never be bored with him. There was a moment a day or two ago when that I thought he was going to propose."

Darcy struggled not to appear overly excited at this revelation. "I must admit I was pleased to see you two together in the foyer. Henry looked like he was about to, ah, to kiss you. Part of me wanted to lock him in the library and interrogate him about his intentions regarding you—but I promised you I would not interfere. Just out of curiosity, has Henry ever . . ."

"No, he has not," Georgiana giggled. "This must be very hard for you, William!"

"It is!" he laughed. "I hope you see that I am trying my best."

"I do. Thank you." Georgiana sighed. "Henry did ask me

for a private audience. But I have not had the heart to allow it just yet. I am not ready for him to propose."

She paused and then looked down at her hands, which Darcy noticed were clenched. She consciously relaxed them.

She took a deep breath as if what she was going to say had some importance. "I cannot say he is the one who will make me the most happy."

Georgiana looked away and bit her lip. Something about her tone and the carefully chosen words made Darcy suspicious. He knew Georgiana would never flat out lie to him, but what did she mean? Every time he saw her with Henry she seemed happy. Maybe not exactly ecstatic, but happy nonetheless.

He waited, but he sensed that was all she intended to say on the matter.

He lifted Georgiana's chin and looked deep into his sister's eyes. Something was bothering her. He wasn't sure if it was Wickham or Henry or something else. Just a few years ago, Georgiana had followed him everywhere, prattling all day long, and telling him all her secrets. But it was different now between them. There was something she wasn't telling him. Something that made her sad.

After a few seconds, her lips started to quiver. He scooted closer to her and guided her head to his chest and wrapped her arms around him. He embraced her with all his might.

Soon, Georgiana's shoulders started to shake, and she was sobbing into his shoulder. She had cried many times over the years, but this was something different. She wasn't just scared or overcome with emotion; there was something deeply painful and morose in her tears. It took much effort to contain the sobs and convulsions. But Mr. Darcy found it took even greater effort not to let his own emotion overcome him.

He knew she was hurting. He didn't know why.

He knew he wanted to help. He didn't know how.

He knew she would tell him eventually. He didn't know when.

He knew it had to do with someone close to her. He didn't know whom.

Darcy dug down deep inside and tried to be strong for her. He knew that no matter what she was worried about, he was going to leave no doubt that he was there for her.

He just held her while she sobbed. He did not pressure her to talk. He did not check his pocket watch to see how long it had been. He did not even adjust his position.

But he did rub her back. He did kiss her forehead. He did dab her tears with his handkerchief. No one besides Elizabeth and David were more important than this sister of his.

He would hold her until she was secure again, no matter how long it would take.

*****

Georgiana felt groggy and entirely spent. Never before had she felt so many emotions all at once. As the room came back into focus, she remembered what had caused the tears to come. When she told William that she didn't think that Henry was the one that could make her the most happy, she was overcome with the reality of what was ahead of her.

Her future would not include Mr. Pastel. She knew he was the one who would make her the most happy, but he did not love her as she loved him.

The thought brought such intense emotion that she could not even make a coherent thought. Her hope had vanished at that moment. It led her down other avenues of thinking as William rubbed her back while she cried.

All Georgiana wanted was to be loved. Although she loved Benjamin, he did not seem to love her. They got along nicely and would have an amiable marriage if she accepted him, but she would never be cherished as Elizabeth and Charlotte were.

Could she live in a marriage where she was the only one that did the loving? Or would a better alternative be to marry Henry, who loved her in his own way and always made her laugh? Henry had been about to propose that morning as they waltzed, she was sure of it. He had been so sweet and tender. She remembered how he had tilted her chin up. Standing so close to him like that, her senses had been filled with his musky scent.

It seemed that all she could do was think about Benjamin. But what if Henry's tenderness and love could help her, in time, to forget about Benjamin? Could she learn to love Henry the same way she loved Benjamin? Henry had plenty of wonderful qualities. She would not be unhappy marrying him; she assured herself of that.

Henry had such a strong personality that he dwarfed others in the room. He had one of those presences that everyone noticed. So, as the tears came, she realized that she would like to marry Henry, if for no other reason but to forget the man who did not love her.

Her brother kissed her forehead again and whispered. "Are you awake now?"

"Yes. Forgive me for losing myself there. How long was I asleep?"

"Well, you cried for about thirty minutes straight, whimpered for another ten before I noticed that your breathing was regular. I would say you slept for about an hour." William's voice was calm and reassuring, but there was no doubt he wanted to ask her more questions.

"William?"

"Yes?"

She sat up and looked him in the eyes. "I want you to know I have made my decision. If Henry asks me to marry him, I think it would not be a bad idea to say yes. I think it will be a very wise decision. But I do not want you to pressure him into it. Do not even bring up the topic to him."

William's eyes narrowed slightly. "And this is what you want, to marry Henry?"

His words hung in the air and seemed to grow tentacles around the ache in her chest, squeezing it till it was about to bleed again. The pain was resurfacing, and she had to answer him as best she could.

The question was not an easy one to answer without disclosing her broken heart. "It is what I need."

She needed to forget Benjamin, and Henry would help her do it.

*****

The rest of the week flew by for Georgiana. It was a series of shopping days with Aunt Catherine, a picnic with Jane and

Henry, endless hours practicing her curtsy for the queen, and hearing about the last-minute changes to guest lists and food for her birthday ball. She had plenty of private moments with Henry, but he never proposed. Knowing him, he was probably planning on making a big ceremony of it all. Georgiana wished he would not. But Henry was Henry, and he would probably do it at the ball tomorrow night.

Jane was due to arrive in the next few minutes, and the butler was to bring her straight to Georgiana's chamber. Georgiana took a moment to read the journal she had been keeping. Reading it had become her weakness. Every little thing that she and Benjamin had done over the last month was documented. She recognized now that she had probably loved him for some time before that morning in the library.

One entry even said, "Benjamin is the perfect gentleman. There is no one in my acquaintance who can match his kindness and thoughtfulness."

Another entry she wrote after the proposal said, "If I could love a man for who he was—without caring anything about his feelings toward me, his status, his connections, or William's approval, or anyone else's approval—I think I would be happier with Benjamin than every man I have ever met. I do not think I shall ever love a man more. Although if William knew I loved him, he would no doubt point out that Benjamin was a solicitor who had earned all his money, rather than inherited it."

Before long, she had reread her journal for the last month and thoughts of Benjamin were fresh and penetrating that organ under her ribs that was beating far too fast.

How could she accept Henry when her heart still loved Benjamin?

It was cruel to even consider accepting him when she still loved Benjamin so much.

What if these feelings for Benjamin never went away?

What if one day, as an old grandmother, she looked at Henry and realized she had settled?

A thought suddenly came to mind. *It is better to love than be loved.*

All along she had wanted nothing else but to fall in love! She was so focused on Benjamin loving her, that she hadn't realized the value of her love for him. She would rather marry the man *she* loved, even if he did not feel the same way. How selfish she had been! Ready to throw all that love away just because Benjamin did not share it! And there was no doubt that Benjamin respected her, even valued her, no more or less than Henry did.

All she had ever hoped for was to fall in love with someone who didn't care a jot about her dowry. Benjamin fit both those requirements!

She had to find William!

She lifted up her skirts and ran from her room. She looked in the nursery first. "Have you seen my brother, Elizabeth?"

"I believe he had some business in the library with his steward. He wanted to start cataloging which books were in London and which ones were at Pemberley."

"Thank you!"

"Georgiana, is there something wrong?"

Georgiana smiled broadly and went and kissed Elizabeth, "No! Everything is just right! Do you know when Benjamin will be coming back?"

"He told William that it would be over a week but that he would try to make it back for your ball."

"Oh dear! We have to get in contact with him. He needs to come back straight away! I made a terrible mistake and need to amend it."

Elizabeth smiled and stated, "You love him."

"Oh, Elizabeth, I love him with all my heart!"

"Well then, go and tell William your decision. I had to convince him more than once not to pressure Henry into proposing this week. I think he wishes for a conclusion as much as you do."

"Oh, I do! I must go find him!"

Georgiana hurried as fast as she could. "William!"

There was nothing that could stop her now. Not the upstairs maid that asked if she needed fresh sheets before nightfall. Not the footman whom she almost knocked down as he carried a heavy load. Not the sound of Charlotte and Richard coming in the front entrance.

She was determined to tell William that she was not going to accept Henry, but was going to marry Benjamin. That is, if he wasn't so hurt that he would not renew his addresses.

What if he didn't renew his addresses? *But he has to!*

She was determined. She would do whatever it took to win Benjamin. She set her goal high, for she wanted to win his heart.

She called out with more urgency. "William!"

Finally she made it to the library and rushed in. The day was coming to a close, making the fading light define the objects in the room with shadows, but it was not so dark that she could not see Henry's broad shoulders wrapped around Lady Jane who was holding tightly to his neck in an intimate embrace.

Jane was being kissed by Henry Darcy! And it was no small kiss!

Before she could work through the emotions—first, relief that she would not be breaking Henry's heart, and then, excitement to know that her best friend just got her first kiss, something they had always dreamed about—she heard William behind her enquire what it was that Georgiana so urgently needed.

But his inquiry was stopped midsentence at the exact moment he entered the library. Obviously, he saw the scene in front of them too.

She turned to look at him. She was shocked to see such intense emotion contorting his features until he no longer resembled the loving brother that he was.

Her brother stepped past her and without hesitation asked the most direct question she could imagine, "Have you no intentions toward Georgiana, Henry?" The couple jumped apart, but then Henry put his arm lovingly and protectively around Jane.

For the first time that Georgiana could remember, Henry was speechless.

William continued his barrage. "Have you no family pride? Did you think you could court Georgiana right under my roof but not be faithful to her honor? And what about Lady Jane's honor? I may not know how things are done in America, but here in England if you kiss a lady like that, you had best be prepared to make an offer.

"And Lady Jane, what do you have to say for yourself? Your father will hear about this. Of all men to have to reveal an indiscretion to, it had to be *your* father! A man who holds propriety and a person's reputation higher than the person themselves! And what about Georgiana? I have watched you, Henry Darcy, smile at her, even wink and flirt your way into her heart. I will have you know that just days ago she admitted she wanted to marry you!"

Georgiana interrupted. "William, please, I never said I wanted to marry Henry."

"You most certainly did!"

"No, Brother, I said I *needed* to."

William looked back at Georgiana and stated, "It means the same thing."

"William," Georgiana pleaded, "I do not love Henry. And if I am not mistaken, I believe that Lady Jane does." Jane nodded her head silently.

"But, Georgie, you said he was going to propose," William said, "that he asked for a private audience with you . . ."

Henry finally released Jane's shoulders and took one of her arms and wrapped it around his, patting it. "Mr. Darcy, my only intention with the private meeting was to get advice on how to propose to Georgiana's best friend. I did not realize that it might be construed differently. Forgive me, Georgiana. I esteem you, but I love Jane."

William was still confused and angry. "That is *Lady* Jane to you, sir!" He then asked, "Is this how it is going to play out? Lady Jane becomes Mrs. Darcy, and Georgiana is left all alone?"

The room fell silent. Jane looked pleadingly to Georgiana. Henry bowed his head and shuffled his feet side to side like a little boy. William's eyes darted to the three people in the room as if keeping his eyes fixed in one spot would blind him. Jane knew Georgiana loved Mr. Pastel, and if Jane knew, it was likely that Henry did too. They were both looking to her to explain things to her brother.

"Well, someone had better give me some answers! Henry, I will talk to you first."

Georgiana considered her words carefully. She did not want to disappoint her brother who had always been so kind and solicitous to her. But she had made her decision and she had to be strong. Georgiana suddenly was reminded of what the gypsy had said, *"There will soon come a time in your life where you must take a stand and come face-to-face with your biggest fear, but it will not be as dangerous as you might think."*

She took a deep breath and reached out for William's

elbow. "No, William, you need to speak to me. I am the one that you need to hear from. I do not want to disappoint you, but I am afraid what I have to say will do just that."

William gently shook her hand off his elbow and then took two steps toward the formerly kissing couple. He raised his finger to Henry's face and said, "Nothing but words until I get back. You were born a gentleman; I expect you to honor your Darcy birthright."

"Yes, sir," Henry said and dropped Jane's arm and took a step to the side.

William walked out the door in somewhat of a huff, and Georgiana followed him out.

Colonel Fitzwilliam's voice boomed through the foyer, "What is for dinner, old man? And how about a game of chess beforehand?" Then Richard must have noticed the serious look on William's face or his hurried pace. He whispered something to Charlotte, who was holding the General, and left her side to follow the two of them down the hall into William's study.

Colonel Fitzwilliam closed the door behind him and asked, "All right, who must I slaughter?"

William just stared wordlessly at Georgiana.

"Good grief, Darcy! The last time I saw that look on your face, it was because of Wickham, and he is already dead! Blast! Sorry, Georgie, you probably did not know about that. I should not have said anything."

"It is all right," Georgiana replied. "I already knew."

"Well then, who dares to cross your path this time? Wait," Richard walked to the cupboard and poured a very tall glass of amber liquid. Handing it to William, he said, "Drink up, then speak."

Georgiana asked Richard if he was going to have a glass.

"No, thank you, I detest the stuff and have for some time."

William took a very long drink and then, when only half the liquid was left, he said, "All Georgiana hoped for can now be discarded and trampled on."

"Oh, no," Richard exclaimed. "Is Mr. Pastel not coming back?"

William looked very confused, "What? No! I do not know. What does he have to do with Henry kissing Lady Jane Andrews in the library like he was going off to war for a year?"

Richard started chuckling. Then he saw William's dark look and self-corrected his merriment. He cleared his throat and asked, "What kind of kiss? On the cheek? Hands do not count, you know. And how long was it? If he was kissing her like he was going to war, how long was he going to be gone, would you say? Was it the kind of kiss that happens only once, never to be reproduced again?" Richard winked at Georgiana, "Because a second and third kiss is never as good as the first. Was it the kind that authors write about, leaving the reader feeling lonely, yet strangely fulfilled?"

Georgiana started to giggle slightly. "Yes, Richard, it was all of those."

"Indeed! Well, congratulations are in order. Where is the happy couple?"

"Stop it! Stop it! Both of you! Do you not see the problem here? Henry is going to be forced to marry Lady Jane, and that means Georgiana is left all alone. He has truly harmed her, simultaneously courting both of them like that." William drank the last of his alcohol and slammed the glass down.

Richard took the glass and refilled it, handing it back to him. "Hmmm, have another drink." He turned toward Georgiana, winking, and mouthed the words, *Play along.*

Richard raised his voice and said, "Georgiana, did you feel Henry was toying with your emotions and that he was not genuine in his affection?"

"Yes, she did!" William shouted. Richard wordlessly moved the glass from William's hip to his mouth and encouraged him to drink.

"Well?" Richard asked Georgiana.

Georgiana said, "I suppose he never gave me reason to doubt his affection."

"See?" William cried.

Richard pushed the drink higher until William drank. "And was that affection ever inappropriate?"

"Of course not! He was the perfect gentleman."

"I see. So a gentleman, a second cousin, no less, led you to believe that you were important to him. And since you are both of marriageable ages, I assume you felt he was paying you, say, special attention?"

"Not exactly. I would not say he paid me any more attention than any other in the household."

Richard winked again, "Not even, Elizabeth?"

"No, I did not feel any more singled out than Elizabeth."

He turned toward her brother. "Yet, Darcy, why did you not assume he wished to marry Elizabeth?"

William just rolled his eyes.

Richard continued. "And, Georgie, during this time of supposed courting, did you find your emotions were engaged? Be completely honest. Were they engaged in any way, towards a man?"

William looked up at her for her answer. Her pause made him drink the last of the glass. She could see where this was going. It was highly likely that Charlotte, who had immediately noticed Georgiana's tender feelings toward Benjamin, had shared her suspicions with her husband. "My emotions were very much engaged during that time to a man."

William groaned, walking toward Georgiana and pleaded with her, "I am so sorry, Pumpkin. I had no idea his character showed such duplicity. To court two ladies at the same time! Only an American would do that! He is not an Englishman, not in my eyes."

Richard probed further. "And would you say you are hurt by this news that Henry has shown affection toward Lady Jane instead of you? Would you have preferred to be on the receiving end of a kiss yourself?"

Georgiana tried not to laugh. Richard clearly knew she loved Benjamin, and he was working her brother into the idea slowly. "I very much would have liked my first kiss. I still have high hopes for it."

Her brother gasped. "What? After what Henry did? You will never be in the same room with him for as long as I live!"

Richard took the glass and refilled it. "Now, now, Darcy, you do not know the whole story yet."

William pointed to Georgiana and said, "She just admitted to wanting to kiss Henry!"

Richard tilted his head toward Darcy and said, "Georgiana, is what Darcy said correct?"

"No, it is not," she giggled. "I never said I wanted to kiss Henry. I said I had high hopes for my first kiss. But truth be told, I have a different person in mind." Richard nodded his encouragement while refilling William's glass.

"Brother, my heart is touched," Georgiana continued, "but not by Henry. I was wrong to have agreed to marry Henry if he asked. It would have been like you agreeing to marry Caroline Bingley when you knew you loved Elizabeth. Elizabeth is your other half. She is who makes you the best person you can be. Once you realized you loved her, did you look at another, even once?"

William was silent for a minute.

"Answer her," Richard ordered.

"No, I never even so much as noticed another. Do you love the solicitor then?"

Richard jumped into the conversation. "Just to be clear, the 'solicitor' in this question is Mr. Pastel, right? Best not to risk any more confusion regarding that point."

"Bugger off, Richard. You have done enough misleading."

Richard chuckled and backed away, swinging his arm and his stump as if he was tiptoeing soundlessly.

Georgiana continued. "Yes, I love Benjamin with all my heart. I want nothing more than to marry him, if he will still have me."

William opened his mouth to speak and then closed it. "Forgive me, I may have had too much to drink." He staggered backwards into a chair. "Why would he not have you? You are Georgiana Darcy. You are beautiful, talented, have the kindest, most innocent heart a lady could have, are entitled to an enormous dowry, and to top it all off, you are loyal and devoted to those you love. You could literally have anyone you want!"

"But I may have missed my chance to have Benjamin."

Darcy rubbed his eyes a bit. "Please, do me a favor? Please call him Mr. Pastel. At least until I have accepted this."

"Of course. Mr. Pastel is who I love. He proposed the night of the theatre, but I refused him."

"He proposed . . . pardon me, you refused him?" William asked.

"You refused him?" Richard repeated with further disbelief.

"Indeed, I did," Georgiana admitted. "He did not profess his love for me in any way, and you both know how dearly I want to have what you have in your marriages. I want a Fitzwilliam Darcy who will return to my sickbed just hours after my refusal and hold me and caress my face. I want a Colonel Fitzwilliam who will take all of my insecurities and make them my strengths. I want what each of you has. I want a man that can make me blush from across the room with a single look."

William smiled for the first time in an hour. "Then that is what you will get. I have an express to write."

CHAPTER 19

Darcy sat at his desk, quill in hand, and hesitated. How did one address a letter like this? What exactly should he say? *"Sorry for judging you unworthy, Mr. Pastel, but it seems you have earned my sister's heart regardless of your being just a solicitor."* That sounded so prideful! He thought he had conquered his pride last spring, after Elizabeth refused him. But it seemed he was just as prideful now as ever. His prejudice against Mr. Pastel certainly seemed to suggest it.

He passed the freshly mended quill from finger to finger, up and down his knuckles from little finger back to thumb over and over again.

The truth was, he was rather relieved. Georgiana loved a good man who seemed to love her back. The fact that she had refused him was likely a good sign.

He chuckled at his next thought. *Every good man needs to be refused once or twice.*

Colonel Fitzwilliam knocked on his open door. "What are you laughing about?"

"I just realized that Georgiana's initial refusal makes an interesting pattern. I was refused by Elizabeth, and, in a way, Charlotte refused you when you tried to kiss her in the rose garden at Pemberley before going off to war! I was just contemplating whether disappointing proposals may be hereditary."

"Goodness, do not remind me!" Fitzwilliam replied. He sat down in a chair next to Darcy. "I assumed Charlotte reciprocated my feelings and was all too eager to come to an understanding." Fitzwilliam's advances toward Charlotte had unfortunately reminded her of her abusive deceased husband, and she fell to the ground, hysterically cowering before him. "At least your refusal did not end with anyone screaming. I think my proposal must be admitted as the worst one of all."

"Well, I think we can agree you are not wholly to blame in

that scenario. Whereas most of what Elizabeth accused me of when she refused me was entirely accurate."

"Minus one or two good stories from a disgraced militia man, of course," Fitzwilliam chuckled.

"Yes, minus that," Darcy replied. "Here I am, trying to decide what to write to Mr. Pastel, but all I can think of is that hopeless feeling I felt when I sat down to write to Elizabeth after she refused me. There was not a stitch of hope. It was like my world had gone black."

Richard asked, "Where is Mr. Pastel anyway? I thought he was trying to get his London office up and going. What was so important that he had to leave for a week?"

"I truly do not know. Georgiana says he went to see an uncle in Kent. My only hope is that his brother, Clyde, will know how to get ahold of him."

His cousin raised his eyebrow suspiciously. "I was under the impression that Clyde Pastel is not trustworthy. In fact, I believe he and Mr. Collins concocted a will that caused Charlotte and myself a great deal of grief."

Darcy looked at the pen in his fingers and then put it down for a moment. He clasped his fingers together rubbing the knuckles as if they had an itch that could not be satisfied. "I do not like it much either. But it is the only way I can think of reaching Benjamin. I just hope Clyde is still in town at the old office."

"Darcy," Richard warned. "Be careful."

William nodded. "I will."

*****

Clyde Pastel looked at the numbers one more time. He always did this on Friday afternoon. He totaled the money coming in as well as the expenses going out. Being busy with filtering the clientele for his brother, as well as packing what needed to go to Liverpool, he had not taken on any new business in over a month. But he had just received final payment from three clients, and so for the first time in three weeks, he was not in the red.

Harold knocked on the door. "Mr. Fitzwilliam Darcy is here."

"Tell him my brother is not here. He should know that."

"Yes, sir."

What was Mr. Darcy doing here? The gall of the man to show up and assume he would be welcomed. Clyde had never seen a man so forlorn as Ben had been last week after Georgiana's refusal. His brother had always been confident and sure of himself. He wanted so badly to be a gentleman, even dressing and acting the part, but he never let that deter his kindness to those who needed him.

Clyde knew his own life was a different story. He had selfishly taken whatever he wanted and resorted to any means necessary, which usually meant under-the-table trades and deals.

Benjamin possessed several virtues that Clyde did not have—well, not until recently. For one, Benjamin was fiercely loyal. Once Benjamin trusted you, you were his friend for life and he would defend you until hell froze over.

Which was exactly what Clyde had seen a week ago. Benjamin had told him about how Miss Darcy had refused him without explanation. He defended Miss Darcy in her refusal, regardless of the fact that he did not understand why she had said no. He even defended Mr. Darcy!

He was taken back to that moment.

"I did not even ask her why," Benjamin said dejectedly.

Clyde tried not to let his mouth drop. "And so you just left her in the library? What kind of negotiation skills do you have? Did Father and I not teach you anything?"

"I am sure she had a good reason. But all she said was, 'I cannot marry you'."

"Cannot or will not?"

Benjamin's eyes looked up. "Cannot. I am sure she said, 'cannot'."

"Then there is still hope for Georgiana. Cannot simply means there is a roadblock, and my guess is it is her brother."

Benjamin drank his coffee and then bowed his head. "Mr. Darcy only wants what is best for her. I am a solicitor, nothing more than a hired hand."

"Damn Darcy!"

"Watch your language. Darcy is a good man and very dear to her. She adores him. I am trying very hard not to blame him for

her refusal, so please do not encourage such thoughts. If I were Darcy and I had a sister like Georgiana, I would . . ." His voice trailed off.

"You can't even finish your thought! You know bloody well—sorry—you know very *well that you would have no objections to a good man who could provide for her, regardless of his station! You would never have done what Fitzwilliam Darcy did!"*

Benjamin rubbed his forehead. *"You are right. I would let my sister follow her heart. I cannot imagine denying her the chance to be happy. But he is her guardian. I must win him over as well as her. I had not realized that until now. All these weeks I have courted Georgiana in my own way. It never occurred to me that I needed to win over anyone else."*

Clyde harrumphed his disagreement. *"You, of all people, deserve a lady like her. If Mr. Darcy does not understand that, then he might be the biggest pig I have ever worked with, and you know that is saying something."*

Benjamin smiled slightly. *"I have never seen this side of you. I did not know you could be so loyal. You have really changed this last month. I am so grateful you gave up drink. A whole knew man has emerged."*

"Don't think the old one is not still in there. I may have taken away the whiskey, but I still have a litany of resources to call upon should you need to set fire to a certain townhouse or—"

"Do not even think about it!" Benjamin laughed outright. *"Angry and loyal! That is a dangerous combination. Goodness, Clyde, you have almost as much fury as a woman scorned! No, do not do anything drastic. My only hope is to find out more about our uncle. Hopefully a birthright will brighten my chances with her. If I was born a gentleman's son, then maybe Darcy will look at me differently. Maybe I will be good enough then."*

"You are good enough *now. Don't let him make you feel differently."*

"Thank you, Clyde. I do not deserve your loyalty, but I certainly appreciate it."

"You will always have it."

Harold's repeated knock brought him back to the present.

"Sir? He insists on seeing you. He says it is very important and that time is of the essence."

Clyde squinted suspiciously. Benjamin would never forgive him if something happened to Miss Darcy and Clyde failed to help. No matter how much he detested Mr. Darcy, he would have to behave and see the man who had ruined his only brother's chance of happiness.

"Show him in."

Clyde had never seen Mr. Darcy before, but when he walked in, he would have been able to point him out in a crowd. He and Georgiana shared the same eyes, although hers were blue and his were brown. They had the same dimple in the chin and high, defined cheekbones. The man was dressed smartly and carried himself just like a fine gentlemen should. His shoulders were squared, and his back was stiff. He brought with him an air of royalty. That alone made Clyde distrust him.

That was until he saw his face. Clyde knew a desperate man when he saw one. After years of gambling, he knew how to read people. Every line on Darcy's face was pleading for help. He needed a savior.

Let us just see how desperate he is.

*****

Clyde Pastel pursed his lips. "The answer is no."

Darcy's brows knit together. *This is not starting off well.* "I have not asked for anything."

"But you are about to, and I will not help you."

Darcy contemplated how to best go about this. He considered everything he and Colonel Fitzwilliam had learned about Clyde Pastel from his Benjamin. There was the gambling, the drinking, the cheating widows out of their inheritance, and not to mention the fact that he had no qualms dealing with lowlifes like Mr. Collins who wanted to punish his poor widow from beyond the grave. That alone should have made him turn around and walk away. Darcy knew that the whole reason that Benjamin was moving to London was to buy out his brother and start clean with new clientele.

Darcy leaned forward and held out his hand. *Respect.*

Every man wants it, whether he knows it or not. Even if it means, in the worst of circles, respect for being the best cheat.

Clyde looked at the offered hand but did not reach for it, nor did he offer him a chair. Clyde remained sitting while Darcy stood in front of his mahogany desk.

Honesty. It is what the world revolves around. "I do have a request."

"And I said the answer is no." Clyde pushed his glasses further up his nose and sat back and crossed his arms. Every bit of his body language spoke of anger and frustration.

Darcy began. "I have a problem."

"And I'm not going to fix it for you, so shut the door on your way out." Clyde looked down at his papers and started shuffling them.

Darcy just held his position and took in the state of the office. There were boxes and piles of papers stacked around the room. He noticed that the piles were very neatly stacked and on top of each of the piles was a very nicely scripted word, saying either, "London", "Liverpool", or "storage".

Order. Every person craves it. "It looks like the exchange of hands has made good progress. I admire your organization."

Mr. Pastel picked up his quill and pretended Darcy hadn't said anything.

Efficiency. A man who can manage his time was a successful man. "I know you are busy. I just need a small moment of your time, sir."

Clyde glanced up from the top of his glasses and then resumed working. The fact that he hadn't thrown him out so far was a good sign. *To be heard.* A basic human need. "May I ask what has prompted the cool welcome?"

Mr. Pastel studied him for a moment. The man who had shown him in earlier came bearing a tray, but Mr. Pastel motioned for him to go away. "Mr. Darcy will not be staying long enough to taste your spectacular coffee, Harold, but thank you for thinking of it."

"Yes, sir." And he left.

Decency. Clyde Pastel was kind to his office help. "You have well-trained staff."

"Flattery will not get you what you want. I told you I will

not help you."

Communication. He clearly defined what was expected and what was allowed.

Mr. Darcy now knew what route that he should take. "I am a desperate man, Mr. Pastel. And I plead with you to hear me out. I do not know the reason behind your cool welcome, and from what I knew of you before coming to this office, I cannot say that I am all too excited about enlisting the help of someone who once served and honored Mr. William Collins." The slightest flicker of recognition flashed through his eyes, so Mr. Darcy continued. "I see you remember the name. His widow married my cousin, Colonel Fitzwilliam, a month ago."

Clyde put down his quill and took off his glasses and leaned back. At least for the moment, it seemed that Mr. Pastel was going to listen to him.

Encouragement. Every man needed it now and again. "I had a chance to read Mr. Collins's will. I must say, it was the finest legal document I have ever seen. But I do not come here to discuss business. I came here to discuss your brother, Benjamin. I have wronged him and would like to make it right."

As he spoke, Darcy continued in his attempts to sketch Mr. Pastel's character. Clyde had the qualities of respect, honesty, order, efficiency, a desire to be heard, decency, communication, and—the final piece of the puzzle fit snuggly into place: *loyalty.*

Darcy could not believe what he was seeing. As soon as Darcy admitted he had wronged his brother, Clyde's entire demeanor had changed. He no longer appeared to be too busy, or put out by Darcy's presence. In fact, Mr. Pastel motioned for him to sit down and then rang the bell.

Harold came in, and Mr. Pastel said, "Coffee, if you please."

"Thought so," Harold snickered as he turned back around and promptly returned with a tray and cups. Harold looked at Darcy and said, "I hope you do not enjoy frilly coffee, Mr. Darcy. Harold's coffee doesn't need any cream or sugar. Trust me."

Harold smiled and poured two cups.

"I will take your word," Darcy agreed.

As Harold left, Darcy contemplated what he had just learned about Benjamin Pastel's brother. The man was loyal, fiercely loyal. Who would have thought? Nevertheless, Darcy dared not lose his chance.

Darcy began, "Are you aware that your brother proposed to my sister, Georgiana, a week ago?"

"I am."

"I was not made aware of this until today. Until an hour ago, to be exact."

Clyde's head tilted slightly as if he was processing the information. "And your first order of business was to come to see me?"

"I believe there were some misunderstandings. I am determined to make it right."

"If I understand correctly, Miss Darcy refused him. She said she 'cannot' marry him. Ben was under the impression that you, sir, were the reason she could not marry him."

"I am not totally sure how that came about. It is true that I want to find a smart match for my sister, and I certainly wanted it to be to her liking, but I have come to realize that I have been rather blinded by my personal preference regarding the kind of man I should like my sister to marry. I thought the decision was mine to make. But Georgiana has plainly made it clear that her only qualification for a husband is that she loves him."

Darcy thought he heard Harold come back in, but both men ignored Harold and continued their conversation.

Clyde Pastel asked, "And does Miss Darcy love Ben?"

"I believe she does. Quite adamantly." Georgiana's words reverberated in Darcy's head again as he thought of his sister. "And I understand her feelings. You see, I have a love match with my own dear wife."

"What exactly did Miss Darcy say about Ben?" Clyde queried.

Georgiana's words were so eloquent that they seemed etched in his mind. Darcy had no trouble repeating them from memory. "She said that she loved how Benjamin—that is what she calls him—has a subtle power, an ability to give support where others do not. His presence in a room calms her to the point that she feels no matter what is asked of her, whether it be to play a concerto or serve tea to her family and friends, she is able to do it with confidence. This sister of mine states that Benjamin is so observant that even when I, her own brother, or her best friend, Lady Jane Andrews, do not pick up on the turmoil in her heart, Benjamin always does. She sounded quite poetic when she said, 'Some days life is all about your dreams, hopes, and visions for the future, but there are a great many more days where it is placing one foot in front of the other and recognizing opportunities that help you reach those dreams. I want Benjamin to be there with me during all these moments.'"

As Darcy finished speaking, Clyde's face slowly softened further. The corners of his lips turned up until he was fully smiling, showing that his two front teeth were missing.

"You see, Mr. Pastel," he continued, "I have learned something over the last few years as I watched myself and many of my family members find love matches. One must first *hope* for love. And to hope for love is to gain *vision* for your future. True vision is having hope in what you want so desperately that you make it come true. And when my sister envisions her future, the only thing she sees is your brother. Mr. Pastel, I am sure her heart has been touched."

Clyde Pastel's smile was slightly unnerving but also encouraging, so Darcy ventured further. "Georgiana says that Benjamin is the first one she wants to see when she wakes up. She cannot play the pianoforte or paint anymore without thoughts of him. She wants to share the best and worst parts of her day with no one other than him. Her thoughts are entirely consumed with him. And that brings me to your office. She says her very happiness lies with Benjamin Pastel."

"You will have to be more specific, Mr. Darcy. What exactly do you need my help with?"

"I need to relay a message to Benjamin that Miss Darcy hopes most sincerely that he return for her ball tomorrow."

"Is that all you wish to tell him?"

"And that I am sorry. I respect the man he has made of himself."

"Am I to assume that you now consider him an adequate suitor, even though he is just a solicitor?"

"I am ashamed to admit I was so prideful as to exclude him as a possibility. I would dearly like to tell him that if he truly loves Georgiana, and will swear with every fiber of his heart to work hard to earn her love each and every day, then he has my permission to marry her. I would like to tell him all those things."

Clyde stood up and bowed. "I am sorry, Mr. Darcy, but I will not give you my uncle's address in Kent for that purpose."

Panic raced through his veins as his last chance to fulfill his promise to Georgiana to find the elder Mr. Pastel seemed to slip through his fingers. "I plead with you. Please help me find him. I promised my sister I would find him."

"And yet I will not relay your message for you."

"But Georgiana's very happiness—" But Darcy was interrupted by a familiar voice from behind him. Darcy whirled around to find Benjamin Pastel with his hat in his hand looking a little sheepish. It was clear he had heard much of what had been said.

"—Georgiana's very happiness lies with me."

*****

Clyde bowed and said, "I will leave you two gentlemen to discuss the matter." Then he left the office.

So many emotions were going through Benjamin's heart. But first and foremost, was hope for Georgiana. Benjamin had indeed heard most of what Darcy had said about Georgiana and himself.

"Did you really mean it?"

Mr. Darcy bowed respectfully and said, "Yes, Mr. Pastel. I have always respected you as a solicitor, but I was too prideful not to see you as a potential suitor. I am sorry. Although I would never have let you spend every morning alone with her if I had seen you as a suitor."

"But that did not stop you from not imposing restrictions on her time with Henry. What is the difference? Do you think I would compromise her to get her dowry? Do you imagine me no better than Mr. Wickham?"

"She told you about that?" Benjamin nodded. Darcy replied, "Then she truly does love you." Even after hearing that Wickham was dead in a very shocking way in front of Henry, she did not reveal anything to him, and Henry knew George Wickham. "I would caution you to—"

"No need to worry about it. I have not told anyone. So you no longer have hopes for Georgiana and Henry?"

"I do not. She says Henry will not make her happy as you will."

"And do you believe this? How can you trust her decisions now when she has made such grievous mistakes before?" Benjamin felt sick questioning Georgiana's abilities this way, but he had to make sure Mr. Darcy was in earnest.

"When she told me she wanted to marry for love, I counseled her extensively. I told her that love is like a mirror. Often, you only see your own feelings. But, make it a window, and a whole new perspective opens up. If she can do this, then there is hope for Georgiana because hope offers vision. She believes you love her. Has she seen something different than the truth? Is she wrong? She admits her vision was fogged over, like a mirror in the hot Roman baths, but now she has a new perspective. I think the only question that remains is whether or not she is correct about your regard. So, I must ask you, Mr. Pastel, do you love her?"

Mr. Darcy looked stern, as usual, but his tone was soft. It was a voice Benjamin recognized from the stories Darcy would tell about how he and Elizabeth fell in love. Nostalgia wafted through his stern, challenging words. Mr. Pastel realized something at that moment. Mr. Darcy was a romantic too. This stern big brother wanted his little sister to find a love match as much as Georgiana did. Benjamin pondered how to answer him.

"I have known many enemies in my life, Mr. Darcy, but I have had no greater foe than myself this last week. My heart was tortured each and every minute with thoughts of Georgiana's refusal. I remember you once telling me how despondent you felt when you finally left Hertfordshire after the Netherfield Ball."

"Yes," Darcy admitted. "I was grateful to put distance between Elizabeth and myself. I prayed that in doing so, her pull on me might be lessened. But it was worse to not have her in my circle of daily acquaintances. Torture. Pure and utter torment for months until I learned that she would be at the Rosings Parsonage."

Benjamin nodded, struggling to find the words to describe his life the last week. He closed his eyes for a moment and relived every second as if it happened all over again.

Benjamin opened his eyes and met Mr. Darcy's impenetrable gaze; their eyes locked as if breaking away would crush Benjamin's fragile composure. It was of utmost importance for Mr. Darcy to understand the depth of his feelings for Miss Georgiana Darcy.

"It was agony to leave her," Benjamin began slowly, looking for words that justified how he felt despite the mounting emotion that pressed at his cravat. "Every part of me buckled as if I were being slowly crushed between two mountains. There was not a moment when I did not ache to know why she had refused me, why I was left to battle colliding mountains without her. Yes, I love Georgiana, desperately so. I cannot be easy until I know why she refused me. For if it was something in my control, you can be assured that the tormenting fault would be remedied before I took another anguished breath."

CHAPTER 20

"The answer that you seek will have to come from Georgiana herself. But from that impressive speech, I believe there is an easy remedy for your colliding mountains," Darcy said.

"Then show me the way," Benjamin replied. He could not lose hope, not now when he seemed so close to happiness.

Clyde bowed respectfully to Mr. Darcy and smiled at Benjamin as they passed.

As they entered Darcy's carriage, the ride was filled with unspoken truths, each making wordless promises to the other in the absence of real conversation.

Mr. Darcy promised to accept Benjamin as an equal, regardless of the fact that he was a solicitor. "You are . . ."

"I know."

Benjamin promised to love Georgiana as fiercely as Mr. Darcy loved Elizabeth. "I will always . . ."

"Of course," Mr. Darcy said,

Mr. Darcy swore he would not meddle in his only sister's care any longer. "I will not . . ."

"I do not doubt it."

Benjamin vowed to make sure Georgiana would always be an intricate part of her brother's life. "She will always . . ."

"I know she will. "

Mr. Darcy begged for validation that he had not ruined things too severely with his pride and prejudice. "I hope I have not . . ."

Benjamin said, "You have not."

Darcy's subtle smile assured him that nothing was lost as of yet.

Mr. Darcy hoped that Benjamin would live up to the legacy Georgiana came from and pass it on to their children. "She has always been a . . . "

"And always will be."

Benjamin was anxious to enlist Darcy's approval of a quick wedding. "If it is not too much to ask . . . "

"Next month is fine."

Mr. Darcy swallowed his pride once more and asked for forgiveness. "I am truly . . ."

Benjamin had already done so. "I know. All will be well."

"Yes, of course it will." Darcy added, "I am glad we had this talk."

"Me too," Benjamin said.

Never before had two gentlemen said so much.

*****

Georgiana fought the urge to pound mercilessly on the ivory and ebony keys. Each time she played the flirtatious crescendo and decrescendo of Bach's Pastorale in C minor, she pressed through them with all the feeling she had. And she had no shortage of feelings at the moment. William had left over an hour ago to see Mr. Clyde Pastel to get an address. How hard could it be to write down directions?

Her fingers worked even harder at the notes dictated on the page. Could there have been trouble in finding Clyde? What if Clyde had already left the office? Where would he have gone? Georgiana had no idea where he lived. What if he had already left for Liverpool? Her exertion showed in the volume as it plateaued. The next part she knew by heart, so she gave free reign to the music as it depicted exactly the turmoil that cursed her insides at the moment.

Note after note, she allowed her emotions to make their presence known. When there was a rest, she paused dramatically and then threw her shoulders into the next note. She let the highest note hang in mid-air, tantalizing the imaginary listener to beg for the reentry. Feeling the emotion of the flirtatious tune filled her somehow, as if Benjamin had never left; as if she had never refused him. In her mind, she danced with him just as her fingers danced on the keyboard.

She thought of Grandpa Jacobs and how he would be so proud of her right now. No one had ever played with so much rubato, adjusting the tempo of the music to help the listener feel the emotion of the music. She had told Benjamin once, after he listened to her play, about Grandpa Jacobs and his devotion to his pupils' education. Benjamin had agreed that his method of teaching was indeed impressive.

Oh, how I wish to impress Benjamin now! I would tell him everything!

"Tell me," a deep, masculine voice huskily said behind her.

Her fingers froze in mid chord. Had she said that thought out loud?

It did not matter, for he had come!

She looked over her shoulder and sure enough, the man she loved the most in the world was smiling at her; his eyes darker than usual but the kindness and love was still there.

"Benjamin!" Georgiana stood up and had not stopped to look around before she flung her arms possessively around his neck, but in looking over his shoulder, she saw her brother swallow hard and back out of the music room, closing the door behind him. William had not only brought Benjamin to her, but had just given his blessing by leaving them alone.

Bless that man! I do not deserve such a good brother. I hope he knows I would do anything for him.

Benjamin nestled his face in her hair and held her securely. She inhaled, and felt the closeness to him more acutely. Relief overcame her, causing the tears to cascade down her cheeks like a spring runoff. The crying waxed and waned. Every time she seemed to gather herself, he squeezed her a bit tighter and she was sobbing again.

"I am so sorry, Benjamin. I was wrong. I was so wrong."

Benjamin loosened his arms and looked down at her face with the kindest toasted almond eyes she had ever seen him possess.

Volumes could be written in the depth of emotion emanating from his eyes, moving her to suck in a ragged breath. His handsome face was strong where a man should be strong, but soft and gentle in the other places, just like the man inside. His hair was slightly disheveled at the moment. The varying browns were like a rainbow of color—it reminded her of the riot of colors in a sunrise.

No one had hair like Benjamin Pastel. She reached her

hand up to his hair and touched it with her palm, then she brushed her finger along his forehead to move the stray curl that rarely was allowed to misbehave. When he did not flinch at her touch, she caressed his cheek with her hand and ran a finger along his jaw.

How odd that there was no awkwardness or unease at her ministrations. She loved this man in front of her. Regardless of the fact that she was a novice, expressing true love came naturally.

But she did not want to be careful. The curl had stubbornly fallen again over his eyebrow and so she daringly took her entire hand and ran her fingers through his hair, combing it backwards, the way he always wore it. The sensation of having him still hold her waist like he was, and his face only inches from hers, was beyond anything that she could have ever hoped for.

Then suddenly something changed. The softness was replaced with a profound yearning that could only mirror of what she was feeling inside. Suddenly she knew what her brother had meant when he said that love could be either a mirror or a window. For at the moment, their hearts and desires were so in step, that it was both! Her exact feelings were reflected in his eyes.

Windows really do offer vision and perspective! Benjamin Pastel loved her just as much as she loved him. Perhaps even more.

His eyes grew darker and she knew, yes, he probably loved her even more. How could she have made it through an entire monologue on his wealth and not seen what he most wanted her to know? He wanted to give her everything, starting with his heart.

He loved her! Hope soared unrestrained in Georgiana's chest, lifting her until she felt she was nearly on her toes.

The yearning and ache deepened for both of them until Georgiana gave her consent with her most welcoming smile. And it was not even half a moment later that Benjamin's lips brushed hers with one long, extended, passionate moment.

He moved when she moved; he held steady when she wanted him to. Everything the other asked for was given without much more than a hint of desire. The intensity of her first kiss simultaneously melted her spine so that she curved into him and accelerated her heart rate to the point of complete abandon. With a gentle pressure on her back, he held her form as close as they dared and caressed her longingly. The moment could have been a few seconds, or it could have been an hour; neither one knew, but the kisses slowed and each, in turn, relished the opportunity to take in a much-needed calming breath.

With his forehead bent to hers, he whispered, "Now that was a nice welcome home."

Georgiana had not regained enough composure to speak yet, so she only murmured her agreement.

He reclaimed her into his arms once again and kissed her hair, inhaled deeply and kissed it again, murmuring, "Jasmine. How I love the way you smell, Georgiana."

His words gave her strength and she clutched his hair again. "I could hold you like this all day, but I am afraid my brother's patience has a short fuse. I have so much to say, and I need to say it or I will lose my resolve."

Benjamin reached his hand up to hers and brought it down to kiss it. "Tell me. I will listen. I suspect your brother will tolerate a great deal at the moment. We had a very good talk in the carriage."

"Did he tell you why I refused you?"

Benjamin led her toward the chaise and they both sat down. "No, he did not. But I need to know. I have to know."

"I have thought on it every waking moment all week. What is it that motivated me to refuse? What was I feeling?" Georgiana looked up at him, and he was the epitome of calm. His eyes were caressing her just as his hands had moments ago. He offered her support as no other person in her entire life had ever done.

The words came out easily, with him listening intently. "I knew what was going to happen before the words came out of your mouth," Georgiana began. "I remember thinking that it was the moment I had been waiting for. Each step along the way to the library was accentuated with my personal hopes and dreams of how romantic it would be to hear you declare your love for me. I probably had run through ten different lines better suited to a ladies novel or some long-dead poet.

"But when I finally tuned into what you were actually saying, I could not believe what I was hearing. All you talked about was your wealth and your capability in providing for me. My heart plummeted. Horribly written love lines from terrible poets would have been more welcome than your discourse on how much you have saved over the years. You cannot imagine how disappointed I was in your proposal."

She saw the pain from his eyes start to furrow his brow, and she quickly went into the next part. "But . . . there is more. Please let me finish." He smiled at her and she regained her courage as usual. "You always do that to me."

Confusion swept through his face. "Do what? Disappoint you?"

She giggled slightly, "No, Benjamin, give me strength when I need it most with a single look." He leaned over and kissed her on the lips, letting his lips linger a bit long. Hungrily, Georgiana asked for more and he did not disappoint.

She kissed him once again and whispered, "At first I was just disappointed in the proposal, but the next morning I was able to define what it was that was missing. You never declared your love to me. It was all about money and security for our future."

"But I did, Georgiana. What are you talking about?"

Now it was her turn to look confused. "No you did not. I would have remembered."

"I started off by saying 'Never again will you have cause to question this man's heart. For you may have it, forever, if you desire. I love you.'"

Her heart started to skip to an entirely different rhythm, an erratic one at that.

His voice got husky and the intensity rose exponentially, as if he was offered a chance to say it all again, and he would not be accosted in his pursuit of her heart this time. "And then I said, 'I will cherish every moment of our tomorrows that I will have with you, just as I have cherished every moment of our yesterdays that I have ever been blessed to partake of with you, Georgiana.'"

Her heart paused, with each expression of love that he shared, picking up momentum as he rolled her name on his tongue.

"Then I ended it by saying, 'Please say you will be my wife and let me feast on a forever's worth of todays.' Georgiana, I did declare myself."

It jumped, then halted as he spoke, and she realized that her heart was playing its own rubato tune. "You said those things? When?"

"Right before I saw your eyes gloss over. I was sure I had already bungled it. I suddenly became nervous, terrified even, that you were going to refuse me. I knew I saw love and adoration in your eyes that morning when your brother interrupted us, but suddenly, there in the library, I was afraid you had changed your mind.

"Clyde told me that if you really loved me, then the only reason you would refuse me was is if you were worried about money. He thought maybe you would want to continue to live like a Darcy, or at least the way you were accustomed. As your eyes distanced themselves, I figured that I had no other choice but to assume Clyde was correct. So, I tried to explain that I have plenty to live on. But one thing led to another, and I could see your body pull away from mine. You pulled your hands from mine. Then you turned your back on me, and I knew I had to say the right thing to convince you quickly. That is when I shared my bank account information. I see now that only made you pull away further."

"You really declared your love for me before debating the merits of your wealth and financial stability?" she asked. Benjamin nodded. "I must have been overexcited, for I remember none of it. But it sounded perfect just now, Benjamin! My heart bounced with rubato just as it should have the first time. Grandpa Jacob could never have taught a better lesson than those precious words you just spoke. Thank you, Benjamin. Thank you for your tenderness. I see my distraction is truly the limiting factor in our future. If I may be so bold as to ask if—"

Before she could finish, she heard the door to the music room open and William poked his head in. "Did I give you enough time?"

They both laughed and raised their voices, "No!"

William chuckled and backed out again and shut the door.

Benjamin smiled at her and said, "You were asking?"

"Yes, if I may be so bold as to ask if I may pretend that retelling of the declaration of love and if the proposal still stands . . ."

"It does. Marry me, Georgiana. I love you more than a man can love a woman."

Her heart skipped and fluttered out of control. She was tired of being shy. Look at what asserting herself had done! Dare she be bold just a moment longer? "I only have one request,"

"Anything. I will give you anything."

"Kiss me with rubato. I want to feel every emotion our music can communicate."

"You may make that request anytime. It is the duty of a husband. But just to be clear, we are engaged now, correct? I would not want your brother coming in and seeing me compromising you in such an energetic way without an understanding between us."

"You are such a stickler for rules and propriety. But I love that about you." She smiled and whispered, "Benjamin Pastel, I am asking you to compromise me and to do it with rubato."

He did not need to be told a third time.

CHAPTER 21

Elizabeth watched as her husband raked his fingers through his hair. His pacing was not unfounded. It had been over twenty minutes, and still the door to the music room remained closed.

"Dear," she began, "I gather from your anxious state that you have reservations about this match?"

He stopped pacing momentarily. "What? No, not anymore. I just know what kind of trouble you and I got ourselves into when we were alone this long. She is my baby sister! I cannot even imagine her wanting to—well, do things that engaged couples do."

She giggled. "Like this?" She closed the gap between them and cupped his jaw tenderly like she first did when she was delirious on her walk to the Son.

He leaned into her hand and murmured, "Hmmmm, yes, like that."

"Or perhaps she will wish to be held, like this." Elizabeth wrapped her arms around her husband's chest and rested her cheek on his shoulder. She felt her husband melt against her as he caressed her back. She then looked up at him and said, "Or maybe she is hoping for a sweet kiss . . ."

Mr. Darcy looked in her eyes and smiled with mischief. "Like this?" He placed his lips on hers, and their lips kept to a rhythm they had practiced for over sixteen months.

Elizabeth relived the moment in her dream state when she had first recognized her walking companion for who he was. Not only did she know the name of the person walking with her, but somehow she had instantly known his true character, or his strength of constitution.

So many times they had talked about what really happened versus what she remembered from her dream. Their memories were quite similar, but his held such longing and meaning. She dared not call it a vision, but in her dream-like state she knew who Mr. Darcy was at his core, both in spirit and in body. Where once she saw a sternness to him that she had always assumed was him passing judgment on those around him, she now understood for what it really was—a silent, methodical processing of the goings on in the world around him.

As they waited in the hall for some indication that things had resolved between the two, Charlotte and Richard entered through the front door.

Richard exclaimed, "What must a man do to get good coffee around here?"

William put a finger to his lips and said, "Georgiana and Mr. Pastel are having a very important *discussion*. Although I do not think a whole lot of words are being used."

"Is that so?" Richard asked. "Well, how long has it been?"

Elizabeth answered, "Twenty minutes."

Charlotte's eyebrow rose and she glanced at William. "And this sits well with you?"

"I cannot exactly say that. Shall we interrupt them?"

"If you do not, I will!" Richard's tone made it quite clear the former soldier was still ready to engage the enemy, or to defend Georgiana to the death if need be.

*****

Georgiana truly felt all the emotion a kiss like that could deliver. It was like coming home to something that she had dearly missed. It was like smelling fresh bread and knowing that the best was yet to come. She had never allowed her thoughts to venture past the first kiss, and yet here, in just a few minutes, she had been kissed several times, each just as stirring as the others.

For the first time, she truly understood the necessity of chaperones. Two kisses were better than one, which meant three were better than two. She could see the cascade of desire quite easily leading to inappropriate choices. She finally saw how two good people could fall to temptation if afforded enough privacy.

She felt the heat rise in her cheeks. And although she hated to do so, she pulled back and gave him one more embarrassed smile before looking away, because surely he could read her thoughts.

At that moment Richard's voice could be heard very loud

just outside the room. "Georgiana, Pumpkin, I am giving you fair warning: if you desire Mr. Pastel to still have two legs to stand on, I suggest you—" The door flung open, and her cousin entered to see them standing a few feet apart. "Oh, I see I was not needed."

Elizabeth followed after him with Charlotte and her brother. Elizabeth said, "Goodness, Richard! What did you expect to find? Mr. Pastel compromising Georgiana?"

At this comment, both Georgiana and Benjamin stifled their individual giggles and chuckles. They exchanged a knowing glance and Georgiana said, "Cousin Richard, I know you share guardianship with my brother. If it makes it easier for you to approve the match, I feel duty-bound to tell you that I *have* indeed been compromised. I simply *must* be made to marry Benjamin."

Richard flashed a look to William, who was trying very hard not to smile. "I thought you said they had only been in here for twenty minutes?"

Elizabeth too picked up on Richard's protectiveness. "Oh, but Richard, you are married now. Think what can happen in twenty minutes!"

Richard turned pink up to his ears and looked to Charlotte, who came and took his arm. "They are teasing you, colonel," Charlotte assured him. "We all know what kind of man Mr. Pastel is, and Georgiana is too innocent to know any different. Perhaps we just need to congratulate them and accept that your little Georgiana will be married. I assume that you two have worked things out?"

Benjamin said, "Indeed we have. Georgiana had accepted my hand."

William pounded Richard on the back and said, "There now, no need to get protective. It was just a proposal, nothing else." He looked to Benjamin and said, "A very verbose proposal that took twenty minutes, am I right?"

They both nodded. Richard raked his hand through his hair and stood up straight. "For a man who has been through battle, I cannot say I much enjoyed thinking of my little pumpkin growing up. But what does this mean for your season? It has not even started! In fact, tomorrow is your birthday ball."

"I had not thought much about it," Georgiana admitted. "But to tell you the truth, I am much relieved that I will not have to endure a season. For what is the point? I have found my love match that I so wanted."

Elizabeth rushed over to Georgiana and kissed her cheeks. "We can make it an engagement ball, darling," she exclaimed. "Would you like that?"

"What a wonderful idea!" William agreed. "Look at all of us. Who would have thought that two years ago, I would have found a woman who challenged me and kept me humble. And you, Fitzwilliam, found someone who sees your potential, and you, Georgiana, found a man who gives you strength. We really are quite lucky to have found three love matches."

"We all have grown so much," Elizabeth said, "and helped each other. Richard, you gave Will hope again when he felt it was gone forever. And Will, you gave Richard strength when he needed it the most. You both took risks and showed just how valiant and loyal friend can be."

Charlotte nodded and smiled. "You too have changed, Elizabeth," she added. "It has been two years since your pride was injured at the Meryton Assembly when Mr. Darcy said you were 'not handsome enough to tempt' him. I remember when you first told me about it, it was clear that your pride had been injured although you laughed it off as best you could."

"Pride, in so many ways has blinded all of us," Benjamin said. Everyone looked at him. "It is true. Even Georgiana was blinded by her pride."

Georgiana gave him a gentle swat on the shoulder. "He teases me so, but he is right. I wanted fireworks and dancing unicorns with rainbow footprints to show me the path to love. I did not see how love was right in front of me in all his humbleness."

Richard said, "Yes, but we should not let Mr. Pastel off quite that easily. He was certainly proud of the man he has made of himself. In fact, judging from Georgiana's account of that botched proposal, he thought his worth was measured in pounds."

"We have worked that out, Richard," Georgiana explained. "Apparently I was too excited and distracted to hear the first part of the proposal in which he did profess his love for me."

"Well, that is good," Fitzwilliam agreed. "Too bad the rest of you were so universally prideful. Glad I had nothing to work on in that area myself."

Charlotte answered with a laugh, "I am sorry to tell you, my dear, but it is just as true for you as the rest of us. You were blinded by pride when you came home a wounded war soldier, ashamed at your meager birthright. You had to learn that a man is no more worthy of a woman's heart if he happens to have both his arms than if he has only one. In fact, the effort it took for you to do anything was doubled, which made it that much more impressive. I think you have come the farthest."

"But the farthest in a good way, right?" Fitzwilliam confirmed. "Not because I was so prideful that I had the most work to do?"

Charlotte laughed at her husband's teasing. "Of course," she smiled.

Richard looked down at Charlotte lovingly and said, "Charlotte learned that just because one person did not see your worth does not mean that no one sees it. She had to let go of her knuckle-white grip on her pride and independence to fully grasp what unconditional love was and how it could heal any scar."

Georgiana said, "And I had to let go of my fear too. I had enough doubt to crumble the Rock of Gibraltar. I wanted so badly to see the end that I nearly lost sight altogether of the loving eyes that looked back at me."

"Yes," William and Elizabeth agreed.

Richard nodded and squeezed Georgiana's shoulder. "Too true," added Charlotte.

"But there is hope for Georgiana now," Georgiana said. She walked to Benjamin and reached a hand out for him. "I see things the way they are now."

Benjamin took both her hands and squeezed them. "Love does that to people."

William cleared his throat, and Benjamin instantly dropped Georgiana's hands and clasped his own behind his back.

"Hope is a unique concept," Charlotte continued. "One can hope for something or one can be offered hope; it can be both a noun and a verb. I remember hoping for Fitzwilliam to come home alive. I was too afraid to hope he might love me, but I found even hoping for that allowed me to put one foot in front of the other. Eventually he taught me that hope in seeing me again was what kept him alive all those months."

"Even though I did not see how a one-armed man could possibly earn the love of the woman I so admired," Fitzwilliam said.

"Just as I did not see how a woman with a thirty-pound dowry and history of poor decisions could ever find true love," Georgiana admitted.

"And I did not see how a man I had refused twice would ever be induced to make another offer," Elizabeth added.

"And I certainly did not see how the woman who had refused me twice could be induced to accept," Darcy said.

"But love *is* hope," Georgiana said with a smile. "And it is a seed, and a mirror, and a sunrise. Like Paul writes to the Corinthians: Love believeth all things, hopeth all things, and endureth all things. Love is the only thing worth hoping for."

Elizabeth cupped her hand on William's jaw, and Georgiana watched her brother melt into it. Benjamin slyly reached over and reclaimed one of Georgiana's hands. She looked at him and smiled.

The butler came in and said that dinner was served. Charlotte was offered an arm by her husband, and they exchanged smiles, and Richard winked at her as if no one was watching. William took the hand on his face and kissed it gently and wrapped his arm around his wife and kissed her forehead.

Benjamin whispered, "May I escort you to dinner?"

"You may escort me anywhere. By the way, I finished your painting of your office building. May I show it to you?"

"How about tomorrow morning? At sunrise?"

"I was hoping you would say that."

*****

Everyone decided to skip the separation of the sexes, which came as a relief to Benjamin. The idea of being separated from Georgiana, even for half an hour, made him anxious.

Henry was in rare form tonight. He was usually in a good mood, but after returning from a visit to Lord Porterhouse and receiving his permission to marry Lady Jane, he was nearly ecstatic.

Henry's voice bellowed over the chatter and startled

Benjamin and Georgiana, who had been enjoying another private moment. "So, Georgiana, it seems my fortune came true!"

Mr. Darcy asked, "What fortune?"

Henry explained, "The three of us had our fortunes read about three weeks ago by a gypsy woman. To tell you the truth I thought she was rather vague and was dicked in the nob or, at the very least, pitching the gammon."

Mr. Darcy looked between the three of them, seemingly genuinely interested. "How so? You said it came true?"

"Yes," Henry replied. "She said I had traveled far to find great fortune and counseled me to seek for that which will keep me unburdened and light. I'd say Lady Jane is a great treasure, and she certainly helps me be unburdened and light. I am in such a merry mood! But Georgiana's came true too! Tell your brother what she said."

"Yes, tell me, Georgiana," Darcy asked.

"Well," Georgiana explained, "she said that there will soon come a time in my life where I must take a stand and come face-to-face with my biggest fear, but it would not be as dangerous as I might think. She said that there would be a big decision I would have to make. One choice will bring a moment of joy, but no lasting happiness. The other will not really be a choice, but the destiny for my soul." Benjamin couldn't help but smile at the how true this ended up being.

Mr. Darcy raised an eyebrow and made eye contact with Benjamin. "And this came true because of the decision to marry Mr. Pastel? He is the destiny of your soul?"

Georgiana blushed brightly and nodded. "There was a moment, after Henry showed such kindness after the incident on the street with Mrs. Younge that I wondered that maybe I could learn to love Henry. I already knew he could make me laugh. But the gypsy told me to follow my heart. She said the stronger I was, the more others would trust my judgment."

"Well that part is true," Elizabeth said. "William was unconvinced when Mr. Pastel told him of your affection. It was only when you stood your ground and told him yourself that he believed you. "

Benjamin said, "Do not leave out how she said your heart is pure and kind, unblemished from the ways of the world.

"Only you would remember that part, Benjamin."

Henry said, "And she said to choose wisely. 'You can choose gaiety, bringing with it a little temporary joy, or you can choose to listen to the language of your heart and be filled with genuine, unabashed happiness for the rest of time.' It is kind of a blow to my pride that you couldn't find 'unabashed happiness' with me! But you see, we are not meant for each other."

Elizabeth laughed and said, "I can see why you would feel affronted. Did she really use those words? Unabashed happiness?"

Henry laughed and then answered. "She certainly did! But there was a part that Georgiana didn't tell you. Didn't she warn you about something too?"

"Yes, she told me I had to be strong because people would try to cast shadows on my decision unless I was strong. I took that to mean that people would not approve of my decision on whom I wanted to marry." Georgiana looked down at her hands. "I actually specifically thought of you, William, and when I realized that I had fallen in love with Benjamin, I knew that part had come true. You did not approve of him because he was not a titled Englishman with land and an estate. He worked for a living, and I feared you would deny him if he asked."

Benjamin looked to Mr. Darcy and wondered how he would answer. "I very nearly did deny him," Darcy admitted. Benjamin was impressed, but not surprised, by his future brother-in-law's honesty. "A solicitor did not meet my standards for you. Not until you told me, so firmly I might add, that your heart was engaged. Then nothing else mattered. Mr. Pastel tried to tell me you loved him, but I did not want to believe it. I was blinded by my hopes for you with Henry. It took Henry being found kissing Lady Jane and you not being hurt by it to realize that I had the wrong perspective. After that, it was only Mr. Clyde Pastel that stood in my way."

"How so?" Georgiana asked.

"Well, I would not have guessed it of the old Clyde, but he has a rather protective and loyal streak to him. He made it quite difficult to find Benjamin." He looked at Benjamin and said, "I hope it is appropriate to call you Benjamin now and again. Georgiana has been doing it long enough that it is rubbing off on me."

"Of course, Mr. Darcy, I would be honored if you call me Benjamin."

"Well, I still prefer Mr. Pastel, but Benjamin will do fine intermittently."

Benjamin wondered if now was the right time or not and gathered his courage. There really was no better time to bring the topic up but the present. "Actually, there may come a time in the near future that you will call me something else." He looked to Georgiana and saw a very confused look on her face. "None of you have asked why I went to Kent."

"I thought it was to see your uncle," Elizabeth said. "Was there another purpose?"

He took a deep breath and said, "I did go to see my uncle. An uncle that I had never met before. He is very ill."

Charlotte asked, "How is it you have never met your uncle before now?"

"When my father was a young boy, my grandparents died in a carriage accident. My uncle nearly died too. My father and uncle were taken in by different relatives and raised separately. My father eventually reconnected with his brother, but there was a falling out sometime before my father married. I learned most of this once upon meeting my uncle, Christian Pastel—"

Colonel Fitzwilliam interrupted, "Christian Pastel is your uncle?"

Darcy looked confused but asked, "Colonel Fitzwilliam, do you know Christian Pastel?"

"Yes, and you do too. He is but a few miles from Rosings. But he does not go by that name. I believe you know him as Sir Christian, the Earl of Kipling."

Mr. Darcy asked, "Sir Christian is your uncle? The owner of Rolling Farms Estate? It is almost as grand as Rosings!"

"Yes," Benjamin answered quietly. Driving past the unassuming gate house and seeing the size and grandiose of the estate was a shock that he would never forget.

Benjamin was most aware that Georgiana had not said anything. He glanced over to her and could only tell that she was contemplating something with her head tilted to the side. He was about to ask her what she was thinking, when Henry interrupted.

"Benjamin, you said your uncle was sick." It was a question more than a statement, but everyone knew what he was asking.

"He is quite ill. And with no children, the title and estate will pass to the next of kin. His younger brother's oldest child, myself."

Georgiana gasped slightly, but the rest of the room fell dead silent. As each of them worked through the meaning of this, he could see the realization arise in their faces. Elizabeth was the first to accept it, and she smiled widely, glancing at her husband. Colonel Fitzwilliam was the next to understand what it meant, and he slapped his knee excitedly before Charlotte put a calming hand on her husband's hand and shushed him. Henry whistled in amazement and let out a chuckle. But the two that he cared most to know their opinion sat dumbstruck.

Finally Mr. Darcy blinked and then looked to Georgiana and asked, "Did you know any of this?"

"No, Brother. I did not even know he had an uncle, let alone an inheritance or a title." Her words hung in the air, and everyone waited for her to say her last thought. Although she was talking to her brother, she was looking at Benjamin. "It does not matter one jot that he will have a title. I would still love him if he were a butcher. He is kind and loving and offers me strength when I need it the most. I am not myself without him. I love him, not his title, nor his estate. I love Benjamin—the honest hardworking solicitor whose work ethic demands respect from everyone who works with him."

Benjamin's heart sped up with each word she used. She had been strong and valiant and loyal to the end. It really didn't matter to her at all that he was not landed gentry. She loved him for who he was. He felt the emotion rise in his chest and fill his throat. Try as he might, he could not suppress his emotions. Relief swelled through him like a tidal wave, and he blinked back the wetness that was sure to emerge if the tingling on the insides of them was any indication. A slow smile formed as he conquered the urge to cry. He knew the truth now with every fiber of his being—Georgiana loved him, was loyal to him, regardless of whether or not he was a gentleman.

"I do not deserve—" Benjamin started to say.

Mr. Darcy said, "Yes you do. If you have won my sister and my entire family's respect without a title or an inheritance, you deserve it more than any of us in this room. And if your uncle dies shortly, you will outrank any of us as well. I am humbled further than I care to admit that I held any prejudice at all against you. Forgive me. I am terribly sorry to have doubted you in any way."

Elizabeth seconded his thoughts. "It is true. You deserve every happiness. You have earned it through blood, sweat, and tears, without any of the things that society deems important."

A knock on the door silenced everyone as the butler came in and said, "Clyde Pastel is here to see Mr. Pastel."

Mr. Darcy's brows furrowed. "At this late hour?"

"I am sorry. Excuse me please," Benjamin explained. He instructed the butler, "Show him to the library. I will be there shortly."

He stood and asked Georgiana if he could have a word with her. She looked to her brother, who nodded, and then stood and followed Benjamin to the corner of the room. Benjamin made sure that the other's conversation picked up before he whispered, "Are you sure you want to marry me?"

"Yes, Benjamin. I love you for who you are, not who you will be."

He smiled and squeezed her hands and brought them to his lips. "Then I am afraid I will be introduced at the ball as Lord Benjamin Pastel. That is the only reason Clyde would have come to Darcy House. My uncle's family said they would contact me only if Uncle Christian passed away. I had planned on returning after the ball to Kent to be at his side. Nothing was going to stop me from dancing with you at your birthday ball, even if you had refused me. There, now I have revealed just how selfish a man I am. I cannot give you up, not for the world."

"Go see your brother. Come back quickly and tell us the news."

He kissed her hand again and left for the library. He found Clyde browsing the books about Italy and France. "Good evening, Clyde."

His brother snapped a book shut and replaced it on the shelf. "My lord, how fairs things with you?"

"So it is as I suspected. They sent word? Our uncle has

passed?"

"Indeed he has. Not more than a few hours after you left."

Benjamin took a deep breath and sank into the stuffed chair.

"So much has changed!" Benjamin marveled. "I feel so upside down. How can I go from the life of a bachelor solicitor in Liverpool, to an engaged, titled, landowner in just over a month?"

"So she accepted you?"

He smiled at his brother. "Indeed she has. I could have been blown over with a flutter of a butterfly's wing when I walked in on Darcy telling you she loved me and wanted me to come home. And now this!"

"Well, my lord, you have been rewarded for your goodness. When I went to church the other day—"

Benjamin looked up briskly, "You went to church?" Clyde sent him a frustrated look and rolled his eyes. "Forgive me, go on."

"When I went to church I was reciting a prayer with the rest of the congregation and I started reading the inscription on the wall under the sculpture of the apostle Luke. Do you know the one I am talking about?"

"No, I do not."

"Well I could only make out a few of the words because it was in Latin but I memorized what it said and came home and looked it all up. Do you know what it said inscribed there? It said, 'And as ye would that men should do to you, do ye also to them likewise.'"

"Luke 6:31. The golden rule."

"The what?"

"The golden rule. Do unto others as you would have them do unto you. It is called the golden rule."

"Well, I got to be thinking about that. It is kind of like the people of India believe, you know, in karma. They think what goes around, comes around. If you dish it out, then you will be served the same treatment. This is why you have found so much success in life whereas I have wrinkles and grey hair and missing teeth to prove where my actions to date have all been.

"I don't want to just give up alcohol, Ben. I don't want to just walk away from those in my life who are disreputable. I want to really change. I want to have an influence for good in the world.

Ever since you bought the practice from me, I have been thinking about what I want to do with the money. I have plenty of money saved up, for Father would have shot me dead in my sleep if I did not handle money with the respect it deserves.

"So, I think I will travel before I return to Liverpool. I would like to see India and learn a bit more about this karma thing. Maybe it is not too late for me. Maybe if I take a year and travel, I will meet a young lady who does not care that I have no front teeth. Maybe the placard on the office in Liverpool will never have to be taken down or changed. Maybe I will have sons and the office name will once again be Pastel and Sons. What do you think?"

Benjamin grinned. "I think that is a fine idea, Clyde," he said. "I have never gone further than France myself, but I heard India is a whole new world."

"My only worry is what to do with our Liverpool clients," Clyde mused.

"Do not worry about a thing. I left them in the charge of a solicitor friend of mine. I will just write him to inform them that you will not be returning for another year. He will be very happy to have the business."

"Thank you, Ben. I hope I can still call you that. I don't like calling you my lord."

Benjamin laughed and said, "Of course you can call me Ben! Take care and have a safe ride home. Is there anything else left to do in the office?"

"Everything is labeled. Harold will pack what goes to Liverpool. The rest you can manage. Good luck."

"Thank you, Clyde. Your loyalty and devotion has not gone unnoticed."

Clyde started walking toward the door, and then looked over his shoulder at Benjamin. "Karma, Ben, karma. I'm only giving you what you've given me all these years. You are a good man. The best man for this job. I could never carry a title. It would all go to my head. But you? You were born for this. And not just because you are the eldest. You have not squandered your birthright like this prodigal son. You have treasured your birthright, and from what it looks like, it is a very valuable birthright."

"What did you say?"

"I said it is a valuable birthright."

"That is what the gypsy said who read my fortune!"

CHAPTER 22

The next morning, Georgiana was up before the familiar gentle knock sounded. She wanted to be dressed and prepared to watch the sunrise with her intended. This time, for the first time, she was going to be able to hold his hand while they watched the sun make its presence known.

She carefully opened the door and made sure it was Benjamin before whispering, "I am ready." The candlelight danced on his smiling face, and she opened the door further to take his offered arm. The mornings were a bit chilly now that they were well into September. Her shawl slipped off her shoulder a bit, and Benjamin paused in walking. One of his hands held the candle and the other was supporting Georgiana so it was impossible for him to adjust the shawl himself, but she saw his intent.

She took the candle from him and allowed him that courtesy, but she had no idea of how it would affect her. His tender ungloved fingers lifted the material, and he rested his hand on her shoulder momentarily, and as he dropped it to his side, she felt the briefest of brushes, sending a current of sensation along with it.

She was acutely aware of the way he smelled; in the morning, his shaving soap still lingered. In the afternoon, all she could smell was his sandalwood and lemon scent. He must have just shaved, because his chin was nearly glowing, leaving his features to present the glorious chiseled jawline that always reminded her of Michelangelo's *David*. And as usual, there was not a hair out of place, not even the stray curl that flirted and winked at the end of the day in its hopes to escape its designated spot.

She was also acutely aware of the heat emanating from his body. She could nearly detect each part of his body as it ebbed and flowed with the natural movements of walking. He allowed her to walk just ahead of him since she now had the candle, but he stayed as close as possible behind her.

She had never examined how he walked, but now as she listened to his gentle footsteps, she sensed that he deliberately placed his feet rather than was walking naturally. She supposed he was trying to be quiet so as not to wake William or Elizabeth. But they had passed their door some time ago and had now reached the main stairway. Some of the vestibule sconces had been lit since the scullery maids were up and tinkering with the fireplaces already. She didn't actually see any of them, which was a blessing; she didn't want to be seen on their way to the library. In the past, Benjamin had woken her with a knock, and gone on ahead to the library without her. She usually arrived a good quarter hour after him. But this morning she had been ready to go with him. And she was ready in more ways than one.

They finally reached the library. They still had some time before the sunrise, which looked to be very promising this morning, so she opted to show him the painting of his office building.

It was covered with a sheet and had been for two days; she didn't want anyone to see it before Benjamin.

She brought the candle with her and stopped in front of the canvas and said, "Here it is. It is fair, no masterpiece for sure, but I do not doubt that the building is at least recognizable." Then she removed the sheet.

For a moment, she stared at it. An element of pride swelled in her bosom. It was probably her best work she had ever done. Benjamin took the candle from her and held it closer to the painting, making the layers of paint come to life. Shadows became deeper, colors brighter, and lines more defined. Georgiana had to admit that seeing it by candlelight gave it a somewhat magical feel.

Finally, after a thorough perusal of the painting, Benjamin lowered the candle and held it up to Georgiana. "It is spellbinding! You have caught the feeling of the building so well, yet somehow you have painted our future there too, with the promise of the sun hiding behind it. I can see us sitting right there at the café eating the apple custard, repeating this moment year after year."

He set the candle down on the table and reached for her hands. "Tell me we will do it, Georgiana. Tell me we will not take our time for granted. Promise me we will have more magical moments like this. I do not want a week to go by that we do not watch the sun rise. These mornings this last week were void of all value watching it without you."

She nodded. "Every time I see a sunrise now, I think of you Benjamin. I always will. It represents all I feel for you."

His voice deepened, and she felt the breath warm her cheeks. "How so? How does a sunrise make you think of me?"

She walked him to the window seat and motioned to have him sit in the far side of the bay window. He did so and then held out his arm beckoning her to snuggle up against him, and she did so. "You always know just what I need."

They adjusted themselves for the briefest of moments until they found a comfortable position with her knees tucked under her making her lean into him and rest her head on his shoulder while still looking out the window. He very naturally enclosed his arms around her, resting his hand on her shoulder. Rhythmically he started running his hand up and down her arm sending a warmth and peace like never before into her soul. His hand stilled, and he pressed her to him one more time.

It was just like him to relish in the silence, but she still wished to answer him. "Elizabeth told me once that falling in love was like watching a sunrise. She said more often than not, the light comes on gradually, adding light and burning off the confusing fog little by little until there comes a time when the light touches all. Love is not some single moment where in a flash you can say, 'Yesterday I did not love him, but today I do.' She said it pervades every thought until it seems only natural to admit to the sensation in your chest."

She turned from the window to look into his eyes. "And that is exactly how it felt falling in love with you. I do not know quite when I started falling in love with you. Perhaps it was at Rosings at Anne's wedding when we were in each other's presence so often. But I rather think it started even before that. I admired your integrity and work ethic since the very first moment I met you."

Benjamin squeezed her shoulder. "I have to tell you, Georgiana, that I wanted so badly to dance with you a year ago when I first met you at Pemberley. But I knew you were not yet out and without being any relation, I felt the impropriety acutely. From the very first moment you stood your ground and so valiantly defended Charlotte and Colonel Fitzwilliam, I saw qualities in you that I had always been looking for."

His voice was soft, and each word caressed her heart. She laid her head on his shoulder and he kissed her head.

"What did you see?" she asked.

The sky was just starting to lighten, and the deep blue and purples were being chased away. Clouds that were once noticeable only because they hid the stars, suddenly started having shadows and their form flirted with the brightness emerging.

Benjamin continued, "I saw the fiercest of loyalties—someone who would defend her loved ones with unwavering faith. I saw someone who loved with a passion and devotion that rivaled anything I had ever seen. I understood your loyalty to the colonel, but you had only known Charlotte since May when she came for Elizabeth and Mr. Darcy's wedding. But there was already a bond between you that you refused to allow to be tarnished or weakened by the elements around you. I wanted that kind of devotion to look back at me. You have a very unique way of looking at those you love."

"What? How so?" Georgiana asked.

"It is a look of adoration that I had been hoping to see for what seemed like forever. I have been craving it more than a few weeks now. I finally saw it mirrored back at me that moment in the library just before your brother interrupted us."

"I so admire you, Benjamin," Georgiana replied. "I never doubted your kindness or honesty. It reflected off you like those rays of sunshine we are seeing." The sky was brightening and the flagrant purples turned into pinks, which gave way to the reds and oranges. They watched the sunrise in silence for a little while.

Georgiana continued. "You know I just realized something. Love, all forms, not just romantic love, but all kinds of love, is like a sunrise. My love I have for my brother allows me to see his good intentions. And even the love I have for little David and the General came on slowly, forming even before they were even born. But once they entered the world, it seemed only natural that they became invaluable. I suppose even loving my acquaintances, like your brother Clyde, allowed me to see his true potential. Love, in all forms, offers us hope and perspective and understanding."

Any moment the first definite signs of the sun were going to peek over the horizon. It was one of her most favorite moments in watching a sunrise.

She could feel his other hand come around and with a touch that could only be fire and ice—its sensation welcomed on her flushed cheeks but stirring it to life with its heat— he took her face and repositioned it so she was looking up at him. She saw the same look of adoration she had seen that morning she first realized she loved him. She realized that look of adoration in his eyes was really a mirror of her own feelings.

Her shawl slipped from her shoulder but she did not even make an attempt to readjust it, regardless of the fact that the air around them was rather chilly.

"Georgiana, would it be welcomed if I kissed you right now?"

"I cannot refuse you, not when it is my own deepest desire."

His eyes darkened, and anticipation prolonged the distance between their lips, but as soon she closed her eyes, his lips tenderly explored hers. She immediately felt the warmth of the rays of the sun warm her back. Warmth permeated every part of her being. The tingle of having his lips so lovingly and passionately travel over hers, quickened her heart. Each kiss brought about a whirlwind of sensation. He was everything to her.

She did not care if they lived in his townhome or in Kent at Rolling Farms, because home was going to be wherever Benjamin was. If he decided to continue working as a solicitor, as she suspected he probably would because he was too industrious not to, or whether he decided to be more involved with the estate, or both, she wanted to be where he was.

She saw that now. Never had she felt more at peace than curled on his lap with the sunrise behind her and her lips intertwined with his. Remembering the look in his eyes made her realize she knew what love looked like.

And tasting the sweetness of his mouth made her realize that she knew what love tasted like too.

As she let out a small moan of pleasure and heard him sigh as well, she knew she knew what love sounded like.

But putting the last month all together, and all she had learned about love, she realized that recognizing love was not hard at all.

All this time she really did know what love felt like, but until she knew what to call it, she had not realized that the feeling was not unfamiliar at all.

Love felt like coming home.

THE END

Other books by Jeanna Ellsworth

Pride and Prejudice variations

Mr. Darcy's Promise
How can an honorable promise become so vexing?

Pride and Persistence
At some point, a good memory is a bad thing.

To Refine Like Silver *
Our trials do not define us; rather they refine us.

The Hope Series Trilogy:

Hope for Mr. Darcy *
Hope is all they have left, will it be enough?

Hope for Fitzwilliam *
For two destined to be together, hope is their only defense.

Hope for Georgiana *
Hope has become vital—*especially* when it comes to love.

Regency Romance

Inspired by Grace *
What started as friendship has evolved into something quite tangible.

Buying the Duke's Silence *
(Sequel to *Inspired by Grace*—Coming September 2017)
Eventually Evelyn learns that Silence is golden.

* Indicates Christian Romance

About the Author

Jeanna Ellsworth Lake entered a new era in her life in December 2015. Through all her single years, she kept searching for a Mr. Darcy, but didn't realize that what she *needed* was a Colonel Fitzwilliam! And she found him: a second son with a passionate heart, who never fails to make her laugh. She is so proud of her three daughters, who have supported her through her writing, and have always been her inspiration.

She absolutely loves her chance to influence lives as a nurse, and currently does so in the northwest. She finds great joy in her many roles she juggles, but writing especially has been her therapy. She claims she has never been happier.

Jeanna fell in love again with Jane Austen when she was introduced to the incredible world of Jane Austen-inspired fiction. She can never adequately thank the fellow authors who mentored her and encouraged her to write her first novel.

She loves hearing from her readers and cherishes the chance to interact with them. For more information on her books and writing, please visit her website:

www.HeyLadyPublications.com.

JEANNA ELLSWORTH LAKE

HOPE FOR GEORGIANA

www.ingramcontent.com/pod-product-compliance
Lightning Source LLC
Chambersburg PA
CBHW020105180626
46812CB00006B/2474